The Substitute Millionaire

Hulbert Footner

Alpha Editions

This edition published in 2024

ISBN : 9789364730969

Design and Setting By
Alpha Editions
www.alphaedis.com
Email - info@alphaedis.com

As per information held with us this book is in Public Domain.
This book is a reproduction of an important historical work. Alpha Editions uses the best technology to reproduce historical work in the same manner it was first published to preserve its original nature. Any marks or number seen are left intentionally to preserve its true form.

1

On a certain morning, just as on six mornings in the week (barring holidays) and fifty weeks in the year, Jack Norman wormed his way into a crowded subway local at Fiftieth street, and, propping himself against the end of a cross seat, opened his paper. But this morning, like everybody else in the train, he approached the headlines with an unusual thrill of interest, for an immense sensation was in process of being unrolled in the press.

Two days before, Silas Gyde, the millionaire miser and usurer, had been blown to pieces in the street by a bomb. The assassin, arrested, proved to be not one of those who had a grievance against the old money lender (there were supposed to be many such) but a maniac of anarchistic proclivities. His name was Emil Jansen. He was already on the way to an asylum for the criminal insane.

The main facts of the case having been given in previous issues, space in the paper to-day was largely devoted to anecdotes illustrating the extraordinary eccentricities of the dead man. It was said that with an income of perhaps six millions a year, he spent no more than six hundred. He bought his clothes at an immigrant outfitters' on Washington street, and even so had not had a new suit in two years. To keep himself from spending money it was his habit to go about with empty pockets, and borrow what few cents he needed from bootblacks, newsboys and applewomen to whom he was well known. But he was scrupulous in repaying these debts. Every day, even when he had become old and feeble, he turned up at the office of a certain corporation for the sake of a free lunch provided to the directors, though he had to walk a mile from the Wall street district where all his business was transacted. It was at the door of this office that he had met his end. And so on. And so on.

Silas Gyde died a bachelor, and had left no kin so far as was known. His wealth was said to be well in excess of a hundred million dollars. The paper gave a tempting list of the gilt-edge securities he was supposed to own; but nothing was known for sure, for though continually engaged in litigation, he had left no personal attorney; he had not sufficiently trusted any man. No one could say, now, where he had kept his wealth or how he had intended to dispose of it.

Young Jack Norman read of the millions with the kind of aching gusto that a hungry man pictures a good dinner. Jack's earnings were twelve dollars a week. He knew little about sociology or economics, but he could not but feel a dim dissatisfaction with the scheme of things that restricted him, with all a youth's capacity for living largely, to twelve dollars weekly, while it provided the old man with the tastes of a hermit crab, with a hundred thousand.

Twelve dollars a week meant that Jack's still boyish appetite daily had to be less than satisfied by the fare of a second rate boarding house; it meant that he had to wear cheap clothes when the instinct of his years was to array himself like Solomon; it meant that his lip must curl with envy as the pleasures of the town passed him by; hardest of all to bear, it meant that the joys of honorable courtship were denied him. A fellow must have money to take a girl out in town.

Jack's case was not peculiar. The same expression of sullen wistfulness might have been read in many a young face on the same train. What distinguished this face from the others was a latent fire in the eyes which suggested that, given the opportunity, the possessor had the capacity to play a larger part in life than twelve dollars a week permitted.

He got off at Worth street and made his way East to Centre where he worked as book-keeper in Fisher's sash and blind factory. Walking the street, like many another young head that morning, his was light with dreams.

"If I had Silas Gyde's money I wouldn't be pounding the concrete like this. I'd be fluffing down to Wall street in my Rolls-Royce. Or my yacht would be putting me ashore at the Battery. Or a special train up from Lakewood. First thing I'd do would be to tell Fisher to go to Hell. Oh, that would be worth a million!

"I'd say to Fisher: 'Who do you think you are, you little two-spot bankrupt carpenter with your business in your wife's name! One would think you were William K. Astorbilt, the airs you give yourself. Why I could buy you out for the price of what I spend for a meal!'"

As he turned in at the door of Fisher's place Jack's eyes involuntarily sought a window in the establishment of the hardware jobber opposite. As present the window was tenantless; later it would be sanctified by a chestnut head bending over a typewriter. Jack's dreams were diverted into another channel.

"If I had Silas Gyde's money she wouldn't have to pay for her own lunch when she eats with me. And I could take her out nights. Oh! Automobile, dress-suit, box seats at the Opera, supper at the Bienvenu and a dance! Lord! And they say old Gyde lived on my salary!"

The offices of the Fisher factory were on the second floor. As Jack turned in from the hall, Fisher himself was standing at the door of his private office; hands in pockets, cigar rolling between thick lips, hat on the back of his head, on his face the customary brutal sneer.

"You're late!" he rasped. "Can't you get out of bed in the mornings?"

This was a regular performance at Fisher's. The boss took his pleasure that way, and the office employees were hardened to it. But at the moment Jack was exalted. In his imagination he was still the master of millions.

"The clock's fast," he said curtly, meeting Fisher square in the eye.

"You lie!" said that gentleman.

By way of answer Jack pulled out his watch and compared it with the wall clock. The glance was not complimentary to Fisher's battered time-piece. Fisher purpled with rage.

"You ——— ———! Don't give me any of your lip!"

"Who do you think you are?" said Jack coolly. The words were fatally ready to his tongue. "You little two-by-four sash and blind maker with your business in your wife's name! Better pay your bills before you talk that way to honest men!"

Behind the fright in the eyes of the thin office-boy and the pale typist, gleamed a wondering delight. Never had such words been heard in that place!

"Get out of here! Get out of here!" roared Fisher on the verge of apoplexy. "Get out before I throw you out!"

"As to that," said Jack, "you're not man enough," and he took a step nearer the boss.

Fisher precipitately retired into his private office, slamming the door behind him. The office boy tittered, and clapped a scared hand over his mouth. Jack turned on his heel, and coolly lit a cigarette—lit it and blew a whole cloud of smoke, there in those sacred precincts! The eyes of the other two regarded him with a kind of adoration.

From behind the partition Fisher was still shouting: "Get out! You're fired!"

"Much obliged," said Jack. "It was worth it."

But even while he spake the brave words his heart was sinking like a stone in deep water. It was Wednesday, and his salary was always spent in advance of course. All he possessed in the world was a dollar twenty and his watch—fortunately out of hock for the time being. By this time, he thought Fisher was probably sorry too, and would take him back at a word of contrition—but with those admiring eyes on him, he could not speak it.

"So long, Kids," he said airily, and started for the door.

"Oh, wait a minute," said the boy. "Here's a letter for you this morning."

Jack thrust it carelessly into his pocket and went on down-stairs. At the street door he stopped at a loss. Turned loose on the street at nine o'clock of a working morning, which way was one to turn? He glanced across the street again, the window was still vacant. Anyway, he couldn't very well see her, jobless as he was. Better just drop of sight. This thought cost him a shrewd pang. He started walking quickly in the direction opposite to that whence she would presently come.

He remembered the letter and took it out. Letters were not so frequent in his life that he could afford to disdain them. This was a business envelope, large, square, and made of thick, fine paper. "National New York Bank" was neatly embossed on the flap. It was addressed in long-hand, an untidy but powerful scrawl.

"Some high-class ad," thought Jack. "Want to sell me bonds, I suppose." He chuckled with bitter humor.

Inside he found this communication in the same hand:

"Dear Mr. Norman:

"Will you please call me up at my office to-morrow morning. I shall arrive there about nine-thirty. The number of my private phone is —— Broad. You will not find it in the book.

"Very truly yours,
 "Walter Delamare."

Jack, being a true American youth, regarded this skeptically. "What kind of a con is he handing me?" he thought. "Who the deuce is Walter Delamare?"

The name rang familiarly in his ears. He glanced at the note head again. Under the name of the bank was printed: "Office of the President." Of course! Walter Delamare, President of the National New York Bank. His name was in the papers every day. It wielded a magic influence in the nation.

Jack still suspected a hoax of some kind, though the expensive note paper and the scrawly, characteristic hand were impressive. He examined the latter with fresh care. It was surely real handwriting, not process work.

"Oh well, it's worth a nickel for a telephone call," he thought. "I have nothing to lose."

He had nearly half an hour to kill before nine-thirty, and no twenty-five minutes ever passed more slowly. He walked down to Wall street and had a look at the outside of the National New York Bank, an imposing colonnade a whole block long. He circumnavigated it three times, and at nine thirty-one, precisely, went into a cigar store and called up the number that had been given him.

After a due interval he heard a voice at the other end of the wire that certainly sounded like that of a man of mark—crisp, serene, potent; humorous and kindly, too.

"Mr. Norman?"

"Yes, sir."

"This is Delamare. You are prompt. Can you come down to see me this morning?"

"Yes, sir."

"Can you come right away? Later I shall be very busy."

"Yes, sir."

"Good! Better taxi down. And by the way, it would be better if you sent in an assumed name. I will explain why when I see you. Call yourself—let me see—call yourself Mr. Robinson."

"Yes, sir."

"Very well. I shall be expecting you. Good-by."

Jack issued from the telephone booth a little dazed. A great captain of finance asking him, the humble bookkeeper, to call! Putting Jack on an equal footing by referring to himself as "Delamare"! A mystery suggested by the use of an assumed name! What could it all mean! On the one hand the skeptic in Jack whispered: "Some one is putting up a game on you!" On the other hand the dear hidden ego in us all that only needs a little appreciation to show its head said: "Why shouldn't Walter Delamare have private business with you as well as anybody?"

Jack had only to walk across the street to the bank. The argument within him showed itself in a kind of defiant sheepishness as he passed the great portal and found himself under the far-flung vaulted ceiling. It had been designed to impress, and impressive it was. With its rare marbles and mural paintings it was more like a palace than a place of sober business. It was not yet the opening hour, but many elegant clerks were already starting to work behind the brass grills. Shabby Jack eyed their cravats and fine linen wistfully.

He asked one of the uniformed attendants the way to Mr. Delamare's office, half expecting a roar of laughter to go up. But nothing of the sort occurred. He next found himself opposed by a silvery-haired old gentleman whose exquisite courtesy was the same to all.

"Whom do you wish to see?"

"Mr. Delamare."

"Mr. Delamare can be seen only by appointment."

"I have an appointment."

The courteous old gentleman permitted himself a glance of surprise. "What name shall I say?"

"Mr. Robinson."

"Very good, sir."

He returned with an air of slightly heightened respect. "Please step this way, sir."

"It is all right," thought Jack. "Nobody is hoaxing me."

He followed his conductor down a mahogany and plate glass corridor.

2

Jack was introduced to a room of truly noble proportions, vast and high, with a row of tall windows with round tops, looking down a narrow street to the harbor. In the center was a flat-topped desk as big as a banquet board and behind it sat a man, dwarfed in size by the vastness of his surroundings—but immeasurably increased in significance. The whole place focused in him.

Jack's silken-tongued conductor announced him, and softly withdrew. The man at the desk raised his head and bent a look of strong interest and quizzical amusement on Jack. It was the face of a man well-assured of his place in the world; serene and careless; a man who consorted on equal terms with labor leaders and kings.

"So this is what you're like!" he said.

The unexpected look of interest and the strange words instead of heartening Jack had the contrary effect. His knees shook under him a little, his mouth went dry.

"Sit down," said Mr. Delamare, indicating a chair opposite him.

Jack obeyed, walking jerkily like an automaton.

"I suppose you're wondering why I sent for you?"

"Yes, sir."

"You have no idea?"

"No, sir."

"I will tell you as soon as you have answered a few questions. I must make sure first that I have got hold of the right man."

He pulled out a drawer, and taking from it a typewritten sheet, read his question from it.

"Your full name?"

"John Farrow Norman."

"Parents living?"

"Both dead, sir."

"Father's name?"

"John Goadby Norman."

"Mother's name?"

"Phoebe Farrow."

"Place of your birth?"

"Cartonsville, New York."

There were other questions of a similar tenor, and Jack's answers were apparently satisfactory to Mr. Delamare. He folded the paper, and searched in the drawer for something else. His next question was an odd one.

"Are you wearing your father's watch?"

"Why, yes," stammered Jack.

It was the one article of value that he possessed. He unhooked it from its chain and passed it over. The banker opened the back of the case as if aware of what was to be found there, and the smiling face of Jack's mother as a bride was revealed. From the drawer he took an old-fashioned cabinet photograph, and compared it with the picture in the watch case.

Jack catching sight of the second picture was startled out of his diffidence. "My mother's picture! Where did you get that?"

Mr. Delamare showed him the two faces side by side. "Not the same photograph, but unquestionably the same woman. You may have both now."

He handed them over. The picture he had taken from the drawer showed Jack's mother at an earlier period, just graduating into womanhood with all the touching innocence of youth about her. Jack's eyes filled.

"What does it mean?" he murmured.

"One more question," said Mr. Delamare. "Give me a brief account of yourself as far back as you can remember."

Jack did so, wonderingly, and the banker checked his story with another typewritten sheet that he held.

"That will do," he said at last. "I'm satisfied."

"How did you learn all this?" asked Jack. "I didn't think anybody in the world was interested what jobs I had or where I lived."

"One never knows," was the smiling answer. "Write your name and I'll tell you."

Jack obeyed. The banker compared it with a signature he had.

"Now then," he said. "How would you like to be rich?"

Jack stared at him in a daze.

Delamare laughed. "Rich beyond the dreams of avarice! Worth eighty million dollars in fact."

"Eighty million!" muttered Jack stupidly.

"As you sit there this minute you are worth eighty million—perhaps more."

"Where—did I get it?" stammered Jack helplessly.

"Silas Gyde bequeathed you all he possessed."

Jack's face was a study in amazement, incredulity—not to say downright alarm. At the sight Mr. Delamare threw back his head and laughed a peal.

"Don't take it so hard! You'll live it down!"

"What was I to Silas Gyde?" murmured Jack.

"I don't know the whole story. Mr. Gyde took no man on earth into his confidence. I judge, though, that he was an unsuccessful suitor for your mother. The affair must have cut deep, for he never married."

"Eighty million!" murmured Jack, unable to grasp the idea of such a sum.

"Nearly five million a year; four hundred thousand a month; say thirteen thousand a day."

The figures had a convincing ring. The color stole back into Jack's cheeks, and a delicious warmth crept around his heart. He had no great difficulty in believing his good fortune, because he had already pictured it to himself in fancy. His first thought was of Kate. "I can buy her anything now!"

For a moment or two he found nothing to say. Delamare seeing his eyes become dreamy, smiled again. "Spending it already, I see!"

Jack blushed and descended to earth. "Please tell me all about it," he said.

"I'll tell you what I know. As I said, I was not in Mr. Gyde's full confidence—no man was. Indeed I knew him but slightly. He was a good customer of the bank, but he did everything in his own peculiar way. He rented a large vault from us, and had the locks changed under his own supervision. I believe he kept the major part of his securities there, but he may have other vaults too.

"Some five years or so ago, he came to me saying he wanted to rent a small lock box in our vaults, the kind that we get ten dollars a year for. He was so insistent upon the necessity for secrecy that we allowed him to have it under an assumed name. Another officer of the bank and myself were taken into the secret. Mr. Gyde left me a duplicate key to this box with instructions to open it if ever a day passed without my hearing from him. I believe he used to visit the box himself to make sure that I had not been tampering with it, but his peculiarities were so well known, one didn't mind that in him.

"Since then, every day of his life he dropped in here, or called me or my secretary on the phone, just to report, he said. In the beginning I often wondered why he had set himself such a task, but as time went on it became a mere form, and at last I forgot how the custom had started.

"When word of his death was brought me day before yesterday, all recollection of the small box had passed from my mind. My secretary brought it back by remarking that the old gentleman's daily report was now at an end. I found the keys and opened the box. The papers were sealed into the box itself, so that they could not be removed without breaking the wax. Very characteristic of Mr. Gyde.

"The contents consisted of his will; detailed instructions to me how to find you and identify you, and several keys which I was directed to hand you. Here they are. And here is the will, a model of clearness and brevity you see."

Jack read: "I, Silas Gyde, being of sound mind and in the full possession of my senses, do hereby devise and bequeath all that I die possessed of to John Farrow Norman, son of John Goadby Norman and Phoebe Farrow, and do appoint the said John Farrow Norman and Walter Delamare, President of the National New York Bank, my executors."

"My instructions state," Mr. Delamare resumed, "that the witnesses to the will were two clerks employed by Mr. Gyde at that time. You see he forgot nothing.

"As to those keys, they are for the various doors in Mr. Gyde's apartment at the Hotel Madagascar. I am told here not to deliver them into any hands but yours, and you are instructed to visit the apartment at once, and alone. Always mysterious, you see. By the way, Mr. Gyde was the sole owner of the Madagascar, and it is therefor now yours."

"I suppose there will be lawyers to see, and so on," said Jack.

"Mr. Gyde had no personal attorneys. He was always suing and being sued, but he retained a new man for every case. Obviously he has made these arrangements on his own initiative. I expect it will be up to you and me to ferret out his properties. I will have my attorney probate the will. You had better have a lawyer to advise you. Have you any one in mind?"

Jack shook his head.

"Very well, I will give you a note to a friend of mine for whose integrity and ability I will vouch. His name is Hugh Brome. He is young like yourself, and this matter will mean a big thing for him—that is if you have no objection to his youth?"

"No indeed!" said Jack.

Mr. Delamare wrote a note and handed it over. "Go and look him over before you commit yourself. If you approve of him the three of us can have a talk here later."

Jack rose.

"Haven't you forgotten something?" asked Mr. Delamare smiling.

"What?" said Jack blankly.

"Well—some money?"

Jack blushed. "I didn't think I could get any yet."

"Certainly! As much as you want. Mr. Gyde left a large balance here. Of course I can't hand that over to you yet, but the bank is prepared to advance you whatever you require. The bank hopes that you will continue to favor it with your patronage."

More than anything Mr. Delamare had said, this last little sentence made Jack feel like a millionaire.

"Here's a pocket check book. Make out your check and I'll send it to the teller with my O.K. You don't want to go out there yourself for the reporters are lying in wait for you. That's why I told you to send in an assumed name. They pester the life out of me. As soon as you're safely out of the way I'll give out the story and be rid of them."

Jack took the offered pen and wrote his check, the banker watching him with a smile. At the line for the amount Jack stuck; he thought of a hundred dollars, five hundred, a thousand; higher than a thousand he dared not go.

"Is that too much?" he asked, gasping a little.

"Not at all!" said Mr. Delamare, laughing. "Merely your income for about half an hour!"

3

So Jack Norman came out of the National New York Bank eighty millions richer than he went in. He left the building walking on air, and being unaccustomed to that form of exercise it is not surprising that he staggered a little, and collided with more than one matter-of-fact Wall Street figure. A delightful insane phantasmagoria whirled through his brain, blinding him to his earthly surroundings. He walked five blocks before he had the least idea where he was going. Here a wild taxi-cab almost ran him down, and he was brought back to earth with a bump.

"Good Lord! suppose I'd been laid out before I had a chance to spend a dollar!" he thought with horror.

He looked at his watch. It was only half-past ten. It had taken him less than an hour to acquire eighty millions. An hour and a half must still pass before he could satisfy his great need of telling Kate what had happened—that is unless he descended on her office and carried her off bodily in a taxi-cab, like young Lochinvar. But he was doubtful how Kate would take this. He was a little afraid of Kate.

In the meantime he had to see his lawyer. But he couldn't very well go and ask a man to take charge of an eighty million dollar estate while he looked like a tramp. Clothes!—enchanting thought; he was able to buy anything in New York that caught his fancy. It need not be supposed that the fair sex enjoys a monopoly of this passion; the young male, being more restricted in his choice, brings to it a deeper, more concentrated passion. The difference in shirt patterns! The design of a cravat of which only four square inches is shown!

He retreated into the shelter of a doorway to consider this matter, watching the passers-by meanwhile for inspiration. But he did not see what he wanted. The young men looked either grubby or flash. Jack discovered that he had a definite taste in clothes that he had never been able to indulge.

He was aware of course of the subtle differences between ready-made and made-to-order. But while he took the time to search out the best tailor in New York he had to have something. Dimly he remembered having heard of a fine old firm that outfitted men from top to toe. It was on Madison avenue. He looked about for the nearest subway station, and then remembered with a delightful start that there were such things as taxi-cabs in the world, and his pocket was full of money.

He held up a negligent finger to a passing cab. He got in and, leaning back luxuriously, wondered how the people who looked at him would look if they knew!

At a few minutes before noon, an elegantly dressed young fellow, conspicuous for his graceful figure and sparkling brown eyes, was walking nervously up and down Centre street; ten paces each way and back. A taxicab waited at the curb beside him. In one hand the young man carried a pair of yellow chamois gloves, and swung a yellow malacca stick in the other. He wore a boutonnière of corn-flowers.

As he waited his nervousness increased. It suddenly occurred to him that to greet Kate with a flourish of the new Fedora, and hand her into the waiting taxi might create a scandal in the eyes of her fellow workers. Indeed he was not at all sure but that she might turn him down flat. At the same time he began to worry about the yellow gloves and the yellow stick—a thought too conspicuous for Centre street, perhaps.

Finally he went to the cab and, unobtrusively dropping the stick inside, paid the man off and let him go. He then thrust the gloves and the boutonnière in his pocket, and felt much better.

When Kate finally did come down-stairs, her first glance overlooked the new clothes entirely, and went straight to his eyes. Seeing the beaming smile there, her eyes fell demurely. Then did she perceive the finery from the feet up, but was too well bred to make any comment. Jack was obliged to ask her very off-hand:

"Notice any change?"

"You look very nice to-day."

"Oh, I got tired going round like a rag-picker!"

She made no further remark, and Jack who had counted on creating more of an effect than this, felt a little aggrieved. You never could get any change out of this girl, he reflected. But just let her wait! She was due to be surprised for once in her young life!

At the corner he held her in talk for a moment, while he searched for a taxi out of the tail of his eye.

"Let's not go to Geiger's to-day."

"Geiger's is all right."

"I'm sick of the joint!"

"It's as good as any of the places around here."

"Let's go down-town."

"But you know I only have an hour."

A taxi came bowling through from the Bowery with its little "vacant" flag raised. Jack held up a finger. It drew up beside them with squealing brakes, and the chauffeur opened the door. Kate who had not observed Jack's signal, turned her back on it.

"Get in," said Jack.

That was when she received her first shock. Her eyes opened very wide. "Why, Mr. Norman!" she began.

"Get in!" said Jack so peremptorily, that in her state of fluster she actually obeyed.

"Café Savarin," said Jack to the chauffeur.

The cab started with a jerk, throwing them back on the cushions. "Let me out!" she said—but not very strongly.

He affected not to hear. There was a delicious satisfaction in seeing the self-possessed little lady overcome with confusion, if only for a moment.

"To-morrow I'll come for you in my own car," he said, nonchalantly.

"Are you crazy?" she murmured, really alarmed.

He laughed. "Can't I have a car as well as anybody?"

"But I thought—that is—you always said——"

"That I was as poor as Job's turkey, eh? Only a stall. I just worked for Fisher for the sociological experience. I don't have to work really."

She looked at him with troubled eyes.

He couldn't resist the temptation to tease her a little. "My old man's a multi-millionaire," he rattled on. "Of course I get sick of that life sometimes, and scout about a bit."

Her eyes became so reproachful his heart smote him.

"Oh, that's only a joke," he said quickly. "Lord knows the poverty was real enough—but it's over for good!" "For both of us," he would have liked to add, but did not quite dare. "Look!" he cried, drawing his hand out of his pocket with the great roll of yellow-backed bills. "My income for half an hour!"

"Where did you get it?" she said aghast

He laughed again. "Honest, I didn't steal it."

"Please!"

He told her at last. The story sounded strange in his own ears. When he came to the end he saw to his astonishment that there were tears in her eyes.

"Why—why, what's the matter?" he cried.

"I don't know," she said smiling through the rain. "Am I not silly? But I suppose it means change. And I hate changes!"

"A change for the better, only. If you knew how I hated poverty!"

Her eyes dropped. "I, too," that meant, but she did not care to tell him so, audibly.

"If you knew how mean I felt every day when we went to that beanery together, and you had to pay for your own lunch!"

"But what was the difference? We both work for our living."

"A man feels differently. Why I never would ask you if I could come to see you in the evenings, because I couldn't take you out anywhere. I was afraid I couldn't keep my end up with your gang."

"I haven't any gang," she murmured.

"Well all that's ended now! Now there's no limit but the sky! And here we are. The lawyer guy told me this was the swellest place downtown."

A fresh panic seized her. "I can't eat in a place like this! I'm not fit to be seen!"

"Nonsense! You always look like a lady!"

Circumstances were too strong for her. She found herself being wafted across the sidewalk, and was delivered into the hands of the maid in the lobby, before she could think of an effective resistance. Indeed they were seated at a snowy little board brightened by an electric candle, before she really got her breath. At Jack's elbow stood a post-graduate waiter with a deferential bend in his back, and at just the right distance an orchestra was discussing the *Meditation* from *Thaïs*.

A sigh escaped Kate, for after all she was a perfectly human girl. "Oh, this is heavenly!"

Jack's eyes sparkled. "Good! I was wondering when you'd begin to let yourself go." He leaned forward. "You should worry! You're the prettiest girl here—and the best dressed!"

Which was true—on both counts. There was no doubt about her prettiness; Heaven had attended to that. Eyes of the deepest blue with a glance steady and deep; an adorable little nose, and a mouth at once firm and most kissable. As for her clothes, it may be they were of cheap materials, but the taste that had chosen redeemed them. The hat, most important item, was of Kate's own manufacture, being copied from the window of a milliner whose name is a household word.

"Don't be silly," said the wearer severely. "The waiter is waiting."

"That's what he's here for! Oh, dear! I wish we could stay all afternoon!"

This was put forth really as a proposal rather than a wish. But Kate was relentless.

"We'll have to hurry," she said firmly.

"Well, we've time for a cup of green turtle, a lobster paté and a coupe St. Jacques," said Jack. A whispered order was added, and one of the yellow backs changed hands. The waiter departed.

"One would think you had been coming here all your life," said Kate demurely.

This was delicious flattery. "I've planned it in dreams," he said.

Presently the waiter returned, smiling from ear to ear, and bearing a bunch of violets almost as big as a cart wheel. Their delicious fragrance filled all the air. With a flourish he placed them before Kate.

She gasped. "Oh! How wonderful! For me!"

"Who do you think?" said Jack.

"But—but what shall I do with them?"

"Put them on. Any woman can wear violets without hurting."

"But what will they think when I get back to the office."

"The worst!" said Jack solemnly.

"Oh, Mr. Norman!"

"Why go back to the office?" asked Jack very offhand.

"Oh, Mr. Norman!" she said again, with a scandalized air.

"My name is Jack," he said unabashed.

She made believe not to hear.

"I can't bear to think of you working even for a day longer in that stuffy hole! Why, my first thought when I heard the news was I can take her out of that! What fun will it be for me to fluff around town spending money when you are still jailed there, punishing the alphabet."

"What do you mean?" she said, trying to look indignant.

"You know what I mean. Or if you don't, look at me and you'll see!"

She did not avail herself of the invitation. "You don't seem to have thought much of me. What *I* might like. Am I nothing to you, but a sort of little follower, a hanger-on to help you spend money!"

"Oh, Katy, that's unjust. Look at me! Katy darling, I love you. Will you marry me?"

"Somebody will hear you," she murmured glancing nervously around.

"That's no answer."

"Why—I scarcely know you!"

"Time will fix that."

"You're not in earnest."

"I am! Look at me! I know you well! For months I have thought of you night and day. Oh, I tried to cut you out at first; I thought I was only storing up trouble for myself. Poor devil of a stool-warmer like me. What chance did I have? But I couldn't help myself! Every time I saw your face at the window I forgot my hard-headed resolutions. You see you had me at a disadvantage. I had an ideal of what a lady was, that I got from my mother—but knocking round in cheap boarding houses, well you don't meet that kind. It was just plumb luck my meeting you. First time I heard your voice you just knocked me out. That was what I had wanted—all my life. Look at me! Don't you think I'm in earnest now?"

"*Please*, not here!" she murmured.

He suddenly realized that a girl *is* entitled to a certain degree of privacy in receiving a proposal. "Oh! I clean forgot where we were!" he said contritely. "I'm sorry. The two things are so mixed up in my mind, I felt I couldn't tell you quick enough."

A silence fell between them. He studied her face wistfully, but could read nothing in the closed lips and downcast eyes.

"Katy, dear, can't you give me one word to go on?"

She shook her head.

"Nothing definite, Katy—but just a hint I can't stand the suspense."

She murmured softly: "My answer is no."

"Oh, Katy!" he said brokenly. "Sometimes I thought you looked at me as if—my mistake, I suppose. Don't you like me, Katy?"

"One doesn't marry on liking. I used to like you as a poor boy; But money changes people's characters. I'll have to wait and see."

4

Having left Kate at the office to which she most unreasonably insisted on returning, Jack bethought himself of the charge laid upon him to visit Silas Gyde's rooms alone. Kate's last words had not been too discouraging, and there was a pleasant suggestion of mystery in this new errand. Jack's spirits were good.

Another taxi-cab whirled him up-town to the Madagascar. Even now, occasionally the feeling came over him that he was living in a dream. He fingered the roll of bills in his pocket for reassurance.

"This is certainly me, Jack Norman," he thought. "And this is my money! The roll's not much smaller either. It must be real money because I have eaten it, drunk it, smoked it and am wearing it!"

He entered the hotel, one of Manhattan's greatest, with an odd little thrill in his breast. "This is mine," he told himself, "all this marble and onyx and plate glass; these tapestries, these Oriental rugs, these tropical plants, all mine! These good-looking bell-hops work for me; the Duke himself yonder at the desk will have to bend his haughty head when he finds out who I am!"

Jack was a little shy of asking to be shown to the late Mr. Gyde's rooms. Having no credentials, he suspected that his story might very well be laughed at, and he himself be shown the door. Anyway, he felt an instinctive repugnance to telling his story to all and sundry. If he could only find out where the rooms were he needn't apply at the desk, since he had the keys.

An attractive young woman at the news counter caught his attention. He bought a magazine from her, and while she made change sought to engage her in conversation.

"They say Mr. Silas Gyde used to live here."

"Yes, he owned this hotel."

"He must have been a queer Dick if you can believe what you read."

"Oh, the half of his queerness hasn't been printed."

"Was he a customer of yours?"

"No indeed. He never bought anything in the hotel. Said he could get it cheaper outside. Got his meals over on Eighth avenue and around."

"I wonder he lived here at all. Did he have a fine suite?"

"No, the cheapest rooms in the house."

"Where were they?"

"On the second floor at the back on the Forty ——th street side."

"He must have been a funny sight here in the lobby with his old hand-me-downs."

"He seldom showed himself here. He went in and out by his private entrance on Forty ——th street."

"So he had a private entrance, eh?"

"Yes, it was a regular thing to see him going in and out carrying his little oil-can."

"Oil-can!"

"Well, you see, when he rented the hotel to the management, he saved out his rooms rent free, but there wasn't anything said about steam heat or electric current, and when the management sent him a bill for heat and light, he made them take out the radiators and the fixtures, and he burned an oil lamp and a little oil heater."

"Here, in the Madagascar! Well, that beats all!"

"It sure does!"

In this little colloquy Jack had learned all that he desired. It was a simple matter to leave the hotel, turn the corner into Forty ——th street and proceed to the private entrance. It was at the extreme end of the hotel building, a modest door with the street numeral painted on it. Adjoining the hotel on this side was a deserted dwelling with boarded up windows below, and blinds pulled down above, the whole bearing the signs of long neglect.

One of Jack's keys fitted the door. Inside he found a single flight of stairs ending on a dark landing with another door. This door was not locked. Opening it he found himself in the sitting-room of the suite, a small room with two windows looking out on the street he had just left.

It was a typical hotel room, furnished by contract expensively but without taste. An amusingly incongruous note was furnished by the oil heater in the center of the rug, and the cheap lamp on the table. The naked ugliness of the latter object was not even mitigated by a shade. There was nothing to suggest that the room had been a man's home for several years, no personal belongings of any description.

Yet it was neat enough, and Jack guessed that Silas Gyde's arrangement with the hotel must have included maid service. From the bedroom there was a door to the hotel corridor, through which servants might have entered. This bedroom and a bathroom, both almost entirely without light or air, completed the suite. Jack had no difficulty in believing that it was one of the least desirable apartments in the hotel.

Jack's first glance around revealed nothing out of the common. The only signs of human occupancy were a few cheap toilet articles on the bureau. But there were several closets. That in the bedroom was locked. Opening it with one of his keys, Jack was faced by his first surprise—a modern and highly efficient steel vault door.

An alluring picture of heaped coin, greenbacks, securities, stored inside, arose before him, but the door was locked of course, and he had no instructions as to the combination. He wondered, not without chagrin, if Silas Gyde had been a practical joker. Why had he been instructed to proceed there alone merely for the pleasure of looking at a locked vault.

He went through the rooms more carefully. In the sitting-room there was a little fancy desk. He had a key to this, and upon its being opened, one of the pigeon-holes yielded up a packet of dusty, faded papers. He went over them one by one; advertisements, unimportant business letters, receipts for small amounts; not until he reached the last envelope of all was he rewarded.

This was sealed, and on it was written in an old man's cramped and tremulous hand:

"For my heir."

It was like a voice from beyond the grave.

But the contents were matter-of-fact enough: no more than this:

"*You are to go to James Renfrew, 120 Broadway, who will hand you a communication from me.*"

This simple sentence revived the lure of mystery, and another taxi-cab was soon bearing Jack downtown. Since the old man's note had been written, the famous office building at 120 Broadway had burned down, and had risen again to five times its former height. The firm of Renfrew, Bates and Meldrum, the eminent lawyers, still had their offices there, and Jack succeeded in seeing the senior member without too much delay.

This testy old gentleman with a snort of scorn for what he termed "Gyde's foolishness" put Jack through a cross-examination similar to that he had undergone from Delamare earlier in the day. Jack's answers being satisfactory, he received another note in Silas Gyde's cramped hand.

This contained a row of cabalistic figures, and further instructions for him to go to Nathan Harris, the well-known banker. At this office the performance was exactly repeated, with the exception that Mr. Harris evinced a good deal of curiosity on his own account. But since it was no part of Jack's instructions to take him into his confidence, he confined himself to polite and non-committal answers.

The note he received here, besides giving him more figures, sent him to the office of Sanford Gair, another eminent lawyer. At this stage Jack was brought to a stand by the information that Mr. Gair had been dead for a year. But Jack's blood was up now: persistent questioning finally elicited the fact that Mr. Gair's son and executor did indeed have a note for him.

This contained another line of figures followed by the word: "Complete." Underneath was written: "You are to enter alone."

"Complete?" thought Jack with knitted brows. "What is complete? What am I to enter alone?"

Then a light broke upon him. "The Vault of course! This is the combination!"

He lost no time in returning to the Madagascar.

It may be remarked here, that when Jack afterwards told Mr. Delamare about these visits the banker laughed heartily. "Isn't that like old Gyde! Renfrew, Nathan Harris and Gair, bitter enemies! He wasn't going to take any chances of their getting together!"

It was about five o'clock when Jack entered Silas Gyde's rooms the second time. He double-locked the door leading to the hotel corridor, and set to work on the combination with a burglarious feeling, which all his assurances to himself that it was his own property could not quite dissipate.

Jack had had no experience with such elaborate locks as this, but after all the principle was the same as that of Fisher's safe where he had been accustomed to keeping his books at night. After a number of false starts and misses, the steel bolts finally rang back, and the great door swung noiselessly outward.

Alas for Jack's expectations! The vault inside was as bare as Mother Hubbard's cupboard. There was not so much as a scrap of paper to be seen, let alone the dazzling stores he had pictured. The wall down each side were lined with shelves on which lay a thick, undisturbed coating of dust.

Apparently there never had been anything kept there; at least not for a long time.

Jack was thoroughly disgusted. All that chasing around town for nothing! Was his benefactor's only purpose in taking those elaborate precautions to make a fool of his heir? Perhaps the old man had been really insane.

But having taken all that trouble Jack did not mean to give up until he had made very sure there was nothing to be gained from it. He examined the vault anew, and presently made a curious discovery in the steel door. Differing from any safe he had ever seen, the handle which operated the bolt ran right through to the inside of the door, also the dial and knob of the combination were reproduced inside.

"What did he want that for?" thought Jack, with perplexed brow. "Almost looks as if he wanted to lock himself up inside."

It was dark within the vault, and Jack lit the oil lamp and carried it in. He had not paid much attention to the back of the vault, for his eye had told him it was flush with the outer wall of the building, but he was now struck by the fact that whereas the sides of the vault were of concrete the back wall was of steel, and there were no shelves covering it.

In short, the lamp revealed the outline of a door in the back wall, a steel door so beautifully fitted that only the tiniest of lines marked its boundaries. In it was a tiny slit that Jack's fourth and last key exactly fitted. When it was pressed home, the door swung towards him on a spring.

Here he received another surprise. Instead of the shallow wall cupboard he expected, for he knew he was against the outer wall of the hotel, the beams of the lamp illuminated a large cupboard heaped with rubbish in the corners. At the same moment he was greatly startled to hear an electric bell start ringing somewhere further within.

He realized of course that he had stumbled on a secret way into the house adjoining the hotel. He remembered the aspect of that house from the street, shuttered, neglected, dirty. What would the inside reveal? The feeble, fretful alarm of the electric bell perturbed him. He closed the steel door and it stopped: he let it swing open and the sound recommenced. For whom was it a warning? Inside the closet on his right there was an ordinary wooden door. It did not help to compose his nerves to hear a soft urgent whining and scratching on the other side of it. The lamp trembled a little in his hand.

However there was nothing for it but to advance. Jack was boy enough to refuse to take a dare. He had been instructed to enter alone, and he was not sufficiently frightened to disobey. There was a kind of fascination in entering upon this voyage of discovery alone. Moreover he had no reason to suppose that a trap had been prepared for him.

Before venturing in, he took a careful survey of the closet. The litter in the corners consisted of old clothes, old boots, newspapers. A musty smell arose from it. His attention was caught by a broad black belt painted on the floor at his feet. Stooping, he touched it, and the black came off on his finger.

"Soot," he thought. He took care to step over it when he entered.

The scratching still continued on the other side of the inner door, but Jack was reassured by the sound of an anxious little bark. "That's not a very formidable animal," he thought, smiling, and opening the door.

His first impression was of a little black and tan terrier, who waited just inside the door with an expression of anxiety, human in its intensity. At the sight of Jack the dog snarled and attempted to retreat, but weakness overcame it and it fell.

"Poor beastie!" murmured Jack.

The little animal, whether reassured by Jack's voice or prompted by his own great need, attempted to make friends. He approached wagging a feeble tail. He dragged himself towards the fireplace, and with piteous, speaking glances, directed Jack's attention to a tin box upon the mantel. A human voice could scarcely have been plainer.

"Is that where they keep it, old man?" said Jack.

In the box were some crusts. He made haste to toss them to the little dog, and filled his dish with water.

Jack found himself in a good-sized room to which no ray of daylight penetrated. His sense of direction told him it must be the second floor rear of the dwelling house. There was no lack of character here. The place was both sordid and piteous, and very eloquent of Silas Gyde's strange life.

"This was his real home," thought Jack, looking around. "The hotel apartment was simply a blind.... Poor old fellow!"

5

Jack as an instinctive precaution returned to close the vault door, and the inner steel door. The latter was provided with a handle on the closet side to draw it to. When Jack closed it the irritating little bell stopped ringing.

"That was to warn him if any one opened it while he was inside," thought Jack. "And the band of soot on the floor was to inform him if his stronghold had been entered during his absence. What a queer old boy to take so much trouble to hide himself!"

Silas Gyde's room in its architectural features was exactly like thousands of second floor backs in the endless rows of houses built from forty to fifty years ago. As Jack stood inside the closet door by which he had entered, two windows faced him, looking out on the back yards he knew, though they were closely curtained. At his right was a fireplace with a composition mantel, at his left was the door leading to the stair hall. The bed was below the hall door: it is always there. And adjoining the room on that side would be the bath room. Jack had lived in many such houses.

The air in the room was heavy, but less foul than might have been expected. Jack found behind the curtains that ventilators had been ingeniously contrived, which could be opened and shut without one's showing oneself at the window. For that matter the glass of the windows was well-nigh opaque with the accumulation of years of dust. The bed was tumbled but clean. Jack suspected that the old man had changed linen with the bed in the hotel. There was a similar oil lamp and oil heater in here.

"Those outside were a plant while these got the oil he carried in," thought Jack.

The room was hideously cheerless. Rubbish was piled everywhere. There was an old flat-topped desk with its back to the windows, and a sort of path had been cleared from the desk to the closet door with a branch to the bed midway. Elsewhere the litter had swamped everything. It was principally newspapers. Jack had never seen so many old newspapers in his life. One corner of the room was filled by a small mountain of scrap books containing faded clippings. When Jack came to examine them he found that all the items related to Silas Gyde, and most of them were abusive.

Yet from the walls of this unlovely room looked down a few rarely beautiful old pictures, and, as Jack was to learn later, they were of almost priceless value. Evidently at some period of his career the old miser had

had generous stirrings. One of these pictures caused Jack a great start. It occupied the space next to the closet door, hence he did not see it until he had come into the room and had turned around.

It was his mother. An enlargement by a talented hand of the wistful girlhood picture Delamare had given him that morning. She looked down on the fusty disarray with pitying eyes: she was startlingly young and alive in that dark place. The tears welled up in Jack's eyes again.

"Think of her presiding over a den like this! I'll give her a sunnier prospect. But he must have loved her well! I'll credit him with that."

A tour of the rest of the house from cellar to garret revealed only emptiness, darkness and a smell of must.

Returning to Silas Gyde's room, Jack went to his desk. This spot alone of all the room was in good order. On it lay a book open and face down at the page where the dead man had left off reading. It was the *Ordeal of Richard Feveril*, and it was open at the page describing the first meeting of Richard and Lucy. Jack read a few lines and wondered that Silas Gyde could have cared for that sort of thing. It didn't seem to go with the rest of him. Jack slipped the book in his pocket, against an opportunity to make its better acquaintance.

There was also a fat red leather note book, a sort of journal, in which Silas Gyde had entered the details of his financial transactions. Jack saved that for his lawyer. Finally there was a manuscript which Death had interrupted in the middle of a sheet. Turning back to the first page Jack was not a little astonished to find that it was a sort of letter addressed to himself. From the dates upon it, it had been started five years before and added to from time to time.

Jack sat down to read it. The little dog, making it clear that he had adopted a new master, lay at his feet.

"To John Farrow Norman:

"Dear Jack:

"Everybody knows old Silas Gyde—or thinks he does. Miser, usurer, skinflint, champion tightwad—I quote from the collection of clippings I have made. What everybody says must be true, I suppose, but it is not the whole truth. There is another Silas Gyde—or there was once, and it is he who writes to you.

"Little did you guess that I have been keeping track of you since you were quite a small boy. I have always from that time intended to make you my heir. I suppose you wonder why I never made myself known to you. There were several reasons. For one thing I have noticed that the relations between a rich man and his heir are seldom happy. I didn't care to read in your eyes that you wished the old fool would hurry up and die and be done with it.

"Another thing, and this is the real reason: as the years pass it becomes more and more difficult for me to make overtures to anybody. It sounds silly for an old fellow of near sixty to confess that he is shy, but such is the fact. And shyness in the old is a torturing thing. They call me queer, cranky, crazy, and the truth is simply that I am shy. I never could run with the herd.

"It is true what they say, that I have not a friend in the world, and now I would not know how to set about making one. Especially a young one. I am afraid of you, my boy; afraid of your terrible, pitiless youthfulness. And so I just imagine you are my friend. I have long talks with you, and give you quantities of good advice, to which you give dutiful heed.

"At the same time I have always kept a sort of watch over you. And if actual misfortune had overtaken you I would have found a way to come to your assistance. A little poverty and hard work will enable you to appreciate riches later.

"By this time you have learned that I was once your mother's suitor. She refused me for the first Jack Norman, your father. I wonder if your mother ever talked to you about me. Probably not. She was never a talker. Well, I hope you will never have such a blow as that was to me. I don't think you will. You have a certain grace (I have seen you), Phoebe's grace, that will endear you to your chosen maiden. As for me, even as a youth I was a dry stick.

"What made it harder for me was that I despised your father as a weaker man than myself. When I let this out to your mother in my anger and bitterness, she retorted that if he was less strong he was certainly more lovable.

"I left Cartonsville in my bitterness. My one idea, like so many galled young men before me, was to do something that would force Phoebe Farrow to acknowledge to herself that she had chosen the wrong man. I resolved to make myself a rich man, the richest in America. To gain this end I was prepared to deny myself everything above the barest necessities of life. Every cent was to be set to work to earn five.

"I succeeded, as every man must, who is bent on a thing so determinedly as I was. I did not return to Cartonsville for fifteen years.

Fifteen years of slavery they were. Those were the years that formed me for life—deformed me I should say. I was already a rich man when I went back.

"I found the situation much as I had imagined it. Your mother was the hard-working wife of a poor man—a man destined to die poor. She lived in a small inconvenient house without any servant, and her pretty hands were red and rough. And I was a millionaire. You were five years old at that time and your parents' only child. Both your elder brothers had died in an epidemic.

"But my triumph did not come off as I had pictured. Phoebe pitied me.

"'No wife nor chick?' she said, with her rare soft smile. 'Poor Silas! How useless your wealth must seem to you!'

"Then I saw as in a great white light that I had only been a fool for my pains. I returned to New York and automatically resumed the business of making money. I could not stop. It was all I knew. It filled my days and kept me from thinking.

"I often wished to change my way of life, but it was too late then. I was already known as Silas Gyde the usurer, and men had hardened their hearts against me. My diffident attempts to make friends were rebuffed. I was forced back into the rut I had worn for myself. There was nothing for me to do but earn the reputation the world had given me.

"I have told you that in fancy I often gave you advice. But it is not as a good example that I desire to hold myself up to you. I urge you to avoid my example. Never let money get the upper hand of you. Old Silas Gyde the miser tells you money is no good except to spend. I have succeeded in creating the incubus of wealth, and in so doing lost my soul. I leave you the harder task of ridding yourself of it, without losing yours.

"Your well-wisher,
    "Silas Gyde."

Under a date two years later the letter was resumed:

"I have opened this to add a warning. When you inherit my money, you are bound to inherit my cares also. Ever since I became rich enough to be notorious, I have been a target for men's envy and hate. I expected it. Indeed, I enjoyed it in a way. I gloated over my books of clippings. Their hatred gave me a sense of being somebody in the world.

"In my daily mail I received, and still receive, hundreds of letters, appealing, threatening, abusive; letters from every kind of crank. I ignore them. But lately a real danger has begun to threaten me in the spread of anarchistic doctrines among the people. And there are not lacking those to turn the justifiable discontent of the people to their own blackguardly advantage. My threatening missives now have an organized hatred behind them.

"The culmination was reached a month ago in the shocking death of Ames Benton, the first tragedy of the kind that has occurred in America—but not the last I fear. I knew the man; I did business with him; I had talked to him the day before his death. What brought it closer home to me was the fact that Benton was what you'd call a popular man; openhanded, affable, of a kindly nature. If they did this to him, what will my fate be!

"The affair may be forgotten by the time you read this, so I will say Benton was a prominent and wealthy man—though not so rich as I—president and director in many corporations. He was blown to pieces in his bed at night by an anarchist's bomb. The man that threw it likewise lost his life in the explosion. How he succeeded in reaching Mr. Benton's bedroom will always remain a mystery. Among Mr. Benton's effects were found threatening letters similar to those I have received. The assassin's accomplices—it is believed that he must have had accomplices—have never been found.

"This affair has not helped me to sleep better of nights. My courage is of the daylight variety. So long as I can have my eyes open and my wits about me, I am willing to take my chances, but at the thought of being attacked in my bed I confess my heart turns to water. So I have taken my measures.

"The Madagascar Hotel which I was building was all but complete. To secure light and air on the West I had already bought the adjoining dwelling on Forty ——th street. I got it cheap because it had been a private insane asylum and was in bad odor in the neighborhood. The transaction had been effected through agents, and it was not known that I was the owner.

"I had an opening cut between the hotel and this dwelling. By distributing the work among many hands I was able to conceal my eventual purpose from all. The people who put in the steel doors thought that the rear door was to give on a shallow cupboard in the wall. When the doors were in I knocked out this cupboard myself and had a clear way through. Nobody who knew thought it at all out of the way that Silas Gyde should put in a steel vault in connection with his suite in the hotel.

"I have installed myself in a rear room of the old dwelling. The front of the house which has been boarded up for years I was careful not to disturb. Here I can sleep in peace. If the ghosts of the poor insane patients stalk through the halls, they do not trouble me.

"But they may get me yet, of course, and I am writing to put you in possession of all the particulars. I am sure now, that there is a devilishly able brain using the anarchistic agitation to further a blackmailing scheme on a gigantic scale.

"For instance, immediately after poor Benton's death I received a letter threatening me with the same fate, and I have reason to believe that many other rich men received similar letters. I promptly put mine in the hands of the police, as did others, with what result? None, except that I instantly received another letter apprising me that my act was known, and that if I did not immediately cease all dealings with the police I would be shot down in the street.

"I ignored this letter, and three days later I got a bullet through my hat in City Hall Square. The newspapers seemed to take the attitude that it was no more than my due. But the other rich men appreciated the significance of the act, and I have no doubt the blackmailing business was much stimulated thereby. Still the police did nothing, and I resolved to have no more to do with those gentry, but to protect myself.

"Now observe. A week after the attack on me I was called upon in my office by a polite young man who handed me the card of the 'Eureka Protective Association.' His proposition in brief was, that for a stated sum paid every month (four hundred dollars was the amount named) his organization would guarantee to protect me against all threats from Anarchists, and would warn me in advance of any plans that were laid to attempt my life. Since the police had failed to suppress the Reds, he said, his people had succeeded in placing their agents in every circle of anarchists, to take note of and report on all their activities.

"Ingenious, was it not? I could well imagine that many of my timorous wealthy acquaintances would fall for it eagerly after all the agitations of the past few weeks. But to me it smelled rank of blackmail. It seemed to me that if I once submitted, the impost would promptly be doubled, trebled, quadrupled, and instead of securing peace I would be letting myself in for a life of continuous alarms. I might as well die at once. Anyhow, I thought, it wasn't possible that every rich man would submit, and they couldn't very well assassinate us all. My chance was as good as another's.

"So I turned the polite young man down, and took my own measures. I closed my office down-town, and carried my business under my hat, as they say. I traded impartially through every broker in town. I have moved into my retreat in the old house, and venture out only by daylight, keeping to the crowded streets. The secret of my sleeping-place is still a secret I am sure. I have had no more threatening letters, and I hope they have crossed me off their lists as a hopeless prospect. But if they do get me, you will know all the circumstances."

The next entry had been made nine months later.

"My dear boy:

"The long evenings are hard to get through. My eyes tire with reading, and my thoughts are not cheering. I have tried playing solitaire, but it seems like the last resource of the feeble-minded. I have got me a little dog for company, picked him up half-starved, but he's a great sleepyhead.

"I think of you more and more. I wish I dared go to you and make myself known. But I have put it off too long. I know now that I shall never go. This is the only medium I can use to communicate with you. You will know me after I am gone. Who knows, perhaps I shall have left a friend here after all."

Several pages of good advice followed here; cynical, humorous, friendly, out of the old millionaire's store of experience. A very different Silas Gyde was revealed from him the world knew. But for the moment Jack skimmed over this part hastily in his anxiety to learn more of the facts bearing on his benefactor's end.

The last entry was only three days old.

"Three years have now elapsed since I told you of the first threats against my life. The threats have been renewed from time to time. That I am still above ground is due to no lack of effort on the part of my enemy, I am sure. More and more I feel that one man is behind it all. One attempt has been made on my life that I know of, and no doubt others. My supposed room in the Madagascar has been entered. But my real abiding-place is still my secret, I believe.

"Now I want to tell you of a new direction their activities have taken.

"About three weeks ago in the flock of begging letters that assail me every day there was one which caught my attention. It purported to be from a young girl struggling to make her way in New York as a visiting stenographer, and asked me if I could give her occasional work. An affecting note of simplicity seemed to distinguish it from the usual type of such letters. 'Why shouldn't even Silas Gyde do a good act?' I asked myself, and sent for her to come to the public writing room of the hotel.

"Previous to that I had been dictating to public stenographers wherever I happened to drop in. They didn't know me of course, and thus my business secrets were safeguarded. So you see it was at somewhat of a sacrifice that I engaged my pretty petitioner.

"She was extremely pretty, and seemingly well-bred. Her modest manner carried out the promise of her letter. Perhaps I am not sufficiently experienced with the sex. No man ever fooled me for long. For two weeks she came every day that I needed her. She was not a very expert stenographer but filled my simple demands. I noticed on her part a willingness to enter into more personal relations with her employer, but I didn't blame her for that, poor girl. A hundred millions I supposed was enough to sugar even such an old pill as Silas Gyde.

"But a week ago in amongst the bundle of completed letters she left with me, had been slipped by chance the page of a letter she had been writing on her own account. The beginning was missing, but the piece I had was sufficiently significant. I will paste it below."

The inserted typewritten page read as follows:

"*—where the old man sleeps. You say you are sure he doesn't occupy his bed in the Madagascar, but I haven't been able to find out anything to the contrary. Apparently he comes down from his room to give me dictation. He never has me up there, though I have complained about the noise down-stairs, etc. I got in touch with the chambermaid that does up his room, as you suggested. She doesn't suspect that the bed is not slept in every night. I understood that she has to make it up in the mornings, like all the other beds. So I think you are mistaken in saying that suite is a blind. Give me a little more time and I will make sure through one of the clerks (with whom I am friendly) if S.G. has another suite somewhere in the hotel.*

M.C.

Silas Gyde's ms. resumed:

"When my young lady came the following day I observed a certain anxiety in her glance. Evidently she was not sure where she had lost that tell-tale paper. She sounded me discreetly. I was careful to show her an unchanged front, and she finally made up her mind that I had not seen it. I continued to give her work just as before, and after several days quietly dropped her. That was yesterday.

"This incident has made me thoughtful of course, showing how close they had come to my secret. They may get me at any time. If they do, they will most assuredly transfer their attentions to you as soon as it is published that you are my heir. Therefore I wish you to be armed with all the information possible.

"The name this precious young lady gave me was Beatrice Blackstone. That means nothing of course. But her good looks were really notable, even to my dim old eyes, and I will try to give you a description that will put you on your guard, should she ever bring her fascinations to bear on you.

"She said she was twenty-three, but seemed in unguarded moments to be a good five or six years older. She was a brunette with lustrous, wavy chestnut hair and hazel eyes of extraordinary size and brilliancy. By hazel I mean gray eyes with a rim of brown around the iris. With me she played a demure part, but there were moments when I saw that she could do the haughty and imperious too. She was tall for a woman, about five feet seven I should say, and of a very elegant figure which seemed slimmer than it was. Weight about a hundred and thirty-five. She walked with a peculiar undulating motion, bobbing her head slightly with each step. When she was taking dictation I noticed on the index finger of her right hand a large pale mole, round in shape and of the bigness of a button on a woman's glove. So much for Beatrice Blackstone.

"I find that the pleasure of writing to you is growing on me and I mean to make a regular thing of it hereafter."

Those were the last words.

6

Jack sat staring at the letter he had just read, deeply stirred by feelings new to him. Youth generally is profoundly unaware of the hearts of the aged. The feeling is that the old have had their day, have cooled off and hardened, and practically ceased to exist. It came with a shock of surprise to Jack to learn that an old man might be misunderstood, bitter, hungry for affection—just the same as a young one.

"Poor old fellow!" he murmured. "He thought of me a lot! He was good to me. And I never knew. If I had known him I might have made his last days easier. I might have prevented what happened."

Hard on these softer feelings rose a slow tide of anger. "Oh, the devils! To think up such a fiend's game! And then to get away with it! It's too much for an honest man to stand! I wish I could pay them off! ... I *will* pay them off. I have power now. That shall be my job. If I live I'll square this account!"

He registered his vow with an involuntary glance upward at his mother's portrait. It seemed to him that the wistful face softened on him in approval.

The impulse to action brought Jack to his feet. Peeping through the curtains he saw that darkness had fallen outside.

"Good Lord!" he thought astonished. "How long have I been here!"

His watch informed him that it was eight o'clock. He picked up the lamp, and with a last look around the strange room turned to leave. He had a feeling that that place marked a turning point in his life. He would never again be quite the light-hearted boy that had entered it.

He had forgotten the dog. The little beast seeing his purpose, and terrified of being left alone again, threw himself against Jack's legs in a desperate appeal to be taken along.

Jack stooped to caress him. "Poor old fellow!" he said. "I wonder how long it is since you saw the light of the sun. I can't take you now, honest I can't. But you be patient. I'll be back to-morrow."

But the tiny animal thrust himself into Jack's embrace and would not be denied. Jack finally picked him up and thrust him in his coat pocket. He settled down quite contentedly, only his nozzle and his bright eyes showing.

"Well I guess you must be accustomed to this mode of travel," said Jack. "I'm going to call you Jumbo because that's not your name."

Carefully locking all the doors behind him, he left the lamp in the hotel sitting-room, and made his way out by the private entrance. His impulse was to seek his own hall bedroom, the nearest thing to home that he knew, and there alone, amidst familiar surroundings, to try to bring some order out of his whirling thoughts.

Jack's boarding house was in the West Forties near Eighth avenue, in the center of that vast colony of boarders. His way from the Madagascar lay up Broadway for three short blocks, then westward for a long one. He passed through the throng hurrying theaterward without seeing anybody; he forgot that he had had no dinner; he forgot that his pocket was full of money and was tempted by none of the alluring show-windows.

The burden of his thoughts was: "It's a big job! A big job! I can't afford to make any mistake at the start!"

In front of a corner newsstand he was brought up all standing by a glimpse of the staring headlines of the night editions.

HEIR TO THE GYDE MILLIONS FOUND IN A HALL BEDROOM

A POOR BOY IS ENRICHED BEYOND THE DREAMS OF AVARICE

Old Romance in the Dead Millionaire's Life Revealed

Jack bought several papers, and standing in a doorway out of the press of the crowd, experienced the first wonderful thrill of finding himself famous. There is nothing else quite like it. How you became famous is a secondary matter. To find yourself on the first page is enough: to see the shape of your name in print. Many a good head has been turned for life by it.

All the papers offered sensational versions of Jack's story, more or less accurate. It had apparently been given out at Delamare's office in the first place, and so far they had it pretty straight. But they went on to embroider it. The more reckless sheets even printed interviews which caused Jack to grind his teeth, they made him out such a fool. One paper printed an alleged photograph, but it was a safely fuzzy photograph that might have been taken for almost anybody. They had discovered the address of his boarding-house, but in his absence his landlady, Mrs. Regan, had refused to be drawn out.

"Good old girl!" thought Jack.

The soberer sheets promised an interview in later editions.

"They're looking for me now!" thought Jack.

Being human, Jack could not but feel a pleasurable thrill, but his head was not quite turned. He glanced at the hurrying passers-by whimsically.

"They wouldn't rush by so fast if they knew this was he," he thought. But he had no intention of calling their attention to the fact. Silas Gyde's reference to the danger of too much publicity was present in his mind.

He turned into his own street keeping a wary eye ahead. Mrs. Regan's boarding house was three-quarters of the way down the block, one of a long row of dwellings with little grass plots in front and iron railings. Sure enough by the light of a street lamp Jack made out the figures of a group of men at her gate. As he came closer he saw that several of them carried cameras with flash light attachments.

His first impulse was to flee, but recollecting that they could not possibly know yet what he looked like, he walked boldly up to the group, and asked the New Yorker's stock question of a street crowd:

"Somepin the matter here?"

One replied: "This where Jack Norman lives. We're waitin' for him to come home."

He was already so famous no further explanation was deemed necessary.

"Gee!" said Jack with a glance at the shabby façade. "I guess he'll soon be moving."

A laugh greeted this witty sally.

"Oh boy!" groaned one youth. "Think of having a hundred millions handed you, just like that. It's too much!"

A photographer said: "Well, I'm gonna ast him for one million. He'd never miss it."

"What like fellow is he?" asked Jack.

"Same aged guy as us."

"Worked for twelve per until this morning. Say his old boss was sore as a pup when he heard what he come in for."

"They say he's a bad actor all right."

"Sure, a whale! They say he's already burned up Broadway from Herald Square to the Circle."

"You're wrong, fellow! I heard his roll's as adhesive as rubber tape. Same as the old man's before him. Wouldn't even pry off a nickel to give the poor boy who told him the news."

"Say, when a guy once gets in the papers, scandal begins!" said Jack disgustedly. Seeing Mrs. Regan at her parlor window, and fearful that she might give him away, he walked on.

From a drug-store on Eighth avenue he telephoned back to Mrs. Regan, asking her to come to him there. "Don't let anything on to those guys at the gate," he warned her. "I want to keep out of sight for a few days."

She came into the store in a breathless state of fluster. She was a good-hearted Irishwoman of considerable energy of character and a racy style of speech. But at present she was considerably overcome.

"Oh, Mr. Norman! Oh, Mr. Norman!" she gasped.

"Easy with my name!" warned Jack. "I'm going to be Mr. Robinson for awhile now."

"Is it true what they say in the papers?"

"More or less."

"Oh law! To think of anything like this happening in my house! And the third floor rear hall at that! But that's always the way ain't it, like a story like? The telephone's been going like a Big Ben ever since twelve o'clock, asking for you. And you such a pleasant ordinary young fellow—not to say ordinary-like, but not stuck up at all, just like one of us!" She paused for breath.

"Easy, Mrs. Regan," whispered Jack. "That clerk's got ears like a water pitcher."

"I'll be careful. What did you want of me, Mr. Nor—Robinson?"

"First, I want you to know my friend Jumbo," said Jack, handing him over. "Let him have my eats while I'm away."

"Laws! Ain't he cute!"

"I'll telephone in every little while for news. Please pack up my things for me. I'll tell you later where to send them."

"You're going to leave!" cried Mrs. Regan. "But of course it's natural," she added quickly.

"Don't you make any mistake," said Jack. "I'm not going to forget any of the friends who knew me when I was poor."

"I done my best for you! But with prices the way they is——!"

"I know. Now I want you to promise not to give out a thing about me, no descriptions of me, no information of any kind. I know it will be hard to resist those taking young reporters, but I ask it as a favor."

"Oh, Mr. N—Robinson! Go on! At my age!— It's little they'll get out of me, I can tell you!"

"I knew I could bank on you. I'll tell you all about it some day. I've got to beat it now."

"Good-by. Oh—wait! I almost forgot. I'm that excited! A messenger boy left a note for you at the door this evening. I brought it along."

Jack took the note and left. Mrs. Regan, a little disappointed at not being taken further into his confidence, turned in the other direction. When she was out of sight, Jack stopped under a street lamp and examined what she had given him.

It was a cheap, flimsy envelope much soiled. The address was scrawled in an illiterate hand. He opened it, and this was what he read:

"*Jack Norman*:

"*We don't call you dear sir, because this ain't no friendly letter. We know all about you. We're the gang what croaked old Silas Gyde, and we're going to get you next, see? You needn't think you're going to be let to blow in his tainted money. You millionaires are a dirty disgrace, and we're going to rid the country of you. You can't hide away from us. We are everywhere. Gun, knife, bomb or dope: it's all the same to us. And if you show this to the police you'll only get yours quicker.*

"*The Red Gang.*"

Jack's young face turned grim. "So it's begun!" he thought. "Well, I'm just as glad they didn't keep me in suspense. I'm ready to start. We'll see who's got the best set of wits!"

7

Jack, forbidden the refuge of his own little room, continued to walk the streets, while he debated how best to meet the complicated situation that faced him. Stumbling at last on Bryant Park in his wanderings, he dropped on a bench. His eyes moved sightlessly over the scene before him.

"Once the newspaper guys get hold of me, and print my picture on the front page, I'm a marked man," he was thinking, "I couldn't walk down the street then, without a crowd following. It would be a cinch for this gang to keep tab on me, and a fat chance I'd have of getting anything on them. So I've got to keep out of the papers if I can. That's decided.

"But it's not going to be so easy. For the more of a mystery I make of myself the hotter they'll get on my trail. A paper like the *Sphere*, I suppose, would spend a hundred thousand to run me down. What I ought to do is to get some harmless young fellow to take the part of Jack Norman, while I lie low and do my work."

"Who could I get in our gang? There's Bill Endicott; good fellow, but too much of a talker, specially with a girl. He'd never do. There's Joe Welland, he's close enough—but too thick. He couldn't take a part any more than a bronze statue. They say Stan Larkin and I look alike. He might do. No! He's too hard-headed. He wouldn't do what I wanted. It's too risky anyhow to let one of the gang in on this. The others would have to know. I'd better keep away from them for the present."

Jack's reflections were interrupted by an appeal from alongside: "Say, fella, can you help a fella to a meal?"

He became aware for the first that he shared the bench with another. It was a fat youth of about his own age with an expression at once piteous and absurd. There is bound to be something ludicrous in the spectacle of a fat beggar. Chubby cheeks were designed to wear a good-natured smile. The shame-faced look that accompanied the appeal did not suggest the professional beggar in this case.

Jack had reached the point where he was glad of a diversion. His thoughts had begun to chase themselves in circles. "What's the trouble, 'Bo?" he asked in friendly fashion.

"Down on my luck, that's all. I'm an actor. Got a job to walk on in a big show called 'Ulysses.' Rehearsed three weeks and then they flivved. I had borrowed every cent I could on the job, and now I dassent be seen where my friends are. I'm done! Ain't eaten since yesterday. Say, it's Hell for a fat man to be hungry!"

Jack laughed. Moreover the word "hunger" started something insistent in his own internals. He dropped a further consideration of his problems until that should be satisfied.

"By Gad! That reminds me I haven't had any dinner myself! Come on, let's see what we can find."

"You mean it!"

"Where'll we go."

"There's Little's over here on Sixth."

"To Hell with Little's! I'm fed up on beaneries. It would take a hundred of Little's little portions to fill me. No, I got money 'Bo! Us for the big eats. Let's try that swell French café on the south side of the square. The French know how to eat."

"Ahh! They wouldn't serve a guy like me in there!"

"Well, the clothing stores over on Broadway are open yet. Let's go and get you an outfit. An actor's got to show his Tuppenheimers they say, before he can pull down a salary."

"Ahh! You're stringin' me!"

"Come along! I got a wad that's burning a hole in my jeans! I might as well blow it on you!"

The fat youth made up his mind that Jack had been drinking. He had an open countenance, and upon it was clearly visible his thankfulness to Heaven for sending such a one his way. As Jack started off he took his arm, either with the idea of guiding his footsteps, or in fear that he might escape. His anxious glance, prepared for any sudden, unfavorable change in the weather, never left Jack's face. He even pretended for the sake of camaraderie to be a little spiffed himself.

Jack was vastly tickled by the whole incident. It gave him a new luxurious sensation of opulence. Besides, he had reached the point where he felt he had to blow off a little steam.

"What a fool I was to worry myself to a standstill! Too much thinking is worse than none at all. If you mull over a thing too long, your thoughts begin to go round like a squirrel in a revolving cage. Here's the whole town open to us! We'll have us a time and forget our troubles!"

The fat youth who had no idea of the nature of these troubles made haste to agree. "You're dead right, fellow! Eat, drink and be merry, as the poet says, for to-morrow the rent falls due!"

"What's your name?" asked Jack.

"Private or professional?"

"Oh, anything you like."

"Well, I'm generally known as Guy Harmsworth."

"Some name, 'Bo!"

However, the really significant names seem to come out of the air. Jack started calling his friend 'Bo. From that it was but a little step to Bobo. In the sound of Bobo there was something subtly descriptive. It stuck. He is Bobo still.

As they entered the big clothing store Jack said: "Get the best. I'll stand for it."

Bobo thus encouraged, proved to have a very nice taste in wearing apparel. They bought hurriedly, for the pangs of hunger were pressing. But when the main articles, suit, hat, shoes, were out of the way both young men plunged in the smaller and more luxurious articles; shirts of heavy silk that crinkled richly between thumb and finger; wonderful cravats that would almost stand alone. Few youngsters attain their desires in this direction, and Bobo and Jack, long denied, fairly wallowed. They each bought a valise to carry away their surplus purchases.

In half an hour Bobo was transformed. To call Bobo fat was merely to indicate his type. He was not all over the place, but a well set-up youngster of a rather melting style of beauty, which promised obesity later perhaps, but in youth was not unpleasing. At least not in his new clothes.

When finally Jack produced the roll of yellow backs to pay for what they had bought, Bobo's look of anxiety disappeared and was not seen again. A little sigh escaped him. It was as if he had said:

"It is not a dream."

Bobo leaving the outfitters was metamorphosed in more than his apparel. He stuck his chest out now, and looked passers-by in the eye. A stage-English accent crept into his unadorned Manhattanese. Jack seeing him cast sheep's-eyes at a stand of walking-sticks, purchased him a yellow malacca, such as his own soul had hankered after earlier in the day. It was the finishing touch. Bobo swung it with a delightful arrogance. He even adopted a certain condescension of tone towards Jack who had no stick.

"I say, old chap, these togs are really not half bad for ready-made, what! Not what a London tailor would turn out of course. But they fit, because I happen to have a normal figure."

"Perfect forty-six," murmured Jack.

They returned for their dinner to the famous café on Bryant Square. It was the first eating-place in New York that dared to veil its interior from the vulgar gaze. Those alluring, closely-drawn pink curtains cause the envious poor to suspect the delightful worst. It is not so well known in the provinces as flashier resorts, but it is certainly the place where most New Yorkers go first when they get money.

When they finally penetrated the mystery the plainness of the interior was rather disappointing, and the place was almost empty for it was half way between the dinner and the supper hours. But the food when it came justified the café's great reputation.

Jack had ordered blindly from the French *carte-de-jour*, choosing the most expensive dish from each subdivision; *Petite Marmite; Cotelotte des Ecrivisses au diable; Filet Mignon au Moelle: pommes de terre Florizel; Choux-fleur hollandaise; plombière*, etc. The result was eminently satisfactory. Bobo groaned with delight. It appeared that Bobo had a special and particular talent for eating.

"Don't wake me! Don't wake me!" he prayed. "Many's the time I've dreamed of this, but it was always snatched away just as I sat down. Say, are we going to have coffee and cigars?"

"Sure thing. Fifty centers."

"O Lord, let me sleep till then and afterwards. You can do what you like to me!"

"You seem to have a nice taste in fancy eats," said Jack.

"A nice taste! I was born with the tongue of an epicure, a delicate tongue, a high-toned tongue! For me to be obliged to eat in lunch wagons and beaneries was a crime against nature!"

"Well, how would you like to keep this up for a while?" said Jack with an offhand air.

"Hey?" said Bobo opening his eyes.

Jack studied him. "He's something of a fool," he thought. "But maybe that's what I need. I couldn't control a hard-headed guy. And he's an actor. He ought to be able to play a part. And he'd be grateful for his meals, I could do what I wanted with him. Anyhow I have to take a chance, and I might do worse."

"What d'ye mean, keep it up?" demanded Bobo.

"This is only a sample," said Jack. "How would you like the real thing for a while; a suite of rooms at the Madagascar; a yacht, a motor car—— Oh, half a dozen motors; all the clothes you wanted from the best tailor in America; as for the eats—all you'd have to do would be press a button and give your order."

Bobo turned a little pale. "What are you getting at?"

"Supposing a man offered you this, would you be willing to put yourself in his hands?"

"Say, if it was on the level, he could do what he wanted with me!" said Bobo fervently.

"All right!" said Jack. "It's a go!"

Bobo stared. "Say, fellow, what kind of a pipe are you giving me? Do you mean you are offering me—— Are you crazy?"

"Did you read the afternoon papers?" asked Jack.

Bobo nodded. "Fellow left his on a bench beside me."

"You've never asked me my name."

"What is it?"

"Jack Norman."

Bobo stared speechless. "On the level?" he gasped.

Jack took a couple of letters from his pocket and showed him the superscriptions.

"Jack Norman!" said Bobo. "Then what were you loafing in the park by yourself for?"

"Trying to get accustomed to the idea."

Bobo had no more to say. He had lost the condescending air.

"Here's the situation," said Jack. "For certain reasons which I will explain to you, I want to keep under cover for a while. I want to keep my picture out of the papers. I don't want to be pointed out and followed wherever I go. Well, the easiest way to escape notice is for me to get some fellow to take my place, see?"

"But everybody who knows you will know I'm not the real guy."

"That's all right. We won't be moving in the same circles as I used to. Want to do it?"

"Do I want to do it——!"

"Wait a minute. It's only fair to warn you that old Silas Gyde was croaked by a gang of blackmailers, and they're after me now."

Bobo paled and hesitated.

"But I mean to meet all their demands until we nail them, so there's not much danger."

Bobo's face cleared. "Will I do it——" he began again.

"Hold on! There are two conditions. You must promise to do everything I tell you. And second, you are not to marry any woman under false pretences."

"I promise," said Bobo.

"Good! It's a bargain. From this moment you are John Farrow Norman, the newly-made millionaire, and I am plain Jack Robinson, your secretary."

They shook hands across the table.

8

As the two young men left the café Bobo said: "Where are we going now?"

"First we must find quarters," said Jack. "We don't want to carry these valises around all night."

To the chauffeur who opened the taxi door for them Jack said: "Hotel Madagascar."

"My God!" murmured the still dazed Bobo.

As they entered the gorgeous lobby of the famous hotel Bobo was overcome with self-consciousness. Bobo had always thought of the Madagascar as the abiding place of remote and exalted aristocrats. He slunk at Jack's heels with the yellow stick trailing limply.

"Buck up! Buck up!" whispered Jack. "Remember you are the cheese, and I'm only the mite that lives off it."

"Sure! Sure!" murmured Bobo, moistening his lips.

He made an effort, but quailed again before the sharp-eyed bell-boys. Jack reflected that since he was only supposed to be the millionaire of a day, this would appear natural enough.

"Sign the register," he whispered. "Remember you are John Farrow Norman, and I am John Robinson."

Bobo accomplished this all right. As the clerk nonchalantly spun the card around and read the name, he caught his breath slightly, and a wonderful silkiness crept into his voice.

"Very pleased to have you with us, sir. In a way I hope it's like coming home."

The other men behind the desk, arrested by the note of exceeding deference, made excuses to sidle past and glance at the register. Instantly a kind of electric current charged the office, and was presently communicated to the bell-boys' bench, whence it spread throughout the lobby. "It's Jack Norman," the busy whisper went around.

"I hope you're going to remain with us permanently, Mr. Norman," added the clerk. "What accommodations will you require?"

Bobo, child of nature, rebounded like a rubber ball, feeling the immense respect conveyed by the whole surrounding atmosphere. Once more the chest went out, and the yellow stick was elevated to the ceiling.

"—Er—my secretary will arrange the details with you," he drawled, turning away languidly. One could see his fingers absently feeling for the monocle which ought to have been dangling against his waistcoat button.

Jack stepped forward, modest and business-like. "Mr. Norman wishes to know if the suite occupied by the late Mr. Gyde is available."

"It's empty, I suppose," was the deprecating reply, "but that is outside my province. I assure you the rooms are very undesirable. Mr. Gyde, you know, was most eccentric."

"But Mr. Norman has been told there was a steel vault in connection, which he thought might be useful."

"Naturally. Naturally. Yes, Mr. Gyde had it installed when the hotel was built. But there are only two rooms in the suite, and it does not communicate directly with any other. Moreover the bedroom is quite dark. It wouldn't do at all."

"Hm!" said Jack. "I suppose not."

"But on the same floor, practically adjoining you might say, there is a magnificent corner-suite of six rooms—the finest in the house. People call it the State suite. Prince Boris occupied it on his recent visit, and the President of Managuay always reserves it."

The apparently indifferent Bobo's ears stretched at this.

"The famous Louis Quinze salon with ceilings by Guglielmetti is included in this suite, and the Dutch dining-room decorated by Troward Handler Misty. Each of the bedrooms is done in a different period. I assure you there is nothing like it in New York. It extends all the way down the south side of the building, and it is only a matter of cutting diagonally across the corridor to reach the late Mr. Gyde's suite, which occupies the back corner of that floor. Those rooms belong to Mr. Norman anyway since they were exempted from our lease. Together with the state suite they would make—but let me have the pleasure of showing them to you."

"What do you think, Mr. Norman?" asked Jack respectfully.

"Oh, take them," said Bobo. "We can change later, if we're not suited." He gave the yellow stick a twirl.

"Certainly, sir."

Having been shown up to their magnificent quarters, Jack firmly dismissed the train of admiring clerks, bell boys and maids who overwhelmed them with attentions. Bobo was bearing himself with admirable nonchalance, but Jack thought he saw signs of a coming crack under the strain. There was something comically disproportionate in the relation of their two little selves and their two little valises to that endless suite.

"Our baggage will come to-morrow," Jack casually remarked.

When they were left alone in the Louis Quinze salon panelled in blue brocade, they looked around, and they looked at each other.

"Some li'l sittin'-room," said Jack.

"My God!" cried Bobo. "An hour ago I was sitting on a bench in Bryant Square with my stomach deflated like a punctured tube!"

"Some rapid rise."

Bobo gravely butted his head against the blue satin brocade. "Sure if I was asleep, that would wake me up."

"Oh, cheer up! We couldn't both be having the same dream together."

"That's true!" said Bobo, looking wonderfully relieved.

"Let's go into the next room," said Jack. "Louis Quinze isn't homelike."

Entering the Dutch room, he said: "This is rather classy. We can have some nice little parties in here."

"I wish it was time to eat again," said Bobo with sudden recollection. "What a lot of time we waste digesting!"

They were presently informed over the telephone that Mr. Pope of the *Sphere* and Mr. Wallis of the *Constellation* requested a word or two with Mr. Norman.

"The news of our arrival wasted no time in leaking out," remarked Jack.

Looking Bobo over thoughtfully, he decided that further coaching was necessary before the pseudo-millionaire could safely be thrown to the reporters. So he sent down word that Mr. Norman was out, and to avoid possible encounters in the lobby, he and Bobo made their way out by the rear door of the state suite and thence by Silas Gyde's private stair to the entrance on the side street.

At the Broadway corner they paused. The sight of the double procession of automobiles started a new train of desires.

"They ought to keep the automobile show-rooms open all night," said Jack. "A fellow wants to buy a car most after dinner. I shan't really believe I am a millionaire—I mean that you are, until we have a snaky red roadster with twelve cylinders and a searchlight."

"I'd rather have a limousine with blue upholstery and a chauffeur in blue livery to take the responsibility," said Bobo.

"Oh, go as far as you like! Where will we go now?"

"How about the Alpine Heights?"

"Lead me to it!"

This place of entertainment was on the roof of one of the theaters. A discreet privacy shrouded the street entrance. They were whirled aloft in an elevator, and a small army of silver-buttoned boys and lace-capped maids relieved them of their outer wear. The restaurant opened before them like a dream, warm with perfume and color and softened light. It was arranged like a shallow bowl. The bottom of it was a velvety dancing-floor, and all around were low terraces of tables. Overhead was a balcony, and one end of the place was closed by a great curtain. When this was lifted a sheet of glittering ice was revealed. The whole place exhaled luxury like the palace of a satrap.

"What a background for the lovely girls!" said Jack. "But the black coats and pants are out of place here."

"Oh, I don't know!" said Bobo, strutting a little.

Jack's sharp eyes perceived that the first and lowest row of tables was by a process of judicious selection on the part of the head-waiter, filled with the elite of the "Broadway crowd," the women exquisite with their bare shoulders and jewels, the men looking bored and superior as is expected of super-men. These people, as the cunning management of the restaurant well knew, formed the real attraction to the soberer folk from out of town, who sat further back drinking it all in with innocent big eyes. They thought these fine folk must be Astorbilts or Vandergelds, whereas they were more likely Follies of the Circus and Handsome Harries in funds.

The headwaiter with a shrewd glance at the two young men started to lead them to an obscure corner (young men unaccompanied do not spend much) but Jack with a cough attracted his attention and with discreet motion effected a transfer to his ready hand. Whereupon after heavy study, the majordomo affected to discover a vacant table in the second row. The rail of the balcony was over their heads.

Bobo seized on the bill-of-fare. "I'm hungry again!" he cried in the tone of one making an unexpected and delightful discovery. "Can I order anything I want?"

"Go to it, son!"

"How about champagne? I never tasted it," he added naïvely.

"What! Never tasted champagne!"

Bobo blushed painfully.

"Well, I never did either," said Jack, grinning. "One bottle because this is a party. But mind you, the limit is always one bottle. We've got head work to do."

"Sure, that's right," said Bobo, but without any great conviction, and Jack reflected that along with his other pre-occupations he would have to keep an eye on his partner's potations.

Bobo went into conference with the waiter, and in due course a little Lucullan feast was spread before them. It may be remarked in passing, that where his stomach was concerned Bobo proved to be an astonishingly apt scholar. Within a week he was a menu-card-sharp, and within a month the intimate friend of every head-waiter on Broadway.

Meanwhile the great curtain was lifted, and enchanting slender-legged damsels, in chiffons and furs, performed amazing and graceful evolutions on the ice. Between times, the diners danced on the waxed floor. The teasing music made Jack think of Kate. He looked across the table with distaste.

"What wouldn't I give to have her there instead of that greedy Bobo," he thought. "Lord! I suppose I'm saddled with him now, by day and by night!"

During a pause in the music a small object dropped on their table, bounced and lay still. It was a piece of paper folded into a pellet.

"A note!" said Bobo excitedly. "We've made a hit with somebody. Is it for you or me do you think?"

"You can have my share," said Jack indifferently.

Bobo eagerly opened the paper, while Jack's attention strayed over the crowd. He wasn't going to allow the writer of the note to see that the receipt of it excited him at all, like the foolish Bobo, whose hands actually were trembling.

Jack's glance was sharply recalled by an odd little sound from his partner. Bobo's ruddy cheeks had paled, and his mouth was hanging open stupidly.

"Read it," he gasped, handing the note over.

It was not what Jack expected. There was no salutation.

"We have picked up your trail now, and don't you think we'll ever let it go. When one of us drops it, there will be another handy to pick it up. When the time comes we'll strike, and there will be another rotten millionaire the less to sweat the poor. You will offer a good-size mark. You needn't think your skinny secretary will be any protection. A hundred like him wouldn't save you.

"The Red Gang."

While the tone of the note was the same as the other, this had been written by an educated hand. Jack looked sharply around the nearby tables. No face betrayed any self-consciousness. Behind them sat an honest couple from the suburbs; in front was a party of eight in evening dress, the men silly from too much champagne, the women bored and listless; at their right was a young couple, wholly and completely absorbed in each other; at their left, across an aisle, a gay old gentleman and a languid lady of the chorus—it seemed hard to credit that the note could have come from any of these.

"What shall we do?" murmured Bobo tremulously.

"Laugh at it, and let the sender see us laughing," said Jack, suiting the action to the word.

"It seemed to drop straight down," thought Bobo.

"The balcony!" thought Jack. He rose without any appearance of haste and made his way up-stairs. He had no difficulty in picking out the table that was just over their heads. It was now empty. The napkins lay where they had been dropped. He summoned the waiter.

"Who sat at that table?"

The man cringed to the authoritative air. "An elderly couple, sir. Never saw them before."

"Describe them."

"Plain people, sir. Quietly dressed. But very genteel and liberal."

This seemed to be about the best the waiter could do, even with the stimulus of a generous tip. He did add that the old gentleman wore a heavy gray mustache and small imperial.

"They have just gone?" said Jack.

"Just took the elevator, sir."

Jack returned to Bobo.

"What shall we do?" said the fat youth again.

"Oh, cheer up! Everything's going fine! Don't you see they've swallowed my bait whole. They think *you're* the millionaire!"

"That's fine for you," said Bobo, looking around nervously, "but where do I get off at?"

9

Next morning the delights of purchasing automobiles had to be put off a while longer to allow of some necessary business to be transacted. Jack wanted to secure Mr. Delamare's approval for his new plans. For obvious reasons he did not care to take Bobo to the bank, so he called up the financier, and asked him respectfully if he would mind coming to the hotel.

A laugh answered him over the wire. "Would I mind! My dear boy! A banker would go to Tallapoosa to oblige a customer with an account like yours!"

While they waited for him they breakfasted in the Dutch room. Bobo's appetite showed no evil effects resulting from his scare of the night before. During the meal the card of a visitor was brought them.

H. J. WHIGHAM
The Eureka Protective Association

"Ha!" cried Jack. "Exactly according to schedule!"

"What's that?" asked Bobo.

"Last night we got the rough stuff, to-day the smooth."

"I don't understand."

"Keep your ears open, and you'll see. Just let your little secretary deal with this gent for you."

Jack asked that Mr. Whigham be sent up. A old-young man was shown into them, a starched and ironed little fellow with an air of self-importance like a cock-sparrow's.

"If this is a dangerous crook," thought Jack, "he's got a dam clever line of comedy. Looks like a neck-tie clerk."

"Mr. Norman?" inquired the newcomer with a bird-like quirk of the head from one to another.

Jack waved his hand in Bobo's direction.

"Mr. Norman, I have a proposition to make to you."

"My secretary will talk to you," said Bobo with the drawl he now affected.

He went on with his breakfast and the reading of the newspaper—but missed nothing of what was said. Jack had been well-advised in keeping from him that there was any connection between Mr. Whigham and the Red Gang. Bobo could scarcely have maintained that air of nonchalance, had he known it.

"What can we do for you?" asked Jack politely "Excuse me if I go on with my breakfast. We were up late last night."

"Don't mention it," said Mr. Whigham. "I am early. I came early on purpose, because I thought later you would be besieged by cranks and triflers of all kinds. I have a genuine proposition to make Mr. Norman. It is one I felt ought to get to him without a moment's delay."

"Open it."

Mr. Whigham talked smoothly, and at considerable length. It had the effect of something well-rehearsed. Jack, as we know, had it all beforehand. Only the essential parts of his spiel need be given.

"Both of you gentlemen are no doubt aware of the great increase of anarchistic activity in this country of recent years."

At the word "anarchistic" Bobo started, and let the newspaper sink to the table.

"The police of this and other cities have worked hard to check this evil. They watch the Reds as well as they are able; close up their meeting-places—when they find them; arrest them on the least shadow of evidence. This is all right as far as it goes—understand, gentlemen, I am not knocking the police; but the fact remains that the horrible outrages continue. I need not speak of the latest one which concerns Mr. Norman so closely."

"The police method is like treating an ulcer with external applications only. You may heal it up, but it will only break out in another place. Now the Eureka Association was formed three years ago to deal with the matter from another angle. Not in opposition to the police, nor in alliance with them, but quite independently. We never inform on the Reds nor prosecute them."

"You make friends with them?" suggested Jack.

"In a way, yes. Our agents become Reds; join their circles, watch them, and report to the main office as to the plots they hatch. Our organization has now been brought to such a point of perfection that we are in a position to guarantee our subscribers absolute immunity from the attacks of anarchists."

"Was the late Mr. Gyde a member?" Jack asked slyly.

"He was not," said Mr. Whigham significantly. "He had rejected our respectful solicitations from time to time. Nevertheless out of pure humanity we warned him of what was about to occur. With characteristic obstinacy he ignored the warning—well, you know what happened."

"But they say that Emil Jansen, his assailant, was not a member of any regular circle."

"'They say!'" said Mr. Whigham sarcastically. "What do 'they' know!"

"What's the damage?" asked Jack.

"Hey?" said Mr. Whigham.

"What does the service cost?"

"Five hundred dollars a month."

Jack whistled. "There's nothing small about you."

Mr. Whigham earnestly pointed out the tremendous expenses attached to the association, including enormous salaries paid to the special agents to recompense them for the risks they ran.

"Why did you say you wanted to get to us without loss of time?"

"We are informed that a plot is already hatching against Mr. Norman. The Reds aim to make a spectacular double play by getting Mr. Gyde's successor."

Bobo gasped and looked imploringly at Jack.

"And if Mr. Norman pays up the five hundred you'll give the plot away?" Jack suggested dryly.

"No, sir," was the instant reply. "My instructions are to give you what information we have in any case. The Eureka is something more than a sordid money-making concern. It supplies a real service to the community. For a reference I am instructed to give you the name of Mr. Walter Delamare, who is well-known to you."

"Hm!" thought Jack. "This scheme is even cleverer than I expected." Aloud he asked: "What is the information you have?"

"That a man will be waiting this morning to attack Mr. Norman on the steps of the New York National Bank. Mr. Norman is advised not to visit Mr. Delamare's office for the time being."

"Good God!" said Bobo.

"What is your pleasure in the matter?" Jack asked Bobo with a respectful air.

"Oh, pay him! Pay him!" was the agitated reply.

A pleased faraway look appeared in Mr. Whigham's eye. He was evidently figuring on how he would spend his commission.

"Will you sign a check?" asked Jack.

Jack and Bobo went into the next room, and presently returned with a check, which was handed to Mr. Whigham. That little gentleman received it with thanks, and bowing, left with a promise to send "the contracts" around as soon as they could be made out.

Jack fell into a study.

"What do you make of it all?" Bobo asked helplessly.

"I may be wrong," said Jack slowly, "but my guess is that Whigham has a nice little wife and baby, and lives in a semi-detached with a neat back yard in Bayonne. I believe he is a member of the men's bible class and the Y.M.C.A., and is in every way a decent little citizen without a suspicion of the real nature of the devilish business he is engaged in. We'll have to look a long way past him for the principal."

"Devilish business!" repeated Bobo. "Don't—don't you believe what he said about the Reds being after you—I mean me, and all?"

"Not a word! Though I think the worthy little man believed it himself."

"But all that—about the man waiting on the bank steps?"

"Stage-stuff. Everybody read in the papers that Mr. Delamare was Silas Gyde's executor. A safe guess that you'd be likely to go to his office to-day. It was just a stall. As a matter of fact, we weren't going anyway. Mr. Delamare is coming here."

"Just the same, I wouldn't go—not for all you've offered me!" said Bobo fervently.

"Sure, that's where the pull of the scheme comes in. Look at it reasonably. If the anarchists really meant to croak a millionaire for the good of humanity, as their letter suggested, would they warn him with a letter? Not on your life! Those letters were simply to pave the way for Whigham. But the beauty of the scheme, the novelty of it, lies in the fact that

Whigham is not in the secret. They use an innocent little Sunday-school teacher to collect their tribute!"

"Then you think there's no danger?"

"Oh, danger enough if we had refused to fork out. There was danger in it for Silas Gyde."

"Well, I'm mighty glad we paid!"

"Sure! Now let me think. This matter will stand a lot of doping out."

They soon began to experience the full effects of newspaper publicity. A crowd of newspaper reporters, solicitors, cranks, high-toned beggars, besieged the hotel, and in every delivery arrived a stack of letters a foot high.

The hotel management designated its most experienced bellboy to wait upon them exclusively. This youth, Ralph by name, was smart and good-looking, but he had too knowing an eye. His knowledge of life, particularly of the seamy side of life, was disconcerting. Jack felt impelled to warn Bobo to be guarded in Ralph's presence. Jack decided they would have to forego the luxury of personal servants. The danger of the betrayal of their secret was too great.

After schooling Bobo for the ordeal, Jack had the reporters up-stairs, but excluded photographers. Bobo acquitted himself well enough in the interviews that followed. True he turned to Jack for aid at every other question, but there was nothing in itself suspicious that the newly-made millionaire seemed to be of a soft and dependent character. Jack could see the eyes of the reporters turn on himself enviously. They seemed to be saying:

"Gee! This guy has fallen into a good thing! He runs the show!"

Mr. Delamare arrived in company with Hugh Brome, Jack's lawyer, and the reporters were politely ushered out. Bobo was introduced to the newcomers, and Jack explained the part he was to play. They stared—then they laughed.

"Is it all right?" asked Jack anxiously. "Do you approve?"

"You're keeping the check signing privilege in your own hands I assume," said Mr. Delamare.

"Certainly."

"Well, as your banker that's all I'm concerned with. As your friend I may say I think it's a good scheme. You will have a close, outside view of a millionaire's life that will be of inestimable service to you when you have to take up that life."

Jack told him of the call of the Eureka Protective Association's representative, and mentioned that his, Mr. Delamare's name, had been offered as a reference.

The banker smote his palm with his fist. "By Gad! it's a fact!" he said. "I had forgotten all about it. I subscribed three years ago, after poor Ames Benton's death when we were all scared, and I suppose the payments have been going on ever since by my orders. At the time I thought the scheme was on the square, and I have never thought about it since. But they didn't tax me anything like as much as you. I suppose their ideas were more modest at the beginning. I must put a stop to my contributions."

"Wouldn't it be better to wait until I have looked into the thing?" said Jack.

Delamare shook his head decisively. "I can't stand for anything like that."

Having obtained the approval of his banker and his lawyer for his plans, Jack felt encouraged to go ahead. As Delamare and Brome were leaving Jack said:

"Can either of you put me in touch with a high police official, a man I can apply to in case of need?"

"I know the third deputy commissioner," said Delamare. "I'll give you a note to him."

When Jack and Bobo started out on the automobile buying expedition they left the Madagascar by the front door.

"The back door must be saved for emergencies," said Jack. "We'll have to get used to running the gauntlet."

However since no photographs had yet been published they were not generally recognized in the lobby. They only had one encounter. That was in that well-known cross corridor behind the lobby, where under the softly shaded lights amidst tropical verdure lovely ladies await their companions for luncheon and tea. As Bobo and Jack passed through one of these, a really dazzling creature in an ermine cape jumped up from her fauteuil.

"Mr. Norman!" she cried, addressing Bobo. "I'm sure I can't be mistaken!"

Bobo fell back in dismay. Jack looked on with a twinkle. It was not up to him to rescue his partner. The lady was of that highly-finished type that defies time—for a long time. She might have been twenty-eight or thirty-eight. For furs, millinery and hairdressing one couldn't see much of the woman God made, except a pair of big blue eyes, the whites slightly discolored from make-up. Her clothes outstyled style—but all was in good taste. It looked like the real thing.

"I am Clara Birmingham that was," she went on. "Don't you remember me?"

"I—I can't say I do," stammered Bobo ungallantly.

She laughed charmingly. "Well, it's not surprising, since we were both children when I used to visit Cartonsville. I recognized you from your likeness to your mother. You must come to see me. I am Mrs. Anson Cleaver now. You'll find me in the 'phone book. By the way, I'm having some people in to-night for music. Can't you come?"

"I'm afraid I—I—Mr. Robinson and I have an engagement."

Mrs. Cleaver turned inquiringly towards Jack.

"Mr. Robinson, my secretary," explained Bobo.

"Bring him with you. I should be charmed!"

With that she sailed away.

As soon as she was out of sight Bobo became very bold and looked at Jack with a doggish air, as much as to say: "That's the way to handle them!" But Jack laughed, and he wilted rather.

"Can we go to-night?" he asked meekly.

"Oh, you want to go now."

"It would be sport, wouldn't it?"

"Well, I'll see."

Later he went into a booth and called up Mr. Delamare.

"This is Robinson," he said.

"Robinson?" came the puzzled reply.

"Mr. Norman's secretary."

"Oh, of course!" with a laugh. "What can I do for you?"

"I come to you in every difficulty."

"That's as it should be. What now?"

"Did you ever hear of a lady called Mrs. Anson Cleaver?"

"Surely! Everybody has heard of Mrs. Cleaver. It's easy to see you don't read the society columns."

"She's the real thing, then."

"Well—not quite. Owing to the publicity she gets, she passes in the mind of the public as one of our leaders. But they say she has rather a strangely assorted crowd at her house, and conservative ladies—like Mrs. Delamare, are a little, what shall I say, leery of her. Nothing against her reputation you understand, but she's considered a little too spectacular in her methods."

"She made out to recognize Bobo from his likeness to my mother, and asked us to a musicale to-night. I thought she was a crook."

"Oh, hardly that! That was only a ladies' lie. Perfectly justifiable under the circumstances."

"What circumstances?"

"My dear fellow! You forget the éclat of a hundred millions! Think what a drawing card you—I mean Bobo—will be at her entertainments. She intends to be the first to exhibit him."

"Then you think it will be all right for us to go?"

"Why not? It will be amusing—and it can't very well do you any harm."

Just the same when Jack hung up the receiver a doubt remained in his mind. "How did it happen she picked on Bobo with such certainty?" he wondered. "No photograph has been published."

There followed a delightful orgy of spending during which Jack threw off all cares. The whole of automobile row from Fiftieth street to Seventy-second seemed to have been forewarned of their coming, and their progress was like a triumphal procession. The sleek, exquisite, expensive cars were put through their paces like willing slaves awaiting a master. Failing to agree on a type they bought both Jack's dashing roadster and Bobo's Imperial limousine.

They spent several hours with a millionaire's tailor, Bobo with ecstatic eyes like a dreamer, choosing suit after suit. Finally they purchased the best ready-made outfit obtainable for the party that night.

10

Jack and Bobo dined in the main restaurant of the Madagascar. By this time they were pretty well known in the hotel, and curious envious glances followed them wherever they went. It was meat and drink to Bobo, though he affected to be much annoyed by it.

"What do you suppose they're staring at," he drawled.

"Your fatal beauty," said Jack.

Evening dress had gone to Bobo's head somewhat. The big white shirt front puffed out alarmingly. Among his new possessions was a fine watch that he drew out to consult every three minutes or so. He could not contain his impatience to get to the party.

"Hadn't we better be moving?"

"Good Lord! It isn't eight o'clock. What do you think this is, an M. E. social?"

"What time are you going, then?"

"About ten, I should say. The later we come, the more effect it will have."

"How will we put in the time until then?"

"I have another date. I'll take you along with me."

Bobo, when he forgot himself, dropped into his usual Tenderloin slang. "Gee! I always wanted to go into society. I felt I was fitted for it. I like everything of the choicest. These common mutts gimme a pain. I'll show the swell guys a thing or two to-night. They'll have to hand it to me."

"You'd better cut out the guys and the gimmes," suggested Jack.

"Oh, I've got a line of classy talk all right when I need it. Wasn't I dresser for Bill Calverly the matinee idol season before last. He used to show me all his mash notes. How's this?"

Bobo screwed an imaginary monocle into his eye, and was suddenly prostrated with languor. "—Er—How-de-do, Mrs. Cleaver. So sorry we were late. But a lawyer fellow turned up just as I was leaving my hotel, and I couldn't put him off. Business is such a bother, isn't it?"

"Great!" said Jack dryly, "but tip me a wink before you begin so I can beat it."

"Oh, you've got to back me up!" said Bobo, suddenly scared and natural. "For the love of Mike don't leave me stranded on the grand stairway."

Bobo's limousine, the perfection of luxury and elegance, was waiting for them in front of the hotel. Bobo in silk hat, evening overcoat, fluffy white scarf, and white kids, with the inevitable yellow stick crooked over his arm enjoyed a wonderful moment standing on the top step of the Madagascar waiting for his car to pull up. He flicked the ash from his cigarette, and the humble pedestrians looked up admiringly.

It is not vouchsafed to many of us so completely to realize our dreams. Bobo's dream was based on the cigarette advertisements in color on the back covers of popular magazines. Jack, similarly attired, watched him with a twinkle from a respectful stand to the rear. In his enjoyment of the situation he was perfectly content to play a secondary part. It was lots more fun, he thought, to pull the wires from behind the scenes.

When they got in the car Jack gave the chauffeur an address on East 69th Street.

"What are we going to Yorkville for?" asked Bobo.

"To see an old friend."

"I hate to leave the white lights."

Bobo insisted on keeping the dome light burning. Jack suspected that the real reason his heart had been set on a limousine was that the wide windows afforded the populace every facility to see him pass in his glory.

They drew up before a cheap apartment house, one of a long row in an untidy street.

"Gee! what a crummy joint!" said Bobo fastidiously.

"It would have seemed plenty good enough yesterday," said Jack coldly.

Jack had no desire to take Bobo up-stairs with him. "You stay here till I come down," he said. "I may be an hour, but you've got plenty of cigars. Take a snooze. We'll be up late."

In the vestibule Jack searched among the double row of labels for the name that made his heart beat faster—Storer. Pressing the bell button, presently an answering click in the door latch informed him that the way in was open. He made his way up four flights of narrow ill-lighted stairs with a dirty carpet. Through the thin doors issued the sounds of incontinent domestic broils, and every landing offered the nose a different smell—but all unpleasant. Jack shuddered—not because he couldn't endure the smells, but at the thought that his dear and dainty Kate was obliged to dwell among them.

Kate opened the door, a rare vision in that grimy frame. At the sight of Jack's regalia she quailed a little, but quickly recovered herself. Jack would have kissed her if she had given him the least opening, but she did not. She invited him in with an air better than Mrs. Cleaver's. Once the door closed the squalor was forgotten. It was a lady's room, however small and poorly furnished.

"How grand we are!" said Kate chaffingly.

Jack explained where he was going later.

"I'll call Mother," said Kate. "She has been anxious to meet you."

"Wait!" said Jack. "You must introduce me as Mr. Robinson."

Kate frowned. "Must? To Mother? I can't do that."

"I'll explain——" began Jack.

But at that moment the old lady walked in.

She was a dear little old lady, the old-fashioned kind of mother, quite rare in a New York flat. She wore a black silk dress many times turned and white at the seams, and a little cap which was never quite straight, giving her a lovable, rakish expression.

Jack looked appealingly at Kate, who hesitated and gulped. "Mother, this—this is Mr. Robinson," she said.

"How do you do, Mr. Robinson," said Mrs. Storer in a voice like a little girl's. She affected to take no notice of Jack's grandeur though it must surely have been a notable sight in that poor little room. "I have not heard Katherine speak of you. Where did you meet Mr. Robinson, Katherine?"

"Mr. Robinson was—was formerly in our office," said poor Kate.

The little old lady made polite conversation for five minutes, and then having established the proprieties, like a thoroughbred mother, she made a transparent excuse to disappear and was seen no more.

"She's a corker!" said Jack.

Kate beamed on him.

Through the open window came the sounds of a violent, vulgar altercation from the flat below. Kate closed the window with an oblivious air.

"I expect you've had an exciting day," she said. "What did the papers mean by saying that you were fat, and that you had a good-looking secretary to whom you turned for everything?"

"I'm the good-looking one," said Jack, grinning.

"I don't understand."

"I'll explain in a minute, but first——"

"*Please!*" she said with an admonishing gesture.

"Kitty, I can't help it! I can't play up to you. If you knew how it hurt to find you living in such a place——"

"We don't have to live here," she said with quick pride. "We're saving our money so we can go abroad."

"That's not true. I know how much they pay in the sort of place where you work, and how much it costs to live. I have been through the mill. It takes every cent you earn to keep up this place. And you're always thinking, what would you do if you got sick or were without a job, even for a week. That's what makes that little line between your dear eyes."

Kate laughed delicately. "Mercy, you're quite a mind-reader!"

Jack floundered on. "And me with all this rotten money! Every cent I spend shames me, thinking of you here—and your mother."

"You haven't spent any since you met Mother, have you?" she suggested maliciously.

"Don't tease me! I'm in earnest. Why will you be so silly?"

"Are you proposing that I accept a gift of some of your new riches?"

"I'm proposing that you accept me."

"I would never marry a man that pitied me."

"Oh, Kate!" he said, graveled and reproachful. "How silly!"

Then he got his wind again. "That's only putting me off. What's pity got to do with it or anything? I just want you!"

"Why didn't you ask me when you were poor?" she murmured.

"How could I? I could scarcely keep myself."

"Then I am just a sort of luxury."

"Oh, Kitty! How unjust! You take a delight in putting me in the wrong!"

"It's no use," she said with a firm shake of the head. "I haven't changed since yesterday. If you insist on bringing this up every day, it will only have the effect of spoiling my naturally amiable temper. Let's change the subject. Tell me all your adventures since yesterday."

He was no match for her. He had to obey.

But if she was cruel in other respects, she made a rare listener. Her eyes sparkled and her soft cheeks glowed with excitement as his tale unfolded. When the devilish workings of the blackmailing scheme were made clear to her, her indignation knew no bounds.

"The wretches! The *beasts*!" she murmured. "Oh, they must not be allowed to go free. That poor, lonely old man! It is fine of you to pledge yourself to run them down. It's a crusade in a way, isn't it—and a dangerous one!" She gave him an extraordinary look through her lashes. "Come to me after you have done your work," she murmured, "and perhaps my answer will be different!"

"Oh, Kate!" he said, reaching for her hand.

She neatly evaded him. "Afterwards, I said. Now tell me what you mean to do."

He told her.

"I wish I could help!" she said involuntarily.

Jack had a dazzling inspiration. It must have been his good fairy that sent him that lovely idea all complete and ready to work. "Why, you can help!" he cried.

"How?"

He made out, of course, that the idea had been in his head all the time. "Listen. As Jack Norman's secretary I'm bound to become a pretty well-known figure around town, and it stands to reason I can't do much sleuthing in that character. I've get to have a disguise. I've got to lead a double life. I'll work while Bobo sleeps."

"Yes, but what has that got to do with me?"

"Listen, I'm coming to that. I've told you about our suite at the Madagascar, and Silas Gyde's two little rooms, and the secret way into the house next door. Now, you see, I'll go to bed in the hotel as Jack Norman's secretary, and in the morning I'll come out of the house next door prepared for work in another character."

"But what am I to do?"

"That house belongs to me, you know, though the deed has never been transferred. You must appear to rent it, furnish it and open it as a first-class boarding-house—no, furnished apartments would be easier for you."

"But"——

"Wait a minute. Then I can rent the second floor rear from you in my new character. I can pass back and forth through the vault as I like, and no one can possibly trace the connection between Jack Norman's secretary and the sober little business man who lives in your house. See?"

"Oh, I couldn't!"

"Why?"

"Mother wouldn't like it. And I—I'm not fitted for that sort of thing."

"You could make a bluff at it. You said you wanted to help."

"But would it be helping? I think you're just trying to make an excuse to get us out of this place."

"Nonsense! I had it in mind before I ever came to-night. It's absolutely necessary to the success of my plans!"

"You're just trying to get around me."

"I'm not! How could I trust anybody else with the secret of that vault?"

Jack had struck the right line at last. She could not resist this subtle form of flattery, and in the end she gave in. "But I warn you I'll make that house pay," she said.

"Oh, go as far as you like."

They discussed their arrangements in detail. Once she had consented, Kate entered into it with a will. In the midst of their talk a clock struck one.

"Half-past nine!" said Jack, starting up. "I clean forgot Bobo downstairs!"

"Why didn't you bring him up?" said Kate. "I'm curious to see him."

"Thanks," said Jack, "but for once I wanted to play first fiddle myself."

At the door he gave her her final instructions. "You will start in to-morrow?"

"Yes," she said promptly. "I know a girl that will be pleased to pieces to substitute for me at the typewriter."

"Oh, you'll never go back there," said Jack.

"We'll see," she said demurely. As a matter of fact her heart was singing at the prospect of release from horrible monotony.

"My lawyer will come here in the morning with the keys and the necessary funds," said Jack.

"Oh, don't have him come here. I'll go to his office."

"Very well, if you'd rather. I'll write down the address. You and I mustn't see each other again, until I come to you to apply for a room. Can you open up in three days?"

"Three days!" she cried, aghast.

"Oh, things are made easy for you, I find, when you have the coin."

"Well, I'll try."

Jack went down the stairs two steps at a time, not at all displeased with himself. Had he not rescued Kate from her squalid surroundings, and made sure of being able to see her as often as he wanted? Let her fight him as she would, she was his partner already. She must come all the way some day soon. It was silly for her to make out she didn't mind poverty. She had given it away, in spite of herself.

The elegant limousine still rested at the curb, the chauffeur fast asleep in the corner of the front seat. The dome light was now out and Jack could not see into the body of the car. He was astonished when he opened the door to find it empty. The chauffeur woke up instinctively.

"Where is Mr. Norman?" demanded Jack, staring at the spot where he ought to have been.

"'Deed I don't know, sir. He was inside, all right, when I dropped off. I heard you tell him to take a snooze, so I thought I——"

"Sure, that's all right," said Jack. "He's big enough to take care of himself."

He looked anxiously up and down the street, but there was no sign of his silk-hatted friend.

11

Jack was at a loss which way to turn. Suddenly at a street level window of the apartment house he had just left, he saw a fat woman resting her folded arms on a pillow on the sill. She looked as if she had been there for hours. He approached, lifting his hat.

"Excuse me, madam, but did you see my friend get out of the car?"

"Sure, I see him," she replied in scornful accents. "Didn't he get out and walk up and down gapping and stretching like he was tired of waiting for you!"

"I'm sorry," murmured Jack. She seemed to expect it. Then: "Which way did he go?"

"Well, a fellow come along from Lexington avenue way, and they got into talk like. The fellow said: 'Fine night, friend.' And your friend said: 'Right you are!' One thing led to another, and the fellow said: 'That your car?' And your friend says: 'One of them.'"

"Oh, the fool!" groaned Jack inwardly. Aloud he asked: "When was this?"

"Half an hour ago, maybe. And the fellow says: 'What make is it?' 'Goodwin twelve, ninety horse,' said the other fellow. And——"

"Yes, I know, but which way did they go?"

But the fat woman was not going to be cheated of the telling of her tale. "I'm coming to that. And the fellow said—I don't mean your friend, but the other fellow, he said: 'She's new, ain't she?' And the other fellow said, that's the swell guy I'm referrin' to, the swell guy says: 'Just out of the shop!' Bye and bye the fellow said: 'Will you drink with me? And your friend says: 'Sure!' And they went in the side door of the saloon on the corner yonder."

"Much obliged," said Jack, darting across the road.

His quarry had flown. There were half a dozen men lined up before the mahogany, but Bobo was not among them. Neither was he in the small sitting-room behind. Jack applied himself to the white-jacketed bar-tender.

"Did a friend of mine come in here about half an hour ago?"

"Fellow dressed like yourself?"

Jack nodded.

"Sure, he come in here with a little guy with a bad eye."

"What d'ye mean, bad eye?"

"Crooked. He had a face you could break rocks on. I thought at the time it was a case of a come-on, but it weren't my place to interfere. 'Specially as your friend seemed sober enough. But he certainly was lappin' 'em up!"

Jack began to get seriously anxious.

"They downed four whiskeys in less'n ten minutes. Least your friend did. Little guy just tasted hisn. Then they left."

"Where did they go?"

"Search me! Little guy says he knows a better place down the Avenue, but I didn't hear the name of it. Swell guy says he can't go because he's waiting for his friend, but little fellow says: 'Ahh, we'll be back in fifteen minutes', and swell guy says: 'He's callin' on a dame acrost the street, so I guess he's good for another half hour.' Then they went out the front door."

One of the regulars of the place who had heard Jack's inquiry took up the story here. "They got in a taxi-cab," he said. "I was watching out of the window. It was Gus Harris' car, it was."

"Gus'll tell you where he took 'em," said the bar-tender soothingly.

"He'll be back in a minute if he don't pick up another fare in the street," the other speaker said. "Just stick around awhile."

By this time everybody present was interested in Jack's quest. "Here he is! Here's Gus!" half a dozen voices cried, as a battered taxi-cab came to a stand before the door. They all followed him out on the pavement.

"Did you pick up a friend of mine here?" asked Jack of the driver.

"You know, Gus. Swell guy with the tile and the wedding fixings," some one added.

"Sure!" said Gus.

"Where did you take him?"

"McGann's, Third near Fifty-Eighth."

The name had an ominous ring. "McGann's?" said Jack. "Hasn't that place a bad name?"

- 69 -

"The worst in town," said Gus cheerfully. "Want me to take you there?"

"Thanks, my own car is around the corner," said Jack.

He hastened to it.

Jack's heart sank at the aspect of McGann's. Never had he been in a place better suited to deeds of evil. In front there was an ordinary bar of the humbler kind. It was empty except for the bartenders busy pouring drinks, which were carried behind a screen at the rear by a waiter whose blotched face and furtive eyes suggested an unimagined degradation. Bartender and waiter stared at Jack with a sneer.

"What, another!" the former said under his breath.

Behind the screen Jack found himself in a big, low-ceiled room set with tables more than half filled with drinkers of both sexes. The walls were dark and greasy, the air thick with the smoke of unspeakable cigars. The strangest feature of the place was the silence that filled it. The drinkers for the most part sat huddled in their chairs with eyes cast down or caps pulled low. When they conversed it was in hoarse whispers. When one wanted more drink he held up a finger. It was a strange scene of merrymaking.

The presiding genius of the place was a head-waiter or "bouncer," who did not soil his hands with serving, but lolled about the place watching his patrons with a hard, ironical eye like an animal-trainer. Jack, instinctively lowering his voice to suit the hushed air of the place, addressed his usual question to this individual.

The man looked him over insolently before replying. A defiant sneer turned the corners of his lips. "He ain't been here," he said curtly. His look said: "Sure, I'm lying. What are you going to do about it?"

Jack flushed, and clenched his teeth. Turning his back on the man, he addressed the room at large with raised voice.

"I'm looking for a friend of mine. Young fellow about twenty-four, full habit, red cheeks, wearing a silk hat, white muffler, black overcoat. Have any of you seen him? I'll pay for information."

Those huddled around the walls stirred in discomfort at the sound of a voice so boldly raised in that place of whispers. None answered Jack. None would look at him directly. The bouncer laughed unpleasantly.

"Are you satisfied? Now you can get out!"

It was galling to Jack's pride, but he saw nothing for it but to obey. He walked out slowly with as much dignity as a man could muster under the circumstances. He was in horrid expectation of a cowardly kick from behind. But he would not turn around.

He paused in front of the place, and looked up and down for a policeman. While he stood there one of the furtive figures slouched out of the doorway behind him, and without stopping, whispered:

"Follow me a little way, and I'll tell you."

The man led him into the shadow of a nearby doorway. There were plenty of people passing, and Jack's own chauffeur was still within hail. He was not under any apprehension of an attack.

"Is it worth a fiver to you?" the man whined. "McGann would half kill me if he knew I told."

Jack displayed a five-dollar bill. "It is worth a fiver," he said, "but I'll hang on to it, until I hear what you have to say."

"That's fair enough. Your friend come into McGann's about half an hour back. He was with a guy that's well known there. Wouldn't do you no good to know his name. He's a friend of the boss and a bad egg. They had one or two and your friend got groggy."

"Doped?" said Jack.

The man shrugged. "I didn't name it. Pretty soon the fellow that brought him there says to Stinger—Stinger's the big guy, the bouncer there—he says to Stinger: 'Me friend's real sick,' he says. 'We better put him to bed.' We all knows what that means."

"What does that mean?" demanded Jack.

"Oh, they was just going to roll him. But just as they was liftin' him up, a stranger come in, old man short and stoutish with a big mustache and a little chin whisker, not to say a swell guy but dressed real decent and genteel-like. He was old, but My God! he had his nerve with him.

"'Put that man down,' says he.

"'W'at the Hell is it to you?' says Stinger.

"'He's a friend of mine,' the old feller says; 'I'll take him home.'

"'The Hell you will!' says Stinger. 'Get out of here before I throw you out!'

"'You won't do that,' the old man says, smiling real polite.

"Then Stinger makes for him. The old guy pulled a police whistle. Stinger slung a chair at him, but he ducked the chair, and blew his whistle.

The guy that brought your friend in, and some other guys that was wanted, beat it out the back way. The rest of us just sat there. Stinger rushed the old guy, but he pulled a gun and backed him off.

"Well, a cop come running in, and here's the funny part. The old guy didn't make out to lay no charge against Stinger, but all of a sudden he made out to be friends with him. The old guy says:

"'Sorry to trouble you, officer, but I had a friend here fightin' drunk, and he tried to make a rough-house when I wanted him to come home. But he's all in now; he won't give no more trouble. Just help me carry him out to my car, will you?'

"Well, the cop on this beat didn't want to get in wrong with McGann, and Stinger didn't want no trouble with the police neither. So it all ended friendly-like. The cop and Stinger carried your friend out between them, and put him in the old guy's automobile. But say, Stinger cursed the old guy good when he was gone.

"You don't know where they took my friend?" Jack asked.

The man shrugged. "Headed downtown," he said. "That's all I know. But I took good note of the car, if it's any good to you. It was one of these here, now, limousines, like yours yonder, but with a long body like a private ambulance, and painted black. It carried a Connecticut license."

"What number?"

"Ahh! I didn't have no pencil to take it down. I forget."

This was all the information Jack could extract. He handed over the bill, and the man scuttled away. Jack returned to his car, and stood with his foot on the running-board, trying to plan out some reasonable course of action.

"Old man, short and thick-set," he thought, "heavy mustache and a little chin whisker; sounds like our friend who dropped us the note last night. Looks like out of the frying-pan into the fire for Bobo. But why should the Red Gang kidnap him when we've paid up? Maybe my whole theory of the case is wrong."

He could think of nothing better to do than go to Police Headquarters and send out an alarm for a long black limousine with a Connecticut license. This would play havoc with his carefully laid plans. Nevertheless he was about to give the order to his chauffeur, when a boy of the street stopped beside him, and with inimitable grinning impudence said:

"Say, fella, you'll find what you're lookin' for at the Hotel Madagascar."

Jack, greatly startled, caught the boy by the arm. "Here, you, give an account of yourself!" he demanded.

The boy wriggled in his grasp and whimpered: "Ahh! I ain't done nottin'!"

"Who told you to tell me that?"

"Old guy in a big black limousine. Lemme go! I ain't done nottin'!"

"Where?"

"At the next corner there. I was just standin' there when the car come acrost Third and stopped beside me. Old guy stuck his head out and ast me did I want to make half a dollar. I says sure. And he gimme it. And he says tell that guy in the silk hat standin' by the car in front of McGann's that he'll find what he's lookin' for at the Hotel Madagascar. Then he spoke to his shuffer and they went on towards the Bridge."

"Was he alone in the car?"

"Sure. Except the shuffer."

Jack was at a loss how much of this to believe. As a matter of precaution, he decided to hang on to the boy for the present. "You come along with me," he said.

The boy obeyed with mixed feelings. He was still scared, but the prospect of such a ride cheered him. His attitude persuaded Jack that his tale was probably true. If he had had any connection with the Red Gang, he would scarcely have yielded himself up to Jack so willingly. Jack gave the word to return to the Madagascar. As they drove off the boy waved his hand to his envious companions in the street. At the hotel, Jack left him in charge of the chauffeur.

He found Bobo safe on his own bed.

Inquiry at the office revealed the fact that half an hour before he had been brought home very much the worse for wear by an elderly friend, who departed as soon as he had put him in his room. Jack dismissed the boy and sent the car to the garage.

Returning to their suite, Jack gazed grimly at the recumbent Bobo, who appeared to have suffered no permanent harm. He lay sprawling on the bed, breathing stertorously. The big white shirt bosom was rumpled and stained. His overcoat lay in a heap beside the bed. Jack was greatly relieved, but indignant, and more puzzled than ever.

"I didn't suspect our friend with the imperial of being a philanthropist," he thought. "His letters certainly didn't read that way. Why the deuce did he take the risk of kidnapping Bobo from McGann's if he only meant to bring him home? It beats the Dutch!"

Suddenly Bobo sat up with a grunt. "Wassa matter?" he asked thickly.

"That's what I'd like to know," said Jack.

Recollection returned to Bobo in a flash, and he clapped his head between his hands. "Lord! But I'm sick!" he groaned hollowly.

"Get up," said Jack coldly. "Go into the bathroom, and stick your head in cold water. I'll send for a pot of coffee for you."

Bobo put a hand to his waistcoat pocket, and seemed about to burst into tears. "My watch is gone!" he wailed.

"You're lucky to be here yourself! A nice chase you've led me!"

"What time is it?"

Jack consulted his watch. "Ten-fifteen. It's been a busy forty-five minutes!"

It was a much chastened Bobo that presently returned to the room. "What happened to me?" he asked.

"I'll tell you. You fell into the hands of the Red Gang, that's all; the same little gentleman with the Imperial that dropped us a line last night. Why, after capturing you, he was content to give you up again, I don't know."

Bobo turned pale, and his knees weakened under him. He dropped in a chair. "The Red Gang!" he murmured. "Oh, my God! Never again! Never again, s'elp me Bob! Never another drop unless you are right there to take care of me!"

Jack grunted scornfully.

Jack picked up the overcoat from the floor. As he did so, he discovered a piece of white paper pinned to the lapel.

"Ha! Maybe this is the key to the mystery!" he cried, pouncing on it.

It was written upon by the same hand that had indited the note of the night before.

"*To the Secretary:*

"*For Heaven's sake try to teach this addle-pate the danger of drinking with strangers. His foolishness to-night almost wrecked all our plans. We have saved him from the worst den of thugs in New York, not from any love of him, you may be sure, but because when the right time comes we mean to get him ourselves.*

"*The Red Gang.*"

"Oh, Lor'! Oh, Lor'! Oh, Lor'!" groaned Bobo. "What's the use! They'll get me anyhow!"

Jack laughed suddenly.

"What are you laughing at? I don't see anything to laugh at."

"Cheer up! This doesn't exactly mean what it says. I see it all now."

"What does it mean then?" said Bobo irritably.

"It means your skin is worth five hundred a month to the Red Gang, and they've no notion of letting McGann's crew damage their property!"

12

Bobo was of a very elastic temperament. The pot of coffee quickly completed his restoration. "Say," he said, "I feel all right now. I've got a clean shirt. It's not too late to go to Mrs. Cleaver's."

"Well!" said Jack. "I was thinking you'd had enough company for tonight."

"She'll be sore if we don't come," said Bobo.

"Well, I don't mind. Put on your things, and I'll telephone for the car to be sent back."

Mrs. Cleaver had a modest little house in the Murray Hill district. When Jack learned more about such things he appreciated her astuteness in thus setting up her banner in the stronghold of yesterday's aristocracy. The great people of day before yesterday still linger north of Washington Square, but they hardly count nowadays. A house on Murray Hill though still gives its owner a cachet of exclusiveness that the grandest mansion uptown may lack.

The modest aspect of Mrs. Cleaver's house was limited to the Park avenue façade. "My little house," she always called it. But once inside one was astonished by the great sweep of salon, hall, music room. Below there was a billiard room; above, a library and a little salon. Strangers wondered where the inmates lived.

Jack and Bobo were not too late, for other cars were still rolling up to the door.

"None sweller than this outfit," Bobo remarked with satisfaction.

They trod a red carpet under a peppermint striped awning.

"Lord! What'll we do when we get inside?" whispered Bobo in a sudden panic.

"Just drift on the current," said Jack. "I expect things will be made easy for us."

And they were. On the entrance floor there were cloak rooms as efficiently run as those in a hotel—indeed, the house was in all ways like a hotel. They presently found themselves mounting the main stairway without having made a break. The whole floor above was thrown into one room, and as they mounted a roar of polite conversation met them like an advancing wave.

A superb major-domo at the head of the stairs threw terror into Bobo's soul by demanding his name. Bobo stared at him dumbly, but Jack caught on and answered for both. Their names were bellowed to the roof.

"Mr. Norman!"

"Mr. Robinson!"

Mrs. Cleaver having allowed it to become known that the amazing young millionaire of a day, New York's latest sensation, might be expected, the sound of his name had an electrical effect. The conversational surf was stilled as if by magic, and every face was turned towards the two young men.

Bobo suddenly discovering that "society" people, of whom he had stood secretly in awe, were no harder to impress than those of the hotel, soared like a balloon. He advanced with languid eyebrows, lacking only the monocle to give a perfect imitation of his hero, the imported actor. Jack followed at his heels, smiling.

Mrs. Cleaver, leaving the greatest persons there, came swimming to meet them. Figuratively they rubbed their eyes at the sight of her. She was one who went in frankly for hothouse effects. Her hair was the color of cherrywood stain, her cheeks tinted to match. Her dress was one of those outlandish creations one occasionally sees in the shop-windows, just for an advertisement, one supposes.

"A beaded bib and a torn piano cover!" Jack described it to himself.

Jack naturally had to content himself with the briefest of nods from their hostess. Her heavy ammunition was reserved for Bobo.

"How good of you to come! I hardly dared hope—on such short notice! I hope I am the first to present you to the great world. Everybody is here to-night. But I'm not going to introduce you to a soul until I've had you to myself for awhile!" etc., etc.

Pausing only long enough to unload Jack on a neglected female sitting in the corner, she carried Bobo off. She was still gushing like the great geyser, and Bobo had nothing to do but fiddle in his waistcoat pockets, and incline a languid, attentive head, a part he played to perfection. Jack had no anxiety on his account. Whatever breaks he made, they would simply call him an "original." Was he not a hundred times a millionaire?

Jack discovered that his companion like many a neglected female was not without spice.

"A queer gang, isn't it?" was her opening remark.

"I don't know," said Jack, "haven't had a chance to give 'em the once over yet."

"You don't look as if you belonged," she said with a sharp look. "You look almost human."

"Oh, you're too discerning. How did you get here yourself?"

"I'm not human. A girl of my attractions can't afford it. I'm Sonia Kharkov."

"I wouldn't have thought it of you."

"Everything's Russian nowadays. I write poems about surgical operations. My last was entitled 'Appendectomy.'"

"How thrilling! Sorry I never read any."

"Oh, I don't publish. I only talk about them. It gets me many a good meal."

"Well, you're a good sport," said Jack.

More than an hour passed before Jack caught sight of Bobo again. In the meantime he was parted from the poetess, and the deafening clamor began to weary him.

"There's enough hot air let out here to fill one of the Consolidated gas-tanks," he had said to the poetess.

"Yes, but it's not illuminating gas," she had retorted.

He reflected that he would most likely run across Bobo in the vicinity of the refreshments, and conducting an investigation, he discovered an excellent buffet supper set forth in one of the rooms below. Sure enough, Bobo presently drifted in here.

"Where have you been?" asked Jack.

"Oh, Mrs. Cleaver took me up to the library where she receives a few of the principal guests," he drawled.

"My word!" said Jack, fixing him with an imaginary monocle.

The sarcasm was lost on Bobo. He exhibited a new preoccupation. He had a faraway gaze, and ever and anon he heaved a sigh. Even his appetite was affected. He ate nothing at all; not a thing except a couple of *vol au vents* of chicken livers, a helping of lobster Newburgh, a handful of sandwiches, a cup of punch or two, and a plate of *petits fours*.

"Come away," he said with his mouth full. "I want to talk to you."

They found an unoccupied corner under the stairs, and lit cigarettes.

"I'm in love!" announced Bobo.

"No!" said Jack.

"'S a fact! The real thing! Bowled me right over! Floored me! I feel—I feel all gone here!" He laid a plump hand on the pit of his stomach.

"You need nourishment," said Jack. "Come on back!"

"Don't josh me! This is serious. I'm completely changed. I feel as if I never wanted to eat again. Her name is Miriam Culbreth."

"Um-yummie," said Jack.

"She's the most beautiful girl in the whole world. The moment I laid eyes on her I knew it was all up with me. No other girl ever made me feel like that. And the wonderful part of it is she took to me right off the bat."

"Hm!" said Jack cynically.

Bobo never heeded. "We started right in talking as if we had known each other for years. We found out that we both like the same things. I never met a girl that understood me so well. She said she admired me."

"Discriminating," murmured Jack.

"Such eyes!" sighed Bobo. "When she looks at you like this, through her lashes, you feel—you feel as if you were going up in an airplane. And she has the nature of a child!"

"What are your intentions towards this sweet child?"

"Intentions! No man could have any but the most honorable intentions towards her!"

"Sure! Then how are you going to support her in the style to which she has been accustomed?"

"Oh, she's well fixed. You should see the way she dresses!"

"Be careful! The best dressers are poor girls. It's a life and death matter with them. This girl is displaying her goods on the basis of a hundred million. You can't honestly accept it for less."

"There isn't a mercenary thought in her head. If she ever marries it will be for love alone. She told me so herself. You don't understand her. She's as simple and natural as—as a wild-flower!"

"I haven't noticed many wild-flowers around here."

"She isn't like these people. She's different from other girls."

"Did she tell you that, too?"

"Why, yes, how did you know?"

"They generally do."

"You must come and meet her. I told her about you."

"What!" asked Jack sharply.

"I mean, I told her I had had the luck to secure a secretary, who was a very clever fellow, and could do everything for me."

"Now that was nice of you!"

"Come on up to the library and I'll introduce you."

"But I'm not one of the distinguished guests."

"That's all right. Mrs. Cleaver said I was to treat the house as if it was my own!"

Bobo paused only long enough to snatch another mouthful or two, and they made their way up two flights of the broad stairs. On the main floor the racket was undiminished, though it was long past midnight. Somewhere in the distance one seemed to be frantically sawing on a violin, but it was impossible to be sure. On the floor above the groups were smaller, and one had a pleasant sense of rising above pandemonium.

Bobo led the way into the front room. In the corner a lovely lady reclined in a low basket chair filled with cushions. Three cavaliers were in attendance. Quick to spot the approach of newcomers, she dismissed the three with charming insolence.

"Run along, boys. I'm tired of you now."

The departing ones greeted the arrivals with no friendly glances.

Jack could not but commend Bobo's taste in beauty. The girl was indeed lovely to look at. She had great brown eyes, capable of working havoc in the most indurated male heart, an exquisite naturally pale complexion, and a glorious crown of chestnut hair. She was enveloped in slinky draperies of black silk, and her ankles were truly poetic.

But when she began to talk, Jack did not feel obliged to alter the opinion he had formed of her in advance. There was nothing simple about her—or rather, her simplicity was the effect of well-nigh perfect art. Jack was not much more experienced in these matters than Bobo, but he had a healthy instinct of incredulity.

Her method with Jack was much more subtle than with Bobo, and she had no objection whatever to letting Jack see that it was. It was part of her system of delicate flattery to allow him to understand that she recognized him at once as of a superior intelligence to Bobo. Jack was flattered of course, but she made a mistake with him at the start that spoilt all her work with him. It never occurred to her that Jack might be honest at heart.

No man, however safeguarded, could escape the effect of her beauty. For Jack there was but one woman in the world, but even his breast was shaken by a sudden lift of the brown eyes. They had a mysterious, haunting beauty, which even this bigness and softness was not sufficient to explain. Jack, when he had an opportunity to look closer, saw that they were not brown at all, but hazel; that is to say gray, with a rim of brown around the iris. It was the effect of these strangely-colored eyes looking through curved black lashes that moved men to reckless deeds.

Her conversation was not clever. It had no need to be. If she had recited the Thirty-Nine Articles Bobo would have hung on her lips entranced. Jack was too busy trying to explore the mystery of her real self to pay much attention to what she chose to give out.

"Hazel eyes!" he was thinking. "Where have I heard of another girl with hazel eyes? Oh, yes, it was the pretty stenographer who tried to spy on Silas Gyde. She had chestnut hair, too, and a mole inside her right forefinger. I don't suppose these tapering fingers ever jarred the keys."

"What are you thinking of, Mr. Robinson?" Miss Culbreth asked in silvery tones. "I declare you are one of those dreadful men that bore you through and through with their eyes and never say a word."

"I'd rather bore you with my eyes than with my conversation."

"Mercy! Clever, too! I'm frightened to death of you!"

"Didn't I tell you he was clever?" put in poor Bobo, without at all appreciating what was going on.

"The worst of it is," said Miss Culbreth, "that the men who won't talk are those who really have something to say."

This was accompanied by the shadow of a disdainful glance in Bobo's direction, and a warm flash towards Jack, the suggestion being: "One has to humor the stupid rich, but one enjoys oneself with the witty poor!"

Jack was flattered through and through, but at the same time he was thinking: "She's a regular man-eater. I'll have to watch out for poor Bobo."

"You don't approve of me," she said, casting down the lovely eyes.

"Indeed I do," Jack protested. "What you mistake for disapproval is quite another feeling."

"And what is that?"

"Instinct of self-preservation!"

"Are women so dangerous?"

"Not all women."

Her bold, pleased glance at Jack said: "We can have fun right under his stupid nose, can't we?"

But Bobo was growing restless, and she turned to him promptly, as befitted a prudent, marriageable girl. "You were gone an awfully long time," she complained.

Bobo grinned like the Cheshire cat. "Did you miss me?"

She answered him with a long glance that visibly made his head reel. This was followed by a flash of intelligence in Jack's direction, signifying: "This is the sort of thing I'm obliged to hand out to them."

"Lord! But she's a conscienceless lovely devil!" thought Jack grimly. "I'd like to teach her a lesson. Anyhow, I'm hanged if I'm going to let her make me a party to her game with Bobo."

So he made a careless excuse and left them. Bobo did not mind, of course, but an ugly shadow flitted over Miss Culbreth's fair countenance.

Jack returned to the lower floor, where he could smoke and watch the crowd undisturbed. He had not been there long before Bobo came downstairs considerably agitated.

"Have you seen her?" he asked.

"Who?"

"Miriam—Miss Culbreth," he said, blushing. "We started downstairs to the refreshment room together, but I lost her somehow in the crowd. Can't find her anywhere."

"She will find herself when she wishes to, I expect," said Jack calmly.

"Maybe she's gone on in," said Bobo hopefully. He disappeared into the refreshment room.

As soon as he had gone a footman who had been standing near approached Jack. "Mr. Robinson?" he asked.

Jack nodded.

"Miss Culbreth sent me for you, sir. Will you please come with me."

It was a point of pride with Jack never to be surprised at anything. With a nod, he followed the man. They avoided the stairs, and were raised to the upper regions in a tiny elevator concealed behind the wainscoting. The young lady was found in still another part of the house, a dainty silk-paneled room at the back, and she was alone there with a tempting supper—spread for two. The footman evaporated.

"I was so hungry," she said, waving him to the seat opposite, "and I couldn't face the crowd downstairs. They paw one so! So I had it brought up here, and sent for you to keep me company."

"You make pretty free in the house," thought Jack.

"I live here," she said, as if she had read his thought. "Mrs. Cleaver is my cousin. Do you mind my sending for you?" she said meltingly.

"Mind!" said Jack. "I most certainly do! I shall return at once." And he sat down.

She laughed. "I like you, you're so unexpected. A little while ago you piqued my curiosity so, I couldn't rest without seeing you again." This was said with the wide-eyed seeming simplicity that was her trump suit. "You so plainly did not like me! And most people do!" This with an adorable, deprecating shrug.

"I did like you!" Jack protested with an inscrutable face. "I liked you so much, I felt I had to be very, very careful!"

"Don't be careful!" she murmured, turning on the full fire of those terrible eyes. "I despise careful men!"

Jack kept a prudent hold on himself. "I have no choice," he said calmly. "How long would I hold my job if I was not—well, careful?"

"You're afraid!" she said with provoking scorn.

He shrugged.

"Is it true he has a hundred million?" she asked idly.

"You can't prove it by me. I'm only his secretary."

"But you do everything for him. He depends on you absolutely. Anybody can see that."

Jack declined to be drawn into a discussion of Bobo.

"How long have you known him?" she asked.

"Oh, quite a while," he said vaguely. He could not tell what mythical details of their past Bobo might have given her.

"What a responsibility it will be on you! Looking after all that money and everything."

"Oh, the executor and the lawyer will take care of all that."

"Who is his lawyer?"

"*What does she want to know that for?*" thought Jack. She had overdone the carelessness with which she asked it. He gave her a fictitious name, and looked at her with a new interest. At the moment her profile was turned towards him, and the way the light fell on it certain lines of weariness were shown up. She looked older than she had seemed at first.

Jack thought: "Mr. Gyde said that, too, of the stenographer who worked for him. This is more than a coincidence. Wouldn't it be amazing if———!"

"What do you think of me?" she asked with a direct challenge. "I can see that you're revolving me in your head all the time."

"Well, you do make a man dizzy," he parried.

"No, I'm serious. How would you describe me if you had to?"

"Honest, I don't know."

"Come now, you're a great reader of character. You're always studying people, and trying to figure them out to yourself."

"Am I?" said Jack. He had a sudden idea. "They say there's more character in people's hands than in anything else," he said carelessly.

"Read mine," she said, extending a white and tapering member. It was the left hand she offered.

"It must always be the right hand."

She gave it him.

"I'll read character until the cows come home if you'll let me hold it."

"Go on. And no nonsense."

"Have you ever operated a typewriter?" he asked slyly.

"No. Why do you ask?" she asked sharply.

"Oh, nothing. This hand looks to be capable of anything."

"But my character?"

"Ambitious, luxury-loving and cruel," he began mockingly.

She snatched the hand away. "Horrible! You're no character-reader!"

But he had had time to see what he was looking for: on the inside of the index finger was a large pale mole, as big as the button on a woman's glove.

13

Though it was near morning when they turned in, Jack was astir early, eager to begin the real work on his case. His surprising identification of Miriam as the former spy on Silas Gyde whetted his zeal. Her present game of course was to secure the supposed millionaire in the bonds of matrimony. Was the Red Gang behind that, or was it a private venture? Jack was inclined to think it was all part of the same scheme. In either case Mrs. Cleaver, notwithstanding her social position, must be Miriam's confederate. It was Mrs. Cleaver who had picked them up. This put the game on a pretty high level. Almost every hour of the past two days had made Jack's problem more complicated—but also more fascinating.

When he was dressed, Jack mercilessly awoke the luxurious Bobo.

"Oh, Lord!" groaned the plump youth. "Do I have to get up?"

"You can sleep all day if you like. But we have to have a little talk before I go out. Sit up and rub the sleep out of your eyes and pay attention."

Bobo obeyed, groaning lugubriously.

"It's about Miss Miriam Culbreth."

"Eh?" said Bobo, suddenly wide awake.

"Do you remember all you told me about her last night?"

"Of course I do."

"Doesn't it seem a little foolish to you this morning?"

"No, it doesn't! She's the most beautiful girl in the world. I love her more than ever!"

"Well, I'm sorry. I didn't take you very seriously last night. I thought it was too sudden. You've got to cut her out."

"Why?" asked Bobo blankly.

Jack deliberated before answering. He decided against telling Bobo the whole truth. It was within the bounds of possibility that the infatuated youth might tell the girl.

"I can't tell you all my reasons now," he said. "But believe me they are good reasons. It has to do with the game we are playing."

"You're not fair to her!" Bobo burst out. "You don't like her. She told me so herself."

"You're right, I don't like her. I have mighty good reasons for it."

"She's the noblest woman on God's footstool!"

"I'm not going to argue that with you," said Jack dryly. "I am speaking for your own good. When you first told me about her, I was afraid the poor girl might be taken in, thinking you were a millionaire. But I'm not worrying about her now. She's able to look after number one. But I tell you if you do not put her out of your head now, before the matter goes any further, you'll regret it till you die. I can't put it any stronger than that, can I?"

"I can't give her up! I *can't*! I love her!" cried Bobo, flinging himself down among the pillows.

"Take my word for it," said Jack earnestly, "she's no good!"

"You're wrong! You're wrong!"

Jack began to lose patience. "Well, if you won't listen to reason you'll have to take an order. Remember our agreement. You've got to give her up. This is an order, now."

"I can't! I can't!" moaned Bobo.

As usual in the display of Bobo's emotions, there was something both ludicrous and pathetic in the sight of the fat tousled head threshing the pillows. Jack grinned and said:

"Oh, go to sleep again. When you get up, have a bang-up breakfast and you'll feel better. I'll look in on you at lunch time."

Jack's first visit upon setting out from the hotel was to the offices of the Eureka Protective Association, at the address on Forty-Second street given on their representative's card.

He found the Association installed in an ordinary suite, neither grandly nor shabbily furnished, but entirely businesslike. The customary staff of a small office was visible at work: bookkeeper, stenographer and office-boy. In fact to the eye it was a wholly conventional establishment; open, aboveboard and prosperous.

Upon asking for the manager Jack was shown to an inner room, where a man of about thirty-five with a mop of lank, blonde hair hanging on his forehead, and what is known as an open countenance, was seated at a desk trimming his nails in unashamed idleness. It appeared that this was Mr. Anderson.

"Dave Anderson at your service," said he good-naturedly. "What can I do for you?"

"My name is Robinson," said Jack, "secretary to Mr. Norman."

The atmosphere became balmier, as always with the mention of that magic name. "Sit down, Mr. Robinson."

Jack obeyed. "Mr. Norman felt that he wanted to know a little more about your association, and sent me around to ask a few questions."

"Perfectly natural!" cried Mr. Anderson. "Fire away! We court the fullest investigation. Certain parts of our business, of course, have to be conducted in secrecy, but as to our responsibility and trustworthiness, go as far as you like."

Jack asked all the natural questions, and Mr. Anderson answered them with every appearance of frankness. The information he gave merely amplified the talk of his representative the day before; the great public service Eureka performed, etc., etc. Jack learned nothing really significant from his talk, nor had he expected to. He asked no searching questions, because he did not want Anderson to guess that his customer was suspicious.

Jack's real purpose was to learn what kind of man was at the head of this branch of the Red Gang's activities, and while Anderson talked he studied him. In the end he had to confess himself baffled. Anderson was anything but what he had expected to find. He seemed like one of those rather slack individuals who represent the average of mankind; neither good nor bad; neither wise nor foolish; an untidy, well-meaning, loose-tongued fellow. How such a one could be trusted to direct an important part of so dangerous an enterprise, Jack was unable to understand—unless it were that Anderson himself did not know what was behind the scheme. But that did not seem credible either.

Jack left him, professing to be entirely satisfied on his employer's account.

Mr. Delamare's promised letter of introduction to the third Deputy Commissioner had come in the morning's mail. Jack's next visit was to police headquarters to present it. He wished to establish a connection there on which he could fall back on in case of need.

He found the deputy an accommodating and capable official. Since he bears no part in Jack's story, it is unnecessary to characterize him further. Jack had no intention of taking him into his confidence just yet. He merely said that he was undertaking a little detective work for his employer, and the Deputy furnished him with a circular letter to all members of the force, instructing them to lend the bearer any assistance that he required. Here, as elsewhere, the wonder-working name of Norman smoothed Jack's way.

While he was there, Jack inquired as to the status of the investigation into Silas Gyde's murder. He found that it was at a standstill. The assassin, Jansen, was confined in an asylum a raving maniac, and nothing of importance had been unearthed concerning his antecedents. If he had been a member of any anarchistic circle the fact had not been established. He appeared to have led a solitary life, moving from one hall bedroom to another. His mind had been gradually undermined by too close an application to his anarchistic studies, and to a book on the subject that he was writing.

The fact of the book was new to Jack. "Have you the manuscript?" he asked.

"It was found in his room," the Deputy said.

"May I see it?"

"Certainly. But you'll find neither head nor tail to it."

It was brought, and Jack was obliged to confess the justice of the Deputy's description. It was the product of an insane brain. One could not read more than a line or two before the head began to whirl. But Jack discovered a clew in the manuscript which had apparently escaped the police. He did not call the attention of the Deputy to it, but made a mental note for his own use. On the first page under the many and fantastic titles of the proposed work was a dedication in two words:

"To Barbarossa"

Jack walked uptown turning over the word "Barbarossa" in his mind. Where had he heard it before? Was it the name of a famous historical character or an ocean liner? The sign of a branch of the Public Library gave him an idea. He went in and consulted an encyclopedia.

This told him two things; firstly, that Barbarossa meant Redbeard, and secondly, that the original Barbarossa was a Turkish sea rover. As he was unable to figure out any connection between the old freebooter and a modern anarchist, he deduced that the old nickname had been re-applied to some new wearer of a red beard.

At the library desk he inquired: "Is there any writer on anarchistic subjects who signs himself Barbarossa?"

"We have very little of that sort of matter," the lady librarian assured him frigidly. "There is no such name in our catalogue of authors."

"Is there a bookstore where they make a specialty of such writings?" asked Jack.

The librarian admitted with strong distaste that there was, and gave him the address.

It was a little basement shop far on the East side. It was presided over by a lanky-haired, spectacled youth, who sneered at Jack's good clothes, and was prepared to hate him on the spot.

"Have you anything by Barbarossa?" Jack asked at a venture.

"Barbarossa's never written any books that I know of," was the surly reply.

Jack thought with satisfaction: "Then there is a Barbarossa!" Aloud he said: "I mean anything he's written."

The youth looked at him suspiciously.

"I heard him speak," said Jack glibly. "I'm crazy to learn more about his ideas."

"Barbarossa writes for the *Future Age* magazine," said the snaky-haired one. "He's one of the editors. How is it you don't know that if you know him?"

"I don't know him," said Jack. "I only heard him speak. Have you got a copy of the *Future Age*?"

The young book-seller produced it. "There's his article this month," he said, pointing to a title in the contents. The author's name given opposite was Arno Sturani.

"Is that Barbarossa's real name?" asked Jack.

"Everybody knows that!" was the scornful reply.

Jack bought the magazine, as well as other anarchistic publications that caught his eye. He told himself it would be a good idea to study up their lingo a little, against a future need.

At a corner drug-store in the neighborhood he purchased a sheet of cheap note-paper and an envelope, and on the counter laboriously composed the following note:

Mr. Arno Sturani:

Dear Sir:

I read some of your articles In the "Future Age." I think they are great, but don't understand them very good. I am only a poor boy without much education. But I like to think about things. I want to force the capitalists to give us a square deal. I want to learn more about your ideas. Will you let me come to see you? Or tell me where you are going to speak next time.

Yours respectfully,
Henry Cassels.

The druggist gave his permission for Jack to receive an answer at his store, so he gave that as his address. He sent the letter in the care of the *Future Age* magazine.

"There's one line started," he said to himself, as he let it fall in the box.

14

Another thing that Jack had in mind was the necessity of disguising himself. Being an entire stranger to the art of make-up, he required instruction. Ralph, their private bell-boy at the Madagascar, had seemed the likeliest person to apply to in such a case. Leaving the hotel that morning, Jack had said to him carelessly:

"I'm invited to a masquerade. Where's the best place to go for an outfit? I want something better than the ordinary costumer."

"Why don't you try Harmon Evers?" was the reply. "All the theatrical people go to him. He's the greatest make-up artist in New York."

"Where's his place?"

"Twenty-ninth street, just east of the Avenue."

Jack now bent his steps in that direction. He discovered a neat little shop on the street level with a sign reading:

HARMON EVERS, WIGS AND THEATRICAL MAKEUP.

In each of the two paneled show-windows one marvelous wig was displayed on its stand, nothing else. The interior was discreetly curtained from view. Opening the door, the pungent odor of grease paints greeted Jack's nostrils. Inside was as neat as out. There was a showcase setting forth cosmetics, and a counter beyond with another wig or two on stands. Back of the counter were tiers of drawers neatly labeled. The wall outside the counter was filled by a collection of small engravings of historical personages with especial regard to their hirsute appendages. Away back in the shop were several curtained alcoves for trying on.

Behind the counter sat a little, dumpy old lady befrilled and befrizzed, who suggested an erstwhile favorite of the boards now retired. Her large, faded eyes fell on Jack with a startled look, which however instantly disappeared in the polite saleswoman, as she inquired what he wished.

It appeared that Mr. Evers was engaged with a customer.

This customer presently issued from one of the alcoves, a dandy of the old school who was obviously much beholden to the wig-maker's art. Evers followed at his heels, rubbing his hands, and proudly surveying his work. Jack had the impression of a stout, rubicund little man of middle-age, clean-shaven and bald as an egg. True to the custom of tradesmen generally, he neglected his trade in his own person.

He was talking volubly as he came: "A very interesting question, sir, the relation of brains to hair. It is popularly supposed that a bald head is the result of great mental activity, but I have not found it so in my practice. Among ordinary men it is about six of one and half a dozen of the other. But I believe that a man cannot rise to real heights of greatness without a good head of hair. Yes, I know, there was Julius Caesar, and I admit it would be difficult to prove my case by historical examples, because wigs have always been procurable, and fashionable portrait painters naturally do not call attention to them. But it is an interesting speculation. Good morning, sir."

Jack asked to speak to Mr. Evers in private, and was shown into one of the alcoves. It was like a theatrical dressing-room, with a mirror surrounded by electric lights, and a shelf beneath.

Jack did not offer to tell who he was, and the little wig-maker, who seemed the soul of discretion, betrayed no curiosity on the subject. Jack came to the point at once.

"Circumstances make it necessary for me to do a little private detective work, and I'm obliged to learn how to disguise myself, well enough I mean, so I can go about the streets without danger of recognition. Can it be done?"

"Certainly," said Mr. Evers. "It is done oftener than you suppose."

"What sort of disguise do you recommend?"

"Let me think," said Mr. Evers, putting a thoughtful finger to his chin.

Jack was sitting facing the mirror, while Evers stood behind him studying his reflection through half closed eyes. Meanwhile Jack took stock of him. In repose the garrulous little man's face showed unexpected lines of resolution. He had a strong eye. That kind of eye may be found in wig-maker or bank president, but whatever the trade of the possessor may be, it is a pretty safe guess that he is master of it. All the visible part of Evers' skin, neck, face, skull, was of a curious angry pink shade—but not unhealthy. He had but a fringe of gray hair around the base of his skull, and his eyebrows were scanty. Certainly, in extolling the superiority of hairy men he had been disinterested.

"It is a good mask," he said—meaning Jack's face. "Good bones, well placed. A promising foundation for me to work on. You are young, too.

No tell-tale lines for me to erase. Your hair is too luxuriant, but I don't suppose you want me to cut it."

"What would be the gain if it altered my usual appearance?"

"True, true! We'll get around that somehow. Difficulties only add zest to the artist's work."

After studying a little longer he said: "Since your purpose is to escape observation, I would suggest making you as insignificant as possible. Say a business man in a small way; industrious but not very bright; of very ordinary taste both in ideas and dress."

"My idea exactly!" said Jack.

"But I must impress upon you that my work here with false hair and pigments is only the beginning. To be successful our character must be constructed from the inside out. Before you leave here I will write out a description of the character as I see it, which I will ask you to study at your leisure. I particularly recommend that you repeat it to yourself just before falling asleep at night. It is the surest way of impressing it on your subconsciousness."

"Fine!" said Jack, more and more taken with the philosophic wig-maker.

Evers began to lay out the implements of his trade. While he worked he talked uninterruptedly.

"I assure you one's subconsciousness is all-important. Most people, unknown to themselves, play an assumed part throughout their lives, a part that has been suggested to the subconsciousness in early life by something they admire in other people or in books. When some great disturbance brings the real self to light people are amazed at what they discover in themselves.—Remove your coat, waistcoat and collar, please."

"Make it simple, please," said Jack. "Something that I can put off and on myself at need."

"The best art is always simple," said Mr. Evers. "First a wash for the entire face and neck. It is very thin and contains no grease to betray you in the sunlight. Its purpose is merely to dim the youthful glow of health that distinguishes you. See! You look fifteen years older already! A slightly darker tone under the eyes gives you a sedentary, slightly bilious look. Next heavy eyebrows, which with round spectacles will give you an owlish expression. Also a stiff, closely cropped mustache. You put on eyebrows and mustache with loose hair and glue which I will furnish you. Comb them out and clip them to the desired length after they are stuck on. The ready-made articles never look natural. You may depend upon the glue. It is my own invention. No amount of heat nor perspiration, nor soap and water can affect it, but it melts at a touch of alcohol. Lastly, pomade your hair liberally, and slick it down hard. See, it makes your hair look thin, and alters the whole shape of your head. There you are!"

"Wonderful!" said Jack, gazing at his strangely altered aspect.

"Oh, we've only just begun!" said Mr. Evers. "Next comes the question of clothes. Its importance cannot be exaggerated. Taste in clothes is of slow growth. The clothes of a youth tell you nothing, but a mature man's attire betrays him unerringly. Let me see! This requires study. We shall probably not hit it exactly at the first trial. I should say first a derby hat of very conservative shape, slightly old-fashioned, and a suit stiffly cut, of good material but ugly pattern of cloth. Shirt and necktie are very significant. They should be of common design and coloring, such as might be picked up at a sale. I have all such things here. The suit may not fit you perfectly, but it will take you as far as a clothing store where you can buy another."

In due course Jack was ready to brave the sunshine in his new guise. The charge was steep, but he could not deny that the work was worth it. He left his other clothes with Mr. Evers since he would have to return to the shop to change. The wig-maker stood off and examined him with satisfaction. Mrs. Evers was called on to admire her husband's work.

"What name would you suggest for my new character?" asked Jack, smiling.

Mr. Evers took the matter with entire seriousness. "Let me see—you look to me as if your name might be——" His face cleared—"I have it! Your name is certainly Mr. Pitman."

"Mr. Pitman it shall be!"

"Mr. Fred Pitman," added Evers.

As Jack left the shop it was a few minutes before twelve, that is to say, just about the time he had designed to try out his new character for the first. He made his way up to Forty-Second street, and took up his station before the building that housed the offices of the Eureka Protective Association.

Here he walked slowly up and down well lost in the crowd hurrying east and west. He found his disguise effective in that the passers-by no longer noticed him. Only when people stopped looking at him did Jack become aware that in his proper person he attracted friendly glances wherever he went. That started a curious speculation in his mind: "How do people know whether they want to look at you or not, if they don't look at you first to see what you are like?"

It was half-past twelve before the man he was waiting for appeared. Mr. Dave Anderson turned east on Forty-Second street at a brisk pace. The pseudo-Pitman followed close at his heels. The chase led across Fifth and Madison and in front of the Grand Central station. Jack began to fear that Anderson lived in the neighborhood, and was bound home.

But at a modest saloon on Lexington avenue, a place with a long-established air, he turned in. After loitering a moment or two outside Jack followed. Behind the saloon was a small glass-roofed "garden" set with tables. The settled familiar style of the waiters and diners suggested that this was a real eating-place. Jack commended Mr. Anderson's discrimination.

The tables accommodated four or six, and none was entirely vacant. It was therefore perfectly natural for Jack to seek one of the chairs at the table occupied by Anderson and another man. They made him welcome. Anderson scarcely looked at Jack.

The bill-of-fare provided Jack with an opening. "Are you a regular here?" he asked Anderson. "What's good?"

"To-day, the pot roast with noodles," was the prompt reply.

It came and it was good. Jack's hearty commendation of the dish led naturally to a further exchange of amenities. When one of any two people has a positive disposition to make friends, the task is usually not difficult. Mr. Anderson discovered in this chance acquaintance a man after his own heart, who thought the same as he on all important matters. They were soon talking like old cronies. They finished eating simultaneously, and left the place together. Anderson, who was of an expansive nature, had already mentioned that he ran a detective agency.

"You don't say!" said Mr. Pitman with an air of strong interest not unmixed with envy. "Well, say, that's more fun than pounding the pavements collecting overdue bills like I do."

"You must come around to my office some time, and let me show you a thing or two," said Mr. Anderson affably.

Jack was careful to accept the invitation as casually as it was given. "I sure will some time," he said.

They parted.

Jack went his way thinking with satisfaction: "There's my second line started, all right."

Mr. Pitman's business was now done for the day, and Jack thought it was high time Mr. Robinson re-embodied himself to look after his employer. But before he changed back he had a strong desire to test his disguise on some one who knew him better than Anderson. He thought of Kate. By this time she must be in the thick of her preparations to open her house.

To think of it was to turn his steps in that direction. In ten minutes he was at the foot of the steps. Sure enough the house was already transformed; wooden shutters taken down, doors and windows flung open, and a small army of workmen and cleaners visible inside.

"Verily, Kate is a wonder!" he said to himself.

Mounting the steps, he rang the bell with twinkling eyes. Kate herself answered the door. Jack, seeing her come through the dark hall, experienced a rush of delight. With her capable, businesslike air she was more adorable than ever. Jack longed to fling his arms around her to see how the business woman would take it—but fortunately restrained himself from an act so rash. She fronted him with a polite, inquiring look. It gives one a queer turn to meet that look on a familiar face.

"Is this Miss Storer?" he asked as polite as herself, though he was bubbling inside.

Kate had stoutly denied the necessity of her taking an assumed name.

She bowed.

"I understand you are fitting out this house to rent furnished apartments."

She seemed slightly surprised. "Yes. But may I ask how you learned of it?"

"Oh, a friend told me."

"What kind of accommodations do you require?"

Jack was hard put to it to keep from laughing in her face. Up till now he had been standing in the vestibule with the light behind him. But as Kate stood aside from the door, he stepped in and turned around, so thus his make-up was put to a full test.

"A room in the back," he, said, "away from the noises of the street. And not too high up. The second story rear would suit me very well."

"I'm sorry," she said soberly, "that room is already taken."

Jack could contain himself no longer. There was no one near. He took off his glasses and smiled his own smile. "Don't you know me?" he whispered.

Kate gasped and fell back a step. "Oh! I wasn't expecting you so soon!"

Jack chuckled.

A charwoman with bucket and brush came through the hall, and they were obliged to pull themselves together quickly.

"The gentleman who said he wanted that room may not come back," said Kate. "I'll show it to you anyway."

She led him upstairs. She had not yet touched Silas Gyde's room, and as they went in she was obliged to close the door after them to keep the people in the house from seeing the strange conglomeration inside.

Jack seized her hand. "Katy, darling, you take my breath away, you're so wonderful!" he said, trying to draw her towards him.

She would have none of that. "Behave yourself!" she said crushingly. "You know very well why I had to close the door! How can I go on with this if you're going to act in such a way! Please remember who you're supposed to be! Do you suppose I'm going to be familiar with my lodgers!"

"Oh, I forgot everything except how sweet you are!" groaned Jack.

"Look in the glass!" she said. "Do you suppose I want that yellow face near mine?"

He frowned and rubbed his chin ruefully, not quite knowing how to take this left-handed compliment. "But—but I shan't be able to see you for ages, except as Pitman," he complained.

"Well, I shall survive it," she said briskly.

"Aw, Katy!"

She changed the subject in her own prompt way. "It's really a wonderful disguise!" she said. "How ever did you do it?"

He told her of his experience with Evers.

"And you," he said, "you haven't let any grass grow under your feet. You can open up to-morrow."

"Hardly that. My greatest problem is this room. How can I let the cleaners in here?"

"You and I had better do this," said Jack, careful not to betray any pleasure in the prospect.

"How can you find time?"

"I'll send Bobo to a musical comedy to-night, and slip in through the vault. That is if you'll be here to-night."

"I've already fitted up a room for Mother and I. We'll be here."

"Good!" said Jack. The prospect of a stolen interview with the demure Kate was unspeakably delightful.

He told her something of his adventures the night before.

"What a fool you have on your hands!" said Kate scornfully. "You'd better hurry back and see what he's up to now."

"But I've heaps more to tell you."

"I'm busy. So are you. Tell me to-night. What will the servants say if we stay in here with the door closed? Run along!"

And she fairly shooed him out of the house.

Jack hastened down to Evers' shop, washed his face, changed his clothes, and returned to the Madagascar. Evers provided him with everything necessary to re-assume the personality of Mr. Pitman when the time came.

Bobo was out. Jack applied to Ralph for information as to his movements. That preturnaturally knowing youth was bursting with it.

"Sure, I seen him go out. 'Bout an hour ago. Young lady come for him."

In spite of himself Jack was betrayed into a startled exclamation.

Thus encouraged, Ralph went on with gusto. "She called him up this morning—that is I guess it was the same one. I was in the room brushin' his clo'es, and I answered the 'phone. I hears a voice like butter creams: 'Is this Mr. Norman?' Umm! But when she found it was me the cream froze."

"Mr. Norman goes to the 'phone, and say, you could see by the smile that tickled his ears that she was feedin' him the Martha Washingtons then. 'Aw'fly good of you to call me up,' says he. 'No, I don't think it was improper at all.' Then she must have ast him to lunch, for he said 'Sure!' in a voice that near cracked the transmitter, and bounced up and down like a kid when it sees its bottle.

"But then he remembered somepin and his joy was turned to grief. 'Oh, I forgot, I can't come,' he says. I heard her voice squeakin' over the wire: 'Why?' He says: 'I got a date with my secretary: very important business.' After that she did most of the talkin'. He only said: 'I can't! I can't! Say, I'm sorry!' And so on. Say, he stuck to it, too, and at last she hung up. Say, he was almost cryin' when he come away. He throws himself down on the bed and never says a word to me."

"Well, what then?" asked Jack.

"About half an hour after I was down in the office when I hear a young lady in a Kolinsky cape ask at the desk for Mr. Norman. A looker?—say, boss, some scenery! I was sent up with her card. On the back she had written:

"I have come for you."

"Did he go?" asked Jack.

"Did he go? Does a chicken run when it hears the corn fall in the yard!"

"Hm! What name was on the card?"

"Miss Miriam Culbreth."

15

In the end Jack had to give up the idea of separating Bobo from the lovely Miriam. For one thing Jack needed Miriam and Mrs. Cleaver in his present business, and Bobo supplied his only excuse for going there. The ladies were not interested in the humble secretary for himself.

So he warned Bobo afresh, and prayed that the infatuated youth might not be led into any irrevocable step before he was able to tell him the whole truth about his inamorata.

Meanwhile one of those tremendous intimacies characteristic of the fluff of society sprang up between the four. Within a few days Bobo and Jack were all but living at Mrs. Cleaver's house. A hundredfold millionaire gets on fast socially. Jack was always included in Bobo's invitations as an understood thing. One witty lady was heard to call him the sugar that coated the pill.

Jack speculated endlessly on the real nature of the relations between Clara Cleaver and Miriam. It was given out that they were cousins, and on the surface they exhibited a formal affection towards each other. But that they did not love each other was very clear. Dislike the same as murder will out. Off her guard Mrs. Cleaver's manner towards Miriam was as to something she was obliged to put up with, and the younger woman in her more natural moments displayed more than a touch of arrogance towards her supposed hostess. Moreover, Mrs. Cleaver was clearly well-born and Miriam just as clearly was not. Not for a moment did Jack believe in the supposed blood relationship.

Jack liked Mrs. Cleaver a lot better than Miriam. The former might be light-headed, vain, luxury-loving, rather silly, but she had a kind heart. Jack could not conceive of her as being engaged in calculated villainy. Yet she must be in the game, too. She and Miriam worked together. The farther he explored this amazing game the greater became Jack's perplexity. The different elements were so incongruous.

"But if I go deep enough I *must* find the link that connects them all!" he told himself. "The decent little gentleman with the imperial; Barbarossa, the anarchist; Dave Anderson, the detective; Clara Cleaver, the well-born lady, and Miriam Culbreth, the adventuress!"

The relation between Jack and Miriam was a complicated one. As in the beginning, she made it clear that while she intended to marry the millionaire she was not averse to having the secretary make love to her.

Jack's indifference piqued the spoiled beauty almost beyond bearing. She longed to bring him to her feet, and she hated him cordially, too, as he learned before he had been visiting Mrs. Cleaver's house many days.

It was the tea hour. Jack had come after Bobo, but found everybody out. They had left word for him to wait, so he drifted up to the library where they usually had tea, and picking up a book he dropped into a chair to read. At his left hand hung a portière dividing the library from the central hall, which ran up through the house.

After a little while Miriam and Bobo came up in the elevator. Evidently there had been a misunderstanding about Jack's arrival—possibly some other servant had admitted them, for Miriam said:

"We'll wait a while for him before we ring for tea."

They dropped into a cozy corner in the hall, a nook favored of couples. It was immediately on the other side of the curtain at Jack's hand and he could therefore hear every word spoken above a whisper. He was debating with himself whether or not the circumstances justified him in playing the eavesdropper, when he heard Miriam say:

"You've never told me how you and Jack met, and how you came to choose him for your secretary."

That decided Jack. He gave no sign of his presence.

Bobo replied: "Oh, I've known him a good while. When I worked in the sash factory down-town, he was there, too."

"What did you do there?"

"Bookkeeper."

"What did Jack do?"

"Oh he—he was a bookkeeper, too. There were two of us. And we were friends outside the office, too. Used to go round together nights. So when I came into my money—why it was natural for me to get Jack to help me to look after it."

"Not bad for Bobo," thought Jack. He pricked up his ears at the next words.

"I don't see how you put up with him!" said Miriam.

"Put up with him!" echoed Bobo. In his fancy Jack could see the blank look that overspread the honest fat face. "Why—why, what's the matter with Jack?"

"The way he runs you, I mean. One would think he was the millionaire, and you the hired secretary."

Bobo made queer, scared noises in his throat. It seemed to Jack that Miriam must suspect that she had hit the nail on the head, but apparently she did not, for her next words were in the same drawling, careless tone.

"He all but tells you how to answer when people speak to you."

"Oh!" said Bobo, somewhat relieved. "But Jack's clever, and I'm not."

"You're not as stupid as he likes to make out," suggested Miriam.

"Devil!" thought Jack.

"Make out!" said Bobo. "Jack doesn't make out anything. He's my friend."

"My poor Bobo!" she said with indulgent tenderness. "You're criminally good-natured! Of course he knows which side his bread is buttered on. He's not going to say anything openly. But *friends*! Oh, how blind you are!"

"Jack and I are friends," repeated Bobo. "Jack's on the square!"

She laughed delicately. Jack guessed that she patted Bobo's hand or something like that. "Oh, well, let's change the subject," she said in a tone that forced him to continue it.

"No," said Bobo, just as she had intended him to. "Tell me what you mean. Does he talk about me?"

"Oh, it isn't what he *says*," she said with seeming reluctance. "But it makes me mad! Always poking fun at you!"

"Liar!" thought Jack.

"Making fun of me!" said Bobo in hurt tones. "Behind my back! I didn't think it of him!"

"There, forget it," she said soothingly. "It doesn't make any difference to your real friends."

"What did he say about me?"

"I shan't tell you. I don't want to make trouble."

Jack grimly smiled to himself.

"But I don't see why you put up with it," she presently went on. "As it is, you daren't call your soul your own. He manages you like a child—you a grown man."

"What can I do?" said poor Bobo.

"Fire him!"

"So that's your game!" thought Jack. "It's foredoomed to failure, lady!"

"Oh, I can't do that!" said Bobo horrified.

"Why not? I guess you can manage your own affairs as well as other men, can't you? Get a lawyer to help you. Everybody would think more of you if you came right out and put Jack in his place. They talk about it, you know. It's unmanly to submit to the dictation of one who is really no more than your servant. Send him away, and see how much better you'll get along with people. He fixes it so that you always show to a disadvantage beside him. That hurts me, because I know what there is in you!"

"Oh, you siren!" thought Jack. In a way, he could not but admire her cleverness.

She went on: "Some day I suppose you'll want to marry." Jack could imagine how modestly she cast down the long lashes when she said this. "I say this for your own good. No woman, you know, would want to put herself in the position of being under the thumb of her husband's secretary."

All Bobo could find to say was: "I'm sorry you don't like him." Jack had to confess to himself that a better man than Bobo might well have been stumped by such a situation.

"Oh, it doesn't matter about me," she said, "but he is openly rude to me. You don't seem to care."

"I do! I do!" cried poor Bobo. "I'll put a stop to that. I'll speak to him!"

"Yes," she said with a kind of plaintive spitefulness, "tell him I told you, and then he'll act worse to me than ever. If you cared about me at all, you wouldn't keep him for another day."

"You just leave it to me, I'll fix it," said Bobo desperately.

"That's what you say every day, but I don't see any change."

"So this is an everyday affair!" thought Jack. "Poor Bobo!"

"It can't go on," she said gloomily. "I think too much of you as a friend to stand seeing another man run you. I'd rather give you up—as a friend. If I've got to put up with Jack Robinson, I don't want to see you any more."

The softest creature, pushed to the wall, shows fight. "I won't fire Jack," said Bobo sullenly. "You're just trying to run me the same way you say he is. If I've got to go, I'll go!"

"Good for Bobo!" thought Jack.

She quickly performed the undignified maneuver known as climbing down. "No, Bobo," she said meltingly. "You are right. I shouldn't have spoken that way. It is none of my business. But I can't bear to see you imposed on. It made me forget myself!"

"I can take care of myself," muttered Bobo.

"Forgive me," she said angelically, "and let's change the subject. Come into the library, and I'll order tea."

It was Jack's turn to be surprised. He judged from her voice that she had already risen, so he had about two seconds to make up his mind how to act. He relaxed completely in the big chair, let his head fall back, closed his eyes and breathed deeply.

She came between the curtains. He heard the swish of her silk petticoat.

"Oh!" she said sharply. Surprise, fear, chagrin, all were blended in the sound.

Bobo at her heels said blankly: "I'll be jiggered!"

Jack opened his eyes sleepily, blinked at the sight of them, and sprang up.

"What's the matter!" he said. "Where am I? Oh—I must have fallen asleep. Please excuse me!"

He flattered himself it was very well done. Bobo at least was completely taken in. As to the girl, he could not be sure. It was likely that being an accomplished dissimulator herself, she would on principle suspect him of dissimulation.

But she gave away nothing in her face. "You're excusable," she said with a light laugh. "They told us you hadn't come. If you could have seen how funny you looked! Come on, let's have tea."

Throughout that ceremony Jack labored with his most light-hearted air to remove any suspicions she might have that he had overheard her talk with Bobo. It was not easy to read that young lady's face, but he believed that he saw her gradually relax and be at ease again.

The sequel to this scene took place later the same night. Jack, Bobo and Miriam went to the theater, and afterwards to the Alpine Heights to sup. Having arrived at the exquisite restaurant, Miriam announced that she had lost a pearl pin in the theater. Poor Bobo had to go back after it, though he had already ordered a *recherché* little supper. Jack offered to go, but Miriam silenced him with a peculiar look, so he sat back and let things take their course.

When they were alone together, Miriam softly said, turning the hazel eyes full on him: "Why can't we be friends, Jack?"

He could have sworn the lovely orbs were big with tears, and in spite of himself his heart leaped; she was so beautiful! "Steady!" he whispered to himself. "It's probably onions or pepper!"

"Aren't we friends?" he said with an air of surprise.

She sadly shook her head. "You know we're not! You distrust me, dislike me; you cannot hide it!"

"It's not so!" said Jack. "I've already explained what it is that you think is dislike. You put a man on the defensive. You've already gobbled up poor Bobo, skin and bones and hymn-book, too! I've got to be careful!"

"Oh, you won't be serious!" she pouted. "And you saw how I lied to get the chance of speaking to you alone."

"Then there wasn't any pearl pin?"

"Of course not!"

"Poor Bobo! I'll be serious. What is it?"

"Oh, it's nothing special! I just wanted to see if I couldn't bring about a better understanding between you and me. It's awfully hard on Bobo, who is such friends with both of us—that you and I can't get on better I mean."

"Let's have a better understanding!" said Jack heartily. Privately he was thinking: "Lovely lady, what are you driving at now?"

"Bobo is such a dear," she went on, "but he's terribly dependent. He depends on you, and now he's beginning to depend on me! Well, it seems to me that we share a pretty serious responsibility, his having all that money and all. We ought to consult about what we should do, and agree on a course of action. If you and I pull against each other, Bobo will be torn in two, so to speak."

Jack looked seriously impressed, but inwardly he was grinning wickedly. "Ha!" he thought, "having failed in her effort to kick me out she is now proposing in diplomatic language that we get together and whack up." Aloud he said: "I expect you're right, though I hadn't thought of it that way. I thought I would take care of Bobo's business affairs, and you would look after his personal character."

"But under altered circumstances it might be difficult," she said darkly.

"Eh?"

"Don't be dense. I suppose you know that Bobo wants to marry me."

Jack never batted an eye. "I can't say that I am exactly surprised. Nor that I blame him," he added gallantly.

"Be serious. Of course I haven't accepted him yet. I have to be sure of my own feelings."

Jack stroked his lip to hide a grim smile.

"Have you any objection to his marrying me?" she asked boldly.

Jack lied quickly. "None whatever."

"Then why did you try to poison his mind against me?"

Jack thought: "Oh, Bobo! Bobo! I'm glad I didn't tell you all." To her he said with seeming astonishment: "I! Poison his mind against you! What an idea!"

"Well, try to dissuade him from—er—paying me attention."

"My dear Miriam, put yourself in my place for a moment. I am Bobo's friend. I do feel the responsibility of looking after him, just as you say. He meets a lovely girl of whom we know nothing, a girl lovely enough to believe the worst of—and he falls head over heels in love. Was it not my plain duty to beg him to go slow, to think what he was doing?"

"What do you mean, believe the worst of?"

"Just a figure of speech. You are really remarkably beautiful. It isn't reasonable to suppose that you have reached your present age without having had—well, exciting things happen to you."

She shrugged. "I wish I had had." She was unable to keep a sharp note out of her voice. "You told him that I—wasn't all that I ought to be."

"I had to say something to make him pull up long enough to give me time to find out."

"Then you haven't got anything against me?"

Jack's eyes were as limpid as a mountain stream. If one is going to lie, one may as well do it artistically. "Nothing in the world, Miriam!"

She leaned across the table and gave his hand a little squeeze. "I'm so glad we've had this talk," she murmured.

They beamed on each other in seeming friendly fashion—but there were hard points of light in each pair of eyes.

"Pleasant little comedy," thought Jack. "I'm willing to keep it up as long as she is."

"We must often consult together, and decide what is best for Bobo," she went on sweetly. "And if he won't do things that you think he ought, I'll add my influence. And then I'll get you to help me with him when I need you."

"Fine!" said Jack. "Poor Bobo!" he silently added.

As was usual with this young lady, her romantic and sentimental scenes generally led up to a very practical climax.

"Has Bobo given you power of attorney?" she asked.

"No."

"Why is it he won't draw even the smallest of checks unless you are there?"

"Oh, that was one of the things we agreed on when I took the job of secretary. He wanted to be saved from throwing it about."

"Very wise," said Miriam. "But now that he has another disinterested friend the situation is altered, isn't it? If I am with him it will be sufficient. I shall tell him that you release him from that part of your agreement." This was said with a charming smile, as a sort of experimental joke.

Jack smiled back no less sweetly. "But I have not released him."

"I thought we were going to work together," she pouted.

Jack still affected to treat the matter as a joke. "You surely don't expect me to yield up the only source of my power!—the hand upon the purse strings!"

She shook an arch finger at him—but there was an angry spark in the hazel eyes. "Beware!" she said merrily. "The power of the faithful secretary is threatened by the adored wife. You'd better accept my offer of an alliance when it is open."

"Oh, when Bobo takes a wife I'll resign," said Jack, laughing.

Bobo came bustling back at this juncture. "I've had a deuce of a time," he grumbled. "The theater was closed. I found the watchman, but he wouldn't let me in. Said he'd find the pin if it was there, and turn it into the box-office. Old fool!"

"It was cruel of me to send you all that way," cooed Miriam. "Sit down and eat a good supper. I shan't be able to eat a mouthful till you say you forgive me!"

"Forgive you!" cried poor Bobo. "I'd go to China and back if it would please you!"

They gazed into each other's eyes, while Jack grimly sipped his wine. "You're clever," he was thinking, "but there's a serious defect in your method. How do you expect me to fall for you, when you let me see you making such a fool of Bobo!"

16

Meanwhile Jack was not neglecting his other "lines." In the character of Mr. Pitman he lunched with Dave Anderson nearly every day, and the intimacy between them ripened fast. After several invitations, Mr. Pitman finally allowed himself to be persuaded to visit Mr. Anderson's office.

They sat in the inner office with their cigars, and discussed crime in all its aspects.

"Anything—er—specially interesting on just now?" asked Mr. Pitman, with a look suggesting that he was not averse to hearing the most horrible details. Jack, under Evers' tuition had developed the character of Pitman to a high degree of artistry.

"No. The fact is I don't go after ordinary business any more; don't have to. I only have one case, so to speak, and that keeps me on Easy street. All I have to do is sit here and take the money."

"What a cinch! What kind of case is it?"

"Did you notice the name on the door?"

"Eureka Protective Association. Whom do you protect?"

"Millionaires!"

Thereupon Jack had to submit to hearing again what a fine concern Eureka was, what a benefit it conferred on the public, etc., etc. Though Anderson was at his ease with his friend, he told it all as seriously as before; there was no suggestion of a tongue in his cheek. Jack listened with well-assumed interest, hoping to get some real light on the subject later.

"How did you get into it in the first place?" he asked.

"Dumb luck!" said Anderson. "I'll tell you all about it some day."

Jack, fearful of spoiling everything by a display of eagerness, let the matter drop for the present. Fate presently rewarded his discretion.

"I haven't a thing to do this afternoon," said Anderson. "And you said you weren't busy. Let's go out and have a drink."

Mr. Pitman did not refuse, of course. They went and had their drink, and had another, and in the course of the afternoon Anderson's tongue was gradually unloosed, and the whole story came out.

"It was three years ago it started. I was doing a general detective business, and just barely making out, week by week. It was the time that big millionaire Ames Benton was killed by anarchists; remember?"

Jack nodded. He had a feeling that the loose ends of his case were now beginning to draw together.

"One day an oldish gentleman called at my office," Anderson went on, "a decent, respectable body, that you would expect to see coming out of church on Sunday morning. His hair was fixed in an old-fashioned way, sort of brushed forward of his ears like, and he wore a heavy mustache and neat little goatee or imperial."

Jack had the pleasant feeling that he was getting "warm" as children say in their game. They were sitting in an alcove of a saloon under the elevated railway, and he was glad of the semi-gloom of the place that prevented Anderson from seeing his face too clearly.

"He didn't give me his name," Anderson went on, "in fact I don't know it to this day. I just call him 'Mr. B.' He told me right off the bat that he was an anarchist, and I was a bit startled, noticing the little black satchel he carried. I remarked that he didn't gee with my idea of a Red, and he explained that he was disguised. So I don't even know what he looks like naturally."

"He went on to tell me that he had experienced what he called a change of heart—sort o' got religion you understand. The murder of Mr. Benton had sickened him, he said, and now he was anxious to do something to make up for the harm he had caused."

"He let on that he was one of the leading Reds of the country, a kid of supreme grand master with the entrée to every lodge. He said he wasn't going to betray any of his comrades, but that with my help, if I was willing, he would draw their teeth, so to speak, by giving warning to their intended victims.

"Well, I wasn't in a philanthropic mood myself, being as I had so much trouble already to make ends meet, and I didn't want to invite trouble with the Reds or anybody else, so at first I was cool to his scheme. But as he talked on I began to wake up to the possibilities.

"Well, sir, we began to dope out the scheme of Eureka right then, or rather, he doped it out and I listened with big ears. He had it all thought out before he came. When he talked about getting all the millionaires to subscribe for personal protection, I saw a happy future opening up. The best of it was, it was absolutely bona fide, and on the level; we really had something to sell them, for my friend, as I say, had the entrée to every anarchistic circle in the country, and was prepared to furnish me with full information of any plot they laid against a rich man."

"The only thing we stuck on was the division of the proceeds. He demanded seventy-five per cent. I tried to laugh him down—but it didn't get across. He wasn't a man you could get gay with. He had an eye that fixed you like a brad-awl.

"'You forget,' he said, 'that I'm the one who supplies the essential thing. I could get any one of a hundred detective agencies for the rest.'

"I tried to bluff him a bit. 'Not after you've opened it to me,' I said. 'I could queer it!'

"'You won't do that,' he said very quiet. And, by Gad, when he fixed me with those eyes, I thought of a dozen horrible deaths I might die, and I knew that I couldn't split on him if I wanted to. A wonderful man. In the end I had to accept his hard terms.

"Well, that's all. From the start it worked like a charm. With the horrible death of Ames Benton fresh in their minds, the millionaires fell all over themselves to subscribe for protection. We started at a moderate figure, and gradually jacked up their dues. You'd open your eyes if I told you the amount of money that passes through this little office every month."

"Give me an idea," said Jack.

"That's something I'll never tell any man," said Anderson with a slightly drunken leer.

"Do you only operate in the city here?"

"Yes. He may have other agencies outside. He may have other agencies right here in town for all I know. It was part of our agreement that I was to approach nobody except the men whose names he furnished. I haven't all the millionaires on my books by a long sight."

"Do you mean to tell me you've been in business with this man for three years and don't even know his right name?"

"It's a fact, and what's more I've never laid eyes on him from that day to this."

"Come off!" said Jack incredulously.

"It's a fact, I tell you. It stands to reason, don't it, that he couldn't be seen around here?"

"You could meet him outside."

"Too risky. If the other anarchists got on to his connection with me, his life wouldn't be worth a plugged nickel!"

"But you know where he lives?"

Anderson shook his head.

"Then how do you send him his share of the proceeds?"

"I send it in cash on a certain day every week. I put it in an envelope together with a statement of the week's business, and send it to a name and address previously furnished me that day over the 'phone. It's always different. Generally to a hotel, to be called for. I send it by messenger."

"Have you never had the curiosity to follow up the messenger?"

"No, sir! I've learned that it's healthier for me to follow instructions. I get my instructions over the 'phone, and by Gad! if they're not carried out to the letter he knows it, and I soon know it from him!"

"He must be a wonderful man."

"He's a marvel! Say it scares you like, the way he knows things. He tells me everything to do: who to see and how to approach him; how to follow him up. And everything always turns out just the way he says. It's like magic!"

Anderson's talk got a little muzzy, and drifted away to other subjects. A perfunctory attention was all he required and Jack's brain was free to ponder on what he had heard. He believed Anderson's story in the main. Incredible as it had seemed beforehand, he no longer doubted that Anderson was an innocent tool in the affair—at least comparatively innocent. The great sums he was making had no doubt helped to quiet an inquiring mind. When one is anxious not to discover an unpleasant fact, one may very easily remain in ignorance of it through all.

It began to look as if the decent little gentleman with the goatee was the guiding spirit in the whole scheme. Jack had made a long step forward in his investigation, but he now found himself opposed by an intelligence of the first class; one before whom Jack's youth and inexperience might well falter a little. He marvelled at the cunning with which the principal used innocent men to further his criminal projects. Apparently he had built up a highly organized business of blackmail, with various departments all working independently of each other. And he gathered up all strings in his own hands.

17

Arno Sturani, otherwise "Barbarossa," answered Jack's note and invited him to call at his house in the evening.

Jack visited Evers' shop as a preliminary, and he was obliged to go in the afternoon before closing hours. He dispatched Bobo to dine with Mrs. Cleaver and Miriam. While Bobo could hardly be said to be safe in that company, still it was some satisfaction to Jack to know where he was.

The astute little wig-maker and his wife, the retired ballet-dancer, greeted Jack like an old and valued customer. Old-fashioned shop-keepers have this art.

"Everything going well?" asked Mr. Evers.

"Splendidly!"

"That little job I did for you; has it served its turn?"

"Couldn't have been better."

"What do you require to-day?"

"A fresh make-up for another purpose."

"Ah! Come back into one of the dressing-rooms."

Mr. Evers was distressed to learn that Jack had put himself out to get to the shop before closing time.

"You can make an appointment by 'phone for any hour of the day or night," he said. "Of course it would be too conspicuous for me to let you in and out of the shop after closing hours, but my apartment is upstairs. Come there any time, and we can get what we need out of the shop."

Jack thanked him. "This time," he said, "I want to look like a mere lad, a poor boy in cheap worn clothes, but a student, a highbrow, full of wild, anarchistic ideas."

"Anarchistic?" said Mr. Evers, elevating the scant eyebrows. "Are you going into that kind of society?"

"Temporarily."

"Beware! I know nothing about such people, but I am told they are like wild beasts. Curious, isn't it, how they run to hair? Disturbs all my theories. Such beards! Such tangled, flowing locks. How is it that men so unbalanced are thus favored?"

"I don't know," said Jack, smiling. "Perhaps they don't have any more than other men to start with, but spare the scissors and the razor."

"I've taken that into account. Even so, you never heard of a bald anarchist, did you?"

Jack admitted that he had not. "Perhaps I can give you some first-hand information later," he added.

Mr. Evers said he would be glad of it.

"Now let me see as to your make-up," he went on. "Your luxuriant hair will now come in handy. Let it fall over your eyes so. A pair of thick glasses this time to make you look short-sighted. I have a pair specially made with lenses of clear glass let in to enable you to see where you are going. Clothes are the principal item. I think I have just what you require."

"It's no trouble for me to make you look like a youth who might frequent such company," he said, "but the question is, can you keep up the character once you get there? I am told those people talk a strange jargon of phrases that the uninitiated cannot understand."

"I've been boning up on their literature," said Jack. "I think I can keep my end up."

"Ah, I see I am not dealing with a tyro," said Mr. Evers with a flattering air of respect.

Jack dined at an humble little restaurant on the East Side, such as befitted his new condition, and afterwards presented himself at the address on East Broadway furnished by Sturani's letter. It was one of those plain old-fashioned dwellings common in the neighborhood. They are occupied by the elite of the East Side; that is to say, doctors, lawyers, politicians, who still find it profitable to live among their clients and constituents.

Barbarossa's house was a combination of residence, school and club. On a brass plate beside the door was the legend: "Sturani School of Social Science." A youth, much the same as the one who had sold him books, let Jack in, and after favoring him with a hard stare, led him to a small room at the back and told him to wait. The house seemed to be full of Barbarossa's disciples. Jack had glimpses of groups in the unfurnished parlors, arguing with fury.

Jack had learned that Barbarossa's position among anarchists corresponded in a way with the description of himself which the mysterious Mr. B. had furnished Anderson, and he naturally inferred that Barbarossa might be another alias of Mr. B.'s. His heart beat fast with excitement as he waited for him, thinking that he was perhaps about to come face to face with his real adversary.

But when the redoubtable Barbarossa plunged into the room, Jack was speedily disillusioned of his hopes. Plunged is the only word to use: the anarchist's movements were like those of a frolicking mastiff—only Barbarossa always affected an air of weighty import. He was enormously fat, and it was genuine fat, as Jack could tell by the shake and sag of him as he flung himself into a chair. By no stretch could he have transformed himself into the neat, decent little gentleman so often described to Jack. This was not Mr. B.

Moreover, Barbarossa had a mass of red hair standing on end around his head like a halo, and a spreading red beard. These were indubitably real, too, and had obviously taken years to produce.

"You're Cassels," grunted Barbarossa.

"Yes, sir."

"Humph! English!"

"English descent, sir."

"We don't get many English boys interested in ideas."

Jack privately hoped this would not count against him. He had considered assuming a foreign character, but had given it up as being too difficult to maintain.

"What do you want of me?" demanded Barbarossa.

"I want to learn," said Jack. "I want to meet men with ideas. I want to take part in the movement."

"Have you any money?"

Jack was somewhat taken aback. "A little. I'm only a working-boy."

"If you can pay, you can come to my school. It's fifteen dollars payable in advance. Afternoon or evening classes. You can come as often as you want."

"I'll come," said Jack. "I'll bring the money to-morrow. Is there some work I could do, too? For the Cause. Can I belong to a circle?"

"Circle?" said Barbarossa with a sharp glance of his little blue eyes—they were at once irascible and short-sighted, eyes of a fanatic. "What kind of a circle?"

"Liberators."

"I don't know what you're talking about. If there is any such thing, I suppose you'll be invited to belong when you've proved yourself worthy. Come to my school and I'll put some ideas into your head if it's not too English."

"Thank you, sir," said Jack rising. This was as far as he supposed he could get on the first meeting.

"By the way, who told you about me?" demanded Barbarossa.

"I read your articles in the *Future Age*."

"Well, then, who told you about the *Future Age*?"

Jack was tempted to try an experiment. "Fellow I used to room with. The hero who croaked old Silas Gyde. Emil Jansen."

It had an electrical effect. Barbarossa was out of his chair with a bound. His ruddy cheeks turned a gray color, on which the network of little dark veins stood out startlingly.

"Silence! Don't speak that name here! Hero nothing! Madman! Fool! What have you got to do with *him*?"

"Why, nothing!" stammered Jack, affecting a great confusion. "Isn't he one of you? Isn't he working for the Cause?"

"I don't know him!" cried Barbarossa. "If he claims to be my friend I repudiate him! Such madmen are like to ruin us all!"

"But——you said in your article that I read, that the capitalistic order must be overthrown at any cost. That he was a hero who gave up his life to accomplish it."

"That's all right in a periodical," said Barbarossa. "They don't care what you write. But murder——!" The fat man shuddered. "I'm a responsible citizen. I've got a wife and four children to think of."

Jack thought: "In anarchy, like other religions, there seems to be a considerable gap between preaching and practising."

"What did Jansen tell you about me?" demanded Barbarossa.

"Nothing particular," said Jack. "He just let on that he admired you, and was trying to live according to your teachings. He read me some out of a book he was writing. He dedicated it to you."

"What!" cried Barbarossa. "In writing?"

"Yes, it was written down."

"And the police searched his room! Oh, my God! I'm done!" He collapsed in his chair.

Jack looked at the collapsed mountain of flesh, and suppressed a smile. Not a very formidable object this.

"Was it my right name, Sturani?" Barbarossa asked anxiously.

"No. He had written: 'To Barbarossa.'"

A little color returned to the big man's face. "Oh, well, the police are stupid. Maybe they won't establish the connection. I expect I would have heard from them before this if they had. That's all, Cassels; you can go."

"And may I come to the school to-morrow?"

"Sure, if you bring the money."

From a public booth, Jack telephoned Harmon Evers that he would be right up to change back to his proper person.

On the way uptown he sought to digest what he had learned.

"Barbarossa is certainly not the man I'm looking for. Just the same, his fright makes it clear that he is at the head of some group that Emil Jansen belonged to. I must join that group. It's hardly possible that Barbarossa himself instigated the attack on Silas Gyde. He's only a paper anarchist. Somewhere back of him I'll find the cagy little 'Mr. B.' again. Lordy! This case lengthens out like a telescope!"

"Well!" said Mr. Evers, "you're back early. Did you see any anarchists? How about their hair?"

"The main guy of all had a bald spot as big as a saucer. Just a hedge of hair all around like the burning bush in bloom."

"Well, I'm relieved to hear that."

18

Jack had not yet succeeded in establishing just where Miriam and Mrs. Cleaver fitted into the jig-saw puzzle he had to solve. Miriam, from the foreknowledge he had gained from Silas Gyde's letter, he had no hesitating in dubbing an out-and-out bad one, but he was less sure about Clara. He set himself to discover more about her.

There was nothing mysterious about her origin, and he had no difficulty in learning the main facts about her from outside sources. She was a poor girl, the daughter of a great physician who had lived beyond his means. She had married before her father's death, the son of a wealthy and prominent family, but he, having run through his fortune, shot himself. She had, therefore, been left penniless, nor had she, so far as was known, received any legacy since his death.

To Jack, therefore, the grand question was, where did she get the money that provided the Park Avenue house, the bands of servants, the magnificent entertainments; the dresses, jewels, furs and automobiles. It was charitably said that she had made it in lucky speculations, but Jack was not satisfied with that. One must have something to speculate with. There had never been any scandal in connection with her name.

These parties of Mrs. Cleaver's offered no lack of food for speculation. In her way Clara was quite the rage, and every element of smart New York society was represented among the guests—except perhaps the most hide-bound exclusives. She always took care to provide, too, a leaven of clever artistic people, "to amuse the rich," she said.

So far everything was usual and explainable, but there was always another element present that mystified Jack. This consisted of various young people of both sexes, always good-looking, perfectly dressed and at least superficially well-bred; often vivacious and charming—but invariably with hard, wary eyes.

These self-possessed youngsters turned up mysteriously, and were as mysteriously lost sight of again. They made a convenience of Mrs. Cleaver's house almost as if it had been a hotel. Mrs. Cleaver introduced them effusively at her parties like dear friends, but at other times she ignored them—and they as frankly returned the compliment. Sometimes they made good independently of her and enjoyed a more or less brief career in society. Sometimes they disappeared and were seen no more.

Mrs. Cleaver was not by any means a prudent, wary woman, and it was not difficult for Jack to learn where she banked. She often took him about with her. She had four bank accounts. Through the good offices of Mr. Delamare Jack next learned from the books of the banks concerned, that she had been in the habit of depositing a thousand dollars weekly. In other words, every Friday afternoon she took a thousand dollars downtown and added it to one of her four accounts.

Having learned so much, the next time Friday came around Jack took care to be on hand early at the Cleaver house. He kept his eyes open for all that took place that morning. Just before lunch a messenger boy delivered a small packet for Mrs. Cleaver. Jack by a casual question or two of a servant, learned that this was a regular happening on Friday mornings, and that the packet was always carried direct to Mrs. Cleaver by her orders.

Jack, who had already learned from Anderson of the large part played by the messenger service in Mr. B.'s operations, guessed that this packet came direct from him. It was a good enough working theory anyway. Fifty thousand a year was no mean price! For that, Jack figured, Mrs. Cleaver lent her name and social position to the blackmailers, and allowed them to use her house as a base of operations. It was likely he thought that she did not know what their game was, and with that handsome sum coming in so regularly, did not care to inquire.

Jack conceived the bold idea of enlightening Mrs. Cleaver, trusting to her better qualities to turn her against her present employer, and ally her with himself.

His opportunity to talk to her alone came that night, when Miriam and Bobo failed to return for dinner. Jack and Clara dined alone.

At the end of the meal she said listlessly: "Where shall we go to-night?"

"Let's not go anywhere for a change," said Jack. "Let's have a fire in the library, and sit and talk."

That struck her as a pleasantly novel idea. "All right. I'm sick of the game to-night. And you're a restful person."

Jack smiled a little grimly, thinking that what he had to say to the lady would not exactly be restful.

When they were comfortably established before the fire, he began to lead up to it gradually.

"This society game is a funny one, isn't it?"

"How do you mean?"

"Well, here you are spending your life rushing around like a mad woman to teas and dinners and dances, theaters, operas, fashionable shows of every kind. What do you get out of it, really?"

"God knows!" she said wearily.

"When you're not tearing around to other peoples' shows you're having one of your own. Lord! what a gabbling mob! To hear them, you'd think they loved each other to death, and positively worshiped you. And as a matter of fact nobody gives a single damn!"

"That's true."

"Then why do you do it? It must cost a heap of money."

"I don't know," she said slowly. "Habit, I suppose. In the beginning it seemed like the only thing open to a woman like me, the only way to get on; to build up a social position I mean, and so be powerful. Now I have it, I find there's nothing in it."

"Then why don't you give it up."

She looked at him in a scared way. "How could I? I'm in the thick of the game. I've got to play it out. What else could I do? Where could I go?"

"You have real friends, I suppose."

"I had once. But after the scramble of the last three years—I don't know——!"

The words "three years" struck Jack with meaning. That corresponded exactly with the period of "Mr. B.'s" activities.

"Any one could begin a new life if they really wished," he said.

She looked at him queerly. "You're not leading up to a proposal of marriage, are you?"

"No," said Jack, smiling.

"It sounded like it," she said, settling back. "I like you ever so much, but of course it wouldn't do."

"I have wondered why you never married again," he said. "So many men——!"

"Oh, they don't mean anything. It's just the fashion to pay me attention. They look on me more as an institution than a woman. The ones who do come to the point of asking me are always horrid—or poor."

"But you have plenty."

"The appearances of wealth are illusory."

"I should think fifty thousand a year———"

She laughed lightly. "Where did you get that idea? I haven't the half of it."

There was a silence while Jack debated how to go on.

"Clara, I would really like to be your friend," he said at last.

"That's nice of you."

"If you only felt disposed to tell me frankly of your situation and your difficulties, perhaps I could help you."

Something in this alarmed her; she favored him with a sharp little glance. "Mercy!" she said, turning it off with a laugh. "I haven't any special difficulties that I know of."

"Who are these mysterious hard-eyed young people that come and go in this house as if they owned it? I mean George Thatcher, Emily Coster, Grace Marsden, and the others. Miriam herself; who is she, and where did she come from? She's no cousin of yours."

Frank terror leaped out of Mrs. Cleaver's eyes. She attempted to mask it with a semblance of anger. "They are my friends! Am I obliged to give you an account of them!"

"Queer friends!" murmured Jack. "You scarcely speak to them unless there are outsiders here."

"What do you mean by taking this tone towards me!"

"I wish to be your friend. Don't force me to believe the worst of you. If your conscience is clear, why should you fear a few plain questions?"

"I'll hear what they are first. I don't like your tone."

"You receive a thousand dollars every week. Where does it come from?"

A fresh terror shot out of her eyes, and again she sought to hide it under a towering anger. "What impudent nonsense is this?"

Jack went on imperturbably: "It is brought to you by a messenger in cash every Friday morning, and every Friday afternoon you carry it to the bank."

"You have been spying on me! And you talk about being my friend?"

"I do wish to be your friend. It is true I have been spying on you, as you call it. I was forced to it by my duty to an older friend. Are you going to answer my question?"

"Certainly not! What right have you to question me about my private affairs! A paid secretary! This is what I get for admitting you to my friendship!"

"To lose your temper and to insult me puts you in the worst possible light, you know. That is how a guilty conscience always acts."

"It's nothing to me what you think of me. You can go."

"I am not going," Jack said quietly. "You and I have got to have this out."

She had now worked herself up to a fine pitch of anger. She laughed, but there was little amusement in the sound. "I've got to have it out with you, have I? With *you*! Oh, this is rich! This is the perfection of impudence! Will you go, or must I call a servant to show you the door?"

She sprang up as she spoke, and her hand approached the bell button. Gone was her listlessness now.

"You will not do that," said Jack quietly.

Her thumb rested on the button. "Why won't I?" she demanded.

"Because you don't know yet how much I know."

Her hand dropped irresolutely. "What is it to me what you think you know. Are you trying to blackmail me?"

"I am not."

"What's your game then?"

"I'll tell you if you don't have me put out," said Jack, smiling dryly.

She agitatedly paced the room.

Jack went on: "I am doing you the credit of supposing that you do not know the true source of the money you spend."

"You are accusing me of dishonesty perhaps," she said haughtily.

"I don't know how honest you are," said Jack simply. "I am not acquainted with the terms of your agreement with Mr. B."

She stopped as if she had been transfixed. She went white to the lips. "Mr. B.!" she whispered. "You know him!"

"I know this much," said Jack slowly. "The thousand dollars a week which he sends you is the proceeds of blackmail—and murder!"

She staggered. He thought she was swooning, and sprang to catch her. But she fended him off, and sank in a chair unaided. It was a full minute before she could speak.

"You are just trying—to frighten me," she murmured huskily.

"I shall prove it before I go."

"What—what do you want of me?"

"I expect when I prove to you the truth of what I say, that you will repudiate Mr. B. and his generous allowance, and help me to hang him."

She did not answer at once, but only stared at him with big eyes.

"You will not accept anything further from him, of course."

Still she did not answer.

"Will you knowingly help to levy blackmail, and to bring about additional murders?"

She burst into tears. "How do I know what to do?" she wailed. "You haven't proved what you say! How do I know what your game is? I have nothing—not a sou! Where am I to go! How could I live?"

Notwithstanding her pretended astonishment, indignation, dismay, Jack saw that she had always been secretly conscious of living over a volcano. She had no doubt resolutely averted her face from it, but had dwelt in daily expectation of this dreadful scene.

"As to the means of existence, you need not worry," said Jack. "I shall take care of that."

"You?"

He saw that he had gone too far. "I mean Bobo of course. It is his game I am playing."

"Who was murdered?" she asked abruptly.

"Silas Gyde for one; Ames Benton for another."

"Anarchists committed those crimes."

"Two poor mad youths were used to carry out the purpose of a devilishly sane brain—our friend Mr. B. in fact."

For the last time she attempted to bluff it out. She yawned elaborately, though the hand with which she covered her pretty mouth still trembled. "Mercy! It sounds like a melodrama! You must excuse me if I cannot swallow it entire. I'm afraid you've been too faithful a student of the movies."

"Shall I describe Mr. B. to you?" said Jack. "His favorite disguise I mean: he probably has many disguises. He is a smallish man but rather heavy; not corpulent, but thick-set. He is always well dressed in a decent, sober style. He has piercing blue eyes, and wears a heavy gray mustache, and a little goatee or imperial. He has an old-fashioned look, due principally to the way he wears his hair; that is brushed forward of his ears in the manner popular fifty years ago. He has very courteous manners and is given to rather bookish, literary turns of speech."

The remnants of Clara Cleaver's courage oozed away. She sagged down in her chair white and shaken. "That is the man," she whispered. "What are you going to do with me?"

"Why does he send you all this money?" asked Jack.

"I don't know," she meekly replied.

"Well, I'll give you my guess. It is to secure your house as a base for the young birds of prey that hunt in society. These are the spies that furnish him with the information about rich people necessary to his blackmailing business."

"It can't be as bad as all that!" she murmured with weak horror.

"How else do you explain George Thatcher and Grace Marsden—and Miriam."

"You are not sure of what you say."

"You know in your heart it is true. As to Miriam, I am sure. Mr. Gyde left us a detailed account of how she tried to spy on him, and a faithful description of her. Ever notice the mole on her right forefinger?"

She shook her head. "Oh, there'll be a horrible public scandal!" she wailed fretfully. "I'll be disgraced forever—though I have done nothing!"

"Except take his money," Jack put in dryly.

"How did I know? Where am I to hide my head now! Oh, I wish I'd never laid eyes on you!"

Jack took a new tack. "Well, I see I can expect no help from you," he said, making as if to go.

"Wait!" she said quickly. "Don't leave me! I shall go out of my mind if I'm left alone! If I tell you everything I know, will you promise to save me from public disgrace?"

"I'll do my best."

"Sit down. I'll have to go back to the beginning. It's a long story."

19

"My father was a famous doctor here in New York," Mrs. Cleaver began. "He was what you call a self-made man; he had risen from obscurity and pulled my mother up with him. I was their only child. When I was growing up my father was making a princely income, and we lived like millionaires. The best people in New York were among his patients, and we went everywhere.

"I married at twenty—the usual fashionable marriage. Mr. Cleaver was the last of a fine old family of wealth and position, and I was considered to have done well for myself. But I loved him in a heedless, unthinking sort of way. He was young like myself, and extremely good-looking.

"My first real experience of life came with the death of my father, four years after my marriage. It was discovered that he had lived up to every cent of his great income. He left nothing but debts and an art collection. The proceeds of that went to purchase my mother a modest annuity. Even that was wasted, for she lived less than a year after my father.

"That left me with no one in the world to turn to but my husband. The tragedy of self-made people is that they have no lifelong friends. My husband was good to me in his way; we got along together well enough, but in his disappointment and chagrin at the disclosure of my father's affairs, I received my first suspicion that all was not well with our own.

"But I closed my eyes to it, and we continued to live as before, denying ourselves nothing. It was the only way I knew how to live. We had our big houses in town and in the country, a mob of servants, automobiles, horses. I knew nothing about business and my husband never spoke of it. One thing that helped to ease my mind was the fact that we were never bothered by creditors as I knew some of my friends were. My husband paid up everything on the nail. It was a point of pride with him.

"When he had spent his last dollar, literally his last, he shot himself.

"Well, there I was. Mr. Cleaver had no near relatives. His cousins had always frowned on our extravagance, and I could expect no aid from them. As for my so-called friends, at the first hint of disaster they began to melt away. I was so helpless I didn't even know how to close up my great house. I couldn't summon resolution enough to discharge the servants. I lived for a while on the proceeds of my dresses and jewels. It is tragic how much such things cost, and how little they bring!

"I was at the end of my rope, driven nearly frantic by worry. The unpaid servants were becoming impudent, and that seemed like the last straw. I have always been so dependent on servants! I was actually considering taking my husband's way out—when this man came to see me.

"He sent up no name. But in the frightful state I was in, one jumps at anything for a moment's distraction. I had him brought up. You have already described him; his silvery hair, brushed in an odd way, his sober, well-made clothes of no particular style. His old-fashioned manner prevented me from placing him socially; he might have been almost anybody. The piercing blue eyes were remarkable. His was most kind and courteous, fatherly one might say.

"Though it is three years ago, every detail of that interview is still fresh in my mind. He thanked me first for my indulgence in consenting to receive him incognito. I would agree, he said, when I had learned the object of his visit, that it were better he should remain unknown. He asked me to think of him simply as 'Mr. B.'

"He went on to say that through mutual friends he had learned of my difficult situation, and had been much moved thereby. It was the hardest case he had ever heard of, he said, and I had his sincerest sympathy. I was too desperate in my mind to even pretend to be indignant at the intrusion of a stranger into my affairs. Indeed I found his sympathy comforting. I hadn't received much. Most people had acted as if my misfortunes were due to my own fault. He soothed me like a nice old uncle.

"He said he was a very rich man, so rich in fact, that his money made him uneasy. He didn't want to die with it, he said, and he was looking around for some honorable way of getting rid of it. He used that very word, 'honorable'; it made me smile. He said it was easier to make a fortune than to get rid of it.

"Fancy how my heart began to beat at this. When one is desperate one cannot be particular. I could scarcely believe my ears. It seemed like the miracle I had been hoping for—like an answer to my prayer. He said that the more popular forms of philanthropy, such as colleges, hospitals, libraries, etc., were distasteful to him, as smacking too much of ostentation and publicity. He wanted to make his distribution in secret.

"'Everybody looks after the poor,' he said, 'and nobody thinks of the rich when they are overtaken by misfortune. They are the worthiest objects of help, and I intend to devote myself to the relief of the impoverished rich. You are my first case. Will a thousand dollars a week be sufficient?'

"I thought I was dreaming. I managed to stammer out a question about what conditions were attached to the loan or gift.

"'No conditions! No conditions!' he said,—'that is only one condition; that you will preserve absolute secrecy concerning it.'

"I promised of course. I scarcely knew what I was saying. I thought perhaps he was harmlessly insane. I certainly never expected anything to come of it. But when he had gone I found on the table a little packet containing a thousand dollars in bills.

"I still thought I had been visited by an amiable lunatic. I used the money to pay some of my most pressing obligations. I discharged the insolent servants, and got others. I didn't expect to hear from him again.

"But one week from that day a messenger boy brought me a packet containing a similar sum, and it has been coming ever since with absolute regularity.

"I can see that you are incredulous about there having been no conditions attached to the gift, but I have stated just what happened. I can see now that I was a fool, but then it was easy for me to believe that I had been relieved out of pure philanthropy. As if there was any such thing!

"At first the money came unaccompanied by any communication, but later, when he knew, I suppose, that I had become absolutely dependent on it, I began to receive instructions. In the beginning he still used the language of philanthropy—he wanted to help this young man or that young woman to gain a footing in good society—but latterly, feeling more sure of me, I suppose, he has become frankly peremptory. Oh! if I had only sent the money back in the first place!"

"What sort of instructions?" asked Jack.

"Principally for me to receive certain young people that he would send me, and introduce them to society; sometimes to introduce them to particular persons. This seemed harmless enough. People will do anything to get into society, you know."

"But when you saw these young people didn't you begin to be suspicious?"

"Oh, I didn't want to be suspicious! Their manners were good enough. They didn't shame me. And nowadays society is such a go-as-you-please affair, nobody held me responsible."

"What other kind of instructions did you get?"

"To ask certain people, generally some well-known rich man, to my house. The hardest thing I ever had to do was to go to the Madagascar and scrape acquaintance with Bobo in the corridor. I nearly died at that, but it was too late to turn back. I was terrified by the way the man always knew instantly when I had not obeyed him."

"The spies he had in your house would keep him informed," said Jack. "How did you know that day which of the two of us was Bobo?"

"He had described him to me."

"Does 'Mr. B.' still come here?"

"No, I have never seen him but the once. He writes to me, and very often he calls me up to learn if I have anything to report. I have no way of communicating with him unless he calls up."

"Now about Miriam?" said Jack.

Mrs. Cleaver sat up, and her tired eyes sparkled with hatred. "That woman!" she cried. "If you knew what I have had to put up with from her! I loathe her! Oh, I would like to see her brought low. What have you got against her? Tell me!"

Jack shook his head, smiling grimly. "All in good time," he said. "You're telling me your story now."

"Oh, Miriam's just another of them. She came the day before I received my instructions to get hold of Bobo. I was ordered to take her into my house, and give it out that she was a cousin. That was the final humiliation!"

"Is that all you can tell me about Miriam?"

She nodded. "We don't confide in each other," she said with tight lips.

There was a considerable silence between the two before the fire.

"What are you thinking about?" asked Mrs. Cleaver nervously at last.

"Just trying to dope out a plan to get him—with your help."

"Oh, I'm afraid!" she wailed. "When my income is cut off what shall I do?"

"I promised you—in Bobo's name—to take care of that."

"To the same amount?" she asked sharply.

Jack smiled dryly. "I'm afraid I'd hardly feel justified in recommending that Bobo keep up all this—but, say, ten thousand a year."

"Ten thousand!" she cried, aghast. "That's nothing!"

A grimmer tone crept into Jack's voice. "Sorry, but we don't owe you anything, you know. If you refuse to help me, I should have to have you arrested."

If she had defied him Jack's position would have been a little awkward, for he was not prepared to go as far as he had said. But Mrs. Cleaver's spirit was broken now. She only shuddered and wept the louder.

"Ten thousand!" she wailed. "I'll have to give up everything that makes life worth living!"

"You told me you were sick of all this."

"I'll have to move into a miserable apartment!"

"Come now, plenty of people have a whale of a time on ten thousand—or even the half of that."

"Suburbanites!" she said with the utmost scorn.

"Has 'Mr. B.' any regular time for calling up?" asked Jack.

"No. Every few days. I haven't heard in nearly a week. I shall probably hear to-morrow."

"Very good. Now listen. When he calls up, make out you're in great anxiety. But don't give him too many details over the 'phone. Suggest that it's not safe to do so. You can let him understand though that it has something to do with Bobo or me. Tell him that you think I am having you watched. Tell him that you must see him in order to find out how to act. Don't ask him to come here; that would surely excite his suspicions. Name some public place; a hotel would be the best."

"Will I have to face him?" she faltered. "I'm afraid."

"I'll be there," said Jack. "You may leave him to me."

20

Jack had no great confidence that Mrs. Cleaver would stand by him unless he were right there to assert his supremacy; she meant well, but she was as weak as water. Therefore he took care to be on hand early at her house next morning, and was prepared to hang around all day if necessary listening for the telephone.

By great good luck the call came while he was in the room with her, so that she had no opportunity to betray him, even if she were disposed to do so. By the instant change in her when she heard the voice over the wire, Jack knew that it was he whom they were expecting.

In dumb play Jack ordered her to hold the receiver an inch from her ear. Then by bringing his head close to hers he was able to hear practically all the man said.

"Good morning. Is there anything you want to tell me?"

Jack thrilled a little hearing the veritable voice of his adversary. It was the nearest he had yet come to him. A familiar quality in the sound tantalized him. But he could not place it.

"Yes," said Mrs. Cleaver. Her breathlessness seemed quite natural. "I'm so glad you called up. I can't explain very well. There's something queer. I'm afraid they may be listening at the switch down-stairs."

"Something in connection with our two young gentlemen?" asked the voice.

"Yes, one of them is acting so strangely."

"The principal one?"

"No, the other. He seems well—suspicious. I could explain better if I saw you. Can I see you?"

"Yes, if you wish," came the calm reply.

"Where?"

"Let me see—you'll have to come at once, because I am leaving town this afternoon. Suppose you come to the Hotel Bienvenu, and meet me in the main lobby."

"Half an hour," Jack whispered to Mrs. Cleaver.

"I'll come just as soon as I can dress," she said over the 'phone. "Can you give me half an hour?"

"Very well. I shall expect you in half an hour."

Jack's heart beat high with hope. He immediately called up police headquarters and got the Third Deputy Commissioner on the wire. After identifying himself to that individual, he asked to have a plainclothes man meet him in the bar of the Hotel Bienvenu in twenty minutes time, to make an arrest. The Deputy Commissioner said he would bring the man up himself, so there could be no possibility of missing Jack.

To Mrs. Cleaver Jack said: "I will go to the Bienvenu now and wait for my men. You leave here in precisely twenty-five minutes. Have your chauffeur let you out at the side door of the Bienvenu, and then walk around by the street to the front door. This will bring you past the windows of the bar, and will give me a chance to point you out to my policeman. Then I'll send him up into the lobby, and I can remain in the background. He will arrive in the lobby at the same moment with you."

All the preliminaries passed off as Jack had planned. The Deputy Commissioner and the plainclothes man turned up in the bar of the Bienvenu at the very moment of the time appointed. They took up their post at a window, and sure enough in five minutes Mrs. Cleaver swam past their ken, regal and languid in her silver fox furs.

"That's the woman," Jack said to the policeman. "Mark her well. Now go up into the lobby. As you get there she will just be coming in the front door. Watch who approaches her. Arrest the man with whom she gets in conversation. He's supposed to be an elderly man, short, stocky, with gray hair brushed forward of his ears, gray mustache and Imperial. But he may be disguised. Arrest any man that goes up to her and engages her in conversation. Watch yourself well, for he's a desperate character."

"We'll wait down here," added the Deputy Commissioner. "If you need help blow your whistle."

The policeman departed upstairs, and Jack ordered the Deputy Commissioner a drink. Jack thought he was perfectly cool, until he became aware of a curious little fluttering in his veins. It became increasingly difficult to sit still. When the drink was brought he forgot all about it. He could not keep his imagination within bounds. He tasted the great glory that would be his when it became known that he, single-handed, had broken up the amazing traffic in blackmail. He saw himself taking his rightful place as John Farrow Norman, and enjoying his riches with an easy mind. He saw Kate relenting at last. Meanwhile his eyes were glued to the dragging minute hand of the clock.

"Something must be the matter with that clock!" he cried. "Oh, this is fierce! If I could only go up there and see what is going on!"

"Give him time," said the Deputy Commissioner soothingly. "He hasn't been gone three minutes yet. Your man may be late."

In five minutes the plainclothes man was back in the bar. One look in his perplexed face told Jack that things had not gone off as he had planned. The bright bubble of his dreams burst.

"What's the matter?" he asked.

The man shrugged. "She wants you, the lady. Told me to bring you quick."

"But the man?" asked Jack as he followed him back.

"Never came. She hadn't any more than sat down when a bell-hop begun paging her. Mrs. Cleaver, he was calling. He had a letter for her. She begun to read it, and jumped up and sat down again quick. I thought she was going to faint, and hung around like. She sees me looking at her and says: 'Are you the policeman?' I nods, and she says: 'Bring Mr. Robinson quick.' That's all."

They entered the lobby, and Jack saw Mrs. Cleaver sitting in one of the big chairs. The brave air with which she had sailed past the window was in eclipse. She looked limp and white. As he came to her she held out an open letter without speaking. He read:

"*Dear Mrs. Cleaver:*

"*So you have decided to turn against me—after spending a hundred and fifty thousand of my money. Well, that's your affair of course. I hope you know where you're going to get more. This was a clumsy trap to expect to take the old fox in. Tell the young secretary he will have to do better than this if he expects to make that great reputation he is dreaming of. Like most young men he is prone to go off at half cock. Tell him that he had better be sure that he has anything against me before he calls in the police. But give him and the Third Deputy Commissioner my regards. They are waiting in the bar.*

"*Cordially yours,*
  "*Mr. B.*"

21

Mr. B's taunting letter was a bitter dose for Jack's pride to swallow. Jack was young and very human, and it was only natural he should have been a little puffed up by his preliminary successes in a task that might well have daunted an experienced detective. And then to discover after all that his crafty adversary had only been playing with him, that he was aware of all his movements—well, Jack ground his teeth a bit. But the effect on the whole was salutary. The letter rebuked Jack's vanity, and steeled his resolution.

"I was a fool!" he told himself. "I didn't give the old boy credit for ordinary horse sense. Well, I won't make the same mistake again. I can't do anything more in my own character, that's certain. He has a perfect line on me as Bobo's secretary. But he doesn't know anything about Pitman yet—or young Henry Cassels, the student at Barbarossa's school. I'll get him yet."

The affair of the letter resulted in the swift break-up of Mrs. Cleaver's establishment. Jack did not see her again. He instructed the bank to pay her two hundred dollars weekly. She rented her house and departed—for an extensive trip through the South, it was given out.

Miriam disappeared too. Jack hoped that his mind would now be relieved of any further anxiety concerning her designs on Bobo. She would naturally suppose Jack thought, that in the general expose her connection with Mr. B. would be made known to Bobo, and she would scarcely have the effrontery to pursue him further. But Jack underrated that young lady's hardihood, as will be seen.

As a matter of fact Jack did not feel that it was necessary to explain to Bobo the whys and wherefors of what had happened. He had no confidence in Bobo's discretion. He ascribed Mrs. Cleaver's sudden departure to her well-known capriciousness. Bobo was a bit dazed by the change in the situation, and broken-hearted at the seeming loss of Miriam.

"Why don't I hear from her!" he cried a hundred times a day. "There wasn't any trouble the last time I saw her. You know, we went to the theater together, and you and Clara had dinner at home. When we got home Clara had gone to bed with a headache, but you were there waiting for us, and the three of us had a rabbit together, all as jolly as possible."

"The next day when I went back to lunch the whole house was upset. Miriam had gone out they said, and Clara wouldn't see me. The butler said she was packing. I hung around a couple of hours, and nobody so much as offered me a bite. At last I had to go away to get something to eat. When I got back Miriam had come in and gone again, gone for good the man said. He had had his wages, and was openly impudent. And she hadn't left me a line! The next day the whole house was closed up. I can't understand it! Did Clara write to you?"

"Just a line to say that she couldn't face the fag of a New York season, and was going South for a rest."

"Let me see the letter, will you?"

"Oh, I didn't keep it."

"What do you suppose has become of Miriam?"

"You can search me."

In his mind's eye Jack had a vivid picture of that final scene between Miriam and Clara. Figuratively the fur must have flown!

"I can't understand it!" said poor Bobo. "I didn't do anything to her. She has my address."

"Forget her!" said Jack.

"Oh, you never liked her!" said poor Bobo.

Bobo instituted a sort of footless search for her, which consisted mainly in mooning around the different places they had visited together. Jack let him alone. It could do no harm he thought, and it kept Bobo occupied.

Meanwhile the poor fellow's appetite suffered. He lost weight and no longer found any zest in spending money. He moaned in his sleep, and cried out Miriam's name. Jack somehow had not suspected that a fat man might be so subjected to love's torments.

And then one night when Jack returned to dinner, after having spent the afternoon with Anderson, he found a change. He first noticed it in the eagerness with which Bobo picked up the menu card. Finding Jack's sharp eyes on him, he dropped it again, and said with a sigh that he couldn't eat a thing. But he did—several things. Bobo had but an imperfect command over his facial muscles. The corners of his mouth would turn up.

"He has seen her," thought Jack. "I'll have to tell him the truth now."

"What'll we do to-night?" said Bobo casually.

"Stay home," suggested Jack.

"If you're tired you'd better turn in early," said Bobo with deceitful solicitude. "I'll go out for a little while. I want to look around one or two places."

"All right. I want to have a little talk with you first."

Bobo's face fell absurdly. "Oh, all right," he muttered.

When they were back in their own rooms Jack said without preamble: "So you saw her to-day."

"Saw who?" said Bobo with innocent wide open eyes.

"Come off! Who is it that makes your eyes shine, and your mouth purse up in a whistle?"

"I don't know what you're talking about!"

"We're wasting time."

"If you are referring to Miss Culbreth," said Bobo on his dignity, "I have not seen her."

"What's the use of lying to me? You're as transparent as window glass!"

"Oh, if you've made up your mind that I'm a liar, what's the use of my saying anything?"

"Look here. Miriam is either what I think she is, or what you think she is. If she's all that's good and pure as you think——"

"As I *know*!" corrected Bobo.

Jack dryly accepted the correction. "As you know. It can't do her any harm to tell me the truth about what happened to-day."

"I can't!" said Bobo obstinately.

"I suppose she made you promise not to tell me."

Bobo was silent.

"Very well. Now listen. When you came with me the first condition of our agreement was that you should obey orders. Isn't that so?"

Bobo nodded sullenly.

"Well, I order you to tell me what happened to-day. That lets you out of any promise you may have made."

Poor Bobo was quite unable to stand out against a stronger nature. "Oh, since you put it that way, I have seen her."

"Where?"

"In the Park. On a bench near that fountain down the steps at the end of the Mall. We used to sit there sometimes in the sun. And I just went back on a chance—well you know!"

"Sure, I know how you feel," said Jack more sympathetically. "I'm sorry to see so much good feeling wasted."

"It's not wasted. While I was sitting there a woman came by heavily veiled. I didn't know her at first, but when she saw me she gave a little cry. It was forced from her. She didn't mean to let me recognize her. She tried to get away, but I stopped her."

Jack concealed his smile.

"It was Miriam," Bobo went on. "And what do you think! Just like me she had been attracted to the spot where we had been happy! Wasn't that wonderful!"

"Very wonderful!" said Jack drily.

"She was so overcome she had to sit down for a moment," Bobo continued. "When I reproached her for not sending me word, she said she had been so shocked at the discovery of Mrs. Cleaver's wickedness, she hadn't known what she was doing. Her one idea was to escape from that woman's house. Why didn't you tell me what she had been up to?"

"Never mind that now. Go on with your story."

"When she collected her wits, she said she didn't think it was any use her writing to me, because she was sure I would think she was mixed up in it too."

"Well that was pretty near the truth," Jack put in.

"She said she was sure you would never let such a chance go by of turning me against her."

"But I didn't use it against her, did I?"

"Oh, I expect you had your own reasons. I didn't know what Miriam was talking about. I begged her to tell me what Mrs. Cleaver had been up to, but she refused to believe that I had not been told. Even when I had convinced her I knew nothing she wouldn't tell me because she didn't want to betray her cousin. Bad as she was, she was still her cousin, Miriam said."

"Bosh!" said Jack scornfully. "No more her cousin than you are!"

"Oh, you never believe anything Miriam says," complained Bobo.

"Let that go for the present. What else happened?"

"Nothing much. She was relieved to find out that I didn't think wrong of her. We talked—but we didn't say much." Bobo got red. "Hang it all, I don't have to tell you everything I say to a girl, do I?"

"No," said Jack grinning.

"In the end I promised her I wouldn't tell you I'd seen her. That's all."

"And you're going to see her again, to-night?"

"Y-yes."

"Where?"

"She's stopping temporarily at the Bienvenu."

"Now let's try and let a little light on this subject," said Jack. "She's always saying that I'm trying to turn you against her, isn't she?"

"Yes, and it's true."

"What reason does she give for my actions?"

"Why—I don't know."

"Think a little. Her idea is that I am afraid of her influence over you, because it may threaten mine, isn't it?"

"Well—yes."

"And that's ridiculous, isn't it?"

But Bobo was obstinately silent.

"Good God!" cried Jack. "Are you my boss or aren't you?"

"No," muttered Bobo.

"Then what possible motive could I have for wishing to turn you against her?"

"I don't know," said Bobo sullenly. "I can't read your mind."

Jack threw up his hands. "You're so stuck on your role of multi-millionaire, that you're always forgetting it's only a role you're playing. Now listen. I'm going to tell you the whole truth about Mrs. Cleaver and Miriam. It's all I can do for you. In the first place Mrs. Cleaver has been in the pay of the old man for three years. It was he who supplied the coin to keep up that house. I caught her with the goods."

"Impossible!" gasped Bobo. "A society woman like that! You're sure you are not mistaken?"

"Read that," said Jack, handing him Mr. B.'s letter to Mrs. Cleaver.

Bobo's hair almost stood on end as he recognized the handwriting, and appreciated the significance of what he read.

"But—but Miriam didn't know anything about this. She said she was stunned when she learned of what her cousin———"

"Please don't give me any more of that stuff. Mrs. Cleaver was only the old man's catspaw, but Miriam is a confidential insider."

"How do you know that?"

"Well, for one thing Mrs. Cleaver told me the old man had sent Miriam to her."

"But you've just said the woman was a crook. That's no proof."

"Oh, that's not all I have against Miriam. It appears that she was practicing her wiles on Silas Gyde before he was killed."

From his desk Jack got the unfinished letter that the dead millionaire had left behind him. To Bobo he read that part of it which referred to Miriam.

Bobo was shaken but unconvinced. "That description might fit dozens of girls," he said.

"Sure," said Jack, "all except the peculiar mole on the inside of her right forefinger. Ever noticed that?"

"N-no."

"Well, I have. If you're going to see her again, I recommend that you look for it."

Bobo was now weakening fast "What do you suppose her game is?"

"That's easy. To marry you and get a strangle hold on your supposed millions. Now I didn't want to tell you all this because it endangers the game I'm playing. But I got you into it, and I don't want your blood on my conscience either."

"My b-blood!" stammered Bobo, white as a sheet.

Jack said simply: "If you let yourself be inveigled into marrying that girl, when she finds out you haven't got a sou, she'll kill you. She's that kind."

Bobo shook as with an ague. "I'll never see her again," he whispered. "I swear it!"

22

Jack—in the character of Mr. Pitman, had now reached a degree of intimacy with Dave Anderson, manager of the Eureka Protective Association, sufficient to enable him to drop into Anderson's private office at any hour during the day without exciting remark. He was careful never to display the least curiosity concerning Anderson's business, but simply kept his eyes and ears open and picked up what he could.

His patience was rewarded at last. One morning as he entered the private office, he found Anderson engaged in tying up a little packet, the significant size and shape of which made Jack's heart beat faster.

"Remittance day," said the indiscreet Anderson carelessly. "Just wait till I get this off to the boss, and I'll go out and have a smile with you."

Jack had instantly made up his mind to follow that packet. "Sorry," he said, "can't stop now. Just dropped in to ask you the number of your cigar-maker on lower Sixth avenue. I've got to go down in that neighborhood, and I thought I'd get some."

"81 Sixth," said Anderson. "Will we lunch to-day?"

"All right," said Jack, "I'll be back in time."

Meanwhile Anderson was writing the address on the packet. Jack after considerable practice had taught himself to read his writing upside down. He now read:

> "MR. PETER FEATHERSTONE,
> Hotel Abercrombie.
> (To be called for.)"

This was all he required. He bade Anderson good-by, and went out. Having plenty of time, he proceeded in leisurely fashion to the Abercrombie, one of the great hotels in the Thirty-Fourth street district. He was filled with a great hope.

"Please God, I'll get him this time. I'm safe against recognition in the Pitman disguise. I won't call on any plainclothes man now, but trust to myself."

Prudence restrained him from premature rejoicings. "No counting of chickens this time!" he warned himself. "Remember you're dealing with a customer as slick as an eel. If he slips through your fingers you've got to be prepared to begin all over to-morrow!"

In the pillared lobby of the Abercrombie Jack bought a newspaper, and planted himself in a chair in such wise, that while appearing to be absorbed in the news, he could command all that went on at the desk.

As he was waiting there little Harmon Evers the wig-maker passed through. Jack, not wishing to be recognized by any one just then, buried himself a little deeper in his newspaper, but Evers stopped beside him, nodding and smiling. His expression approved the Pitman make-up as put on by Jack.

"Couldn't have done better myself," he said.

Jack couldn't help but be flattered. "One becomes expert with practice," he said.

"You're on your business and I'm on mine," Evers said with a sly smile, indicating a little satchel that he carried.

"I didn't know you had to go out to yours," said Jack.

"Oh, yes, there's an elderly matinee idol lives here, who wouldn't dare leave his room until I have renovated him. If there was an alarm of fire before I got here, I believe he'd burn up."

Jack laughed.

"But I see you have serious affairs on your mind. Au revoir. Come down to my place when you can, and we'll talk philosophy."

With a nod and a smile he went on to the elevator.

Meanwhile Jack had missed nothing of what went on at the desk. In a short while a messenger boy came in carrying the packet he had seen in Anderson's hands. It was receipted for at the desk and tossed in the pigeonhole marked "F" of the division for letters to be called for.

For twenty minutes thereafter Jack watched the comedy of "The Hotel Desk" being played before him. Unfortunately his mind was at too great a tension to permit him to enjoy the finer shades of comedy. He silently swore at the crowd and the confusion which made it well-nigh impossible for one pair of eyes to follow all that was going on.

He concentrated on the letter box marked "F," and watched it until his eyeballs seemed ready to crack.

Finally the hand of one of the clerks shot out to that box, and hastily shuffling the contents, picked out the packet again. Jack's heart gave a jump. He hastily scanned the row in front of the desk at the moment, but there was no figure among them that answered to the descriptions of "Mr. B." At the end of the row was another messenger boy. The clerk handed the packet to him.

"Of course he wouldn't come himself," thought Jack.

Jack followed the messenger out of the hotel. Boy-like, he shambled up the street, whistling vociferously, tossing the packet in the air and catching it again, careless of the pedestrians he collided with in his exercise. Presumably had he known the contents he would have treated the packet with greater respect.

He turned West in Thirty-Fourth street, stopping to gaze in every window that attracted his attention. Jack was hard put to it to accommodate himself to the snail-like pace without being conspicuous. At the Madison avenue corner an automobile had broken down. The boy hailed this diversion with glee, and Jack, too, had to stand around until the youngster had gazed his fill.

Suddenly the boy aimlessly darted across the street like a bird—or a boy, threading his way among the cars hurrying in both directions. Jack almost lost him then. He finally picked him up on the other side, engaged in converse with another messenger. An argument developed and hostilities were threatened.

"I kin lick you wit' one hand behind me."

"You're anutter!"

"Want to see me do it?"

"Ya-ah!"

"You jus' say any more and you'll see!"

"I ain't askeered of yeh, yeh big stiff!"

"You say that again!"

"Ahh! I dare yeh to touch me! I dare yeh!"

And so on, and so on. Jack, feeling very foolish, had to make out to be studying the pattern of a rug displayed in a nearby window. Anybody who knows boys knows that these discussions are apt to be kept up a long time without getting anywhere. But they end as suddenly as they begin. Having exhausted their powers of repartee they parted, instantly forgetting each other. Jack's quarry continued around the corner and up Fifth avenue.

There were other interruptions; a man was painting a sign; another was dressing a window. Jack almost despaired of arriving at any destination. He wondered if the old man was as impatiently awaiting his packet. Finally it began to rain, and the boy mended his pace a little. He led Jack into the Public Library, and Jack with an accelerated beating of the heart wondered if the rendezvous were here. But the boy went out again by the Forty-Second street door, and it appeared he had only been taking advantage of the long corridors to walk dry shod.

The messenger darted across Forty-Second street in his usual reckless style, and Jack found himself back in the vicinity of the Eureka offices. To his astonishment, the boy turned into that very building. Jack went up in the elevator with him. He got put at the fourth floor, and entered the Eureka offices.

Jack lingered in the corridor, biting his lips in chagrin. All his trouble amounted to this, that he had been led back to the point he started from. He wondered if it were possible that the seemingly heedless Anderson had turned a clever trick on him. He felt that he had to find out at whatever risk. He had a good excuse to enter, for he had said he would be back. He entered, passing through the outer office into Anderson's room as he was accustomed to do.

Anderson was in the act of receipting for the packet. He greeted Jack without the least departure from his usual careless air, and Jack felt relieved. The boy went out, already pursing up his lips to whistle. It all meant nothing to him.

Jack ventured to say with an indifferent air: "Why, when I left you, you were just sending out a packet like that."

"It was the very same package," Anderson replied. "Funny thing, half an hour after I sent it the boss called up again, and said he'd changed his mind and wanted it at the Hotel Madagascar. He never did that before. I sent after it, but the boy was so long coming back, I went to the bank and drew more. 'Tain't healthy to keep the boss waiting too long. I just sent off the second lot."

"Madagascar!" thought Jack. "My own hotel! He has a nerve. Maybe there's a chance to get him there!"

"Ready for lunch?" asked Anderson.

"Sorry, I can't go with you to-day," said Jack. "I've had a hurry call from the house to go up to Yonkers. Just dropped in to tell you not to wait."

"Oh, too bad!" said Anderson. "See you to-morrow?"

"Sure!"

23

While he descended in the elevator Jack thought quickly. His thoughts were not altogether pleasant ones. Evidently "Mr. B." or one of his agents had seen him watching in the Abercrombie and had taken warning. If this were so his disguise had been seen through. Jack did not so much mind the fact that his adversary had given him the slip again, but he had counted heavily on that disguise. And now the whole structure that he had built upon it was crumbling.

But he was far from being discouraged. "Mr. B." had had the nerve to choose the Madagascar. Very well, he would try to call his bluff there. Since it was his own hotel he didn't have to waste the time to get there. He could telephone ahead. He hastened to the nearest booth.

He got the desk at the Madagascar. Establishing the fact that the voice on the wire was that of Baldwin, a clerk well known to him, he said:

"This is Robinson speaking, Mr. Norman's secretary. Do you recognize my voice?"

"Yes, sir, certainly, Mr. Robinson."

"Listen carefully. There's a crook trying to pull a little game on Mr. Norman, and I've framed up a plant to get him with the goods. Do you get me?"

"Yes, sir."

"There's just been a package delivered to the desk there, or will be delivered in a few minutes addressed to Mr. Peter Featherstone, to be called for. No, wait a minute! That name may have been changed—but I'm sure about the package. It's a small flat package the size and shape of a bundle of greenbacks laid flat. It's wrapped in a sheet of white typewriter paper, and tied with a green string. Look and see if you have such a package there now. I'll hold the wire." Presently the answer came: "Yes, sir, we have such a package, but it's addressed to Mr. Amos Tewkesbury."

"That's all right," said Jack. "The name doesn't signify. Now I want you to keep Connolly the house detective within call, and have him arrest, as quietly as possible, whoever calls for that package. Keep the man in the room behind the office until I can get there. I'll go in by the side door and telephone down to you from our suite. Is that all clear?"

"Perfectly, sir."

Jack hailed a taxi and had himself carried home, that is to say to Kate's house, where Mr. Pitman had his ostensible domicile. It was not the sober Mr. Pitman's habit to employ taxis, but this was an urgent case. Jack had to remove the Pitman make-up, of course, before he could show himself around the Madagascar.

He hastily changed to the more elegant attire of the millionaire's secretary, and then made his way through the vault into Silas Gyde's old rooms, thence across the corridor to the rear of the state apartments. Something less than half an hour had elapsed since he had called up Baldwin.

Bobo was there, moping in a dressing-gown while he waited for lunch time, the only thing that relieved his heavy hours. He brightened a little at the sight of some one to whom he might pour out his troubles.

"I wish I were dead!" he groaned.

Jack was in no mood to listen to him then. He ran to the telephone, and snatched the receiver from the hook.

"What's up?" said Bobo, infected with his excitement.

"Give me Mr. Baldwin at the desk," Jack said to the operator.

"Hello, Baldwin. This is Robinson. Have you got my man?"

"Yes, sir, we've got him all right!"

"Thank God! Have him quietly brought up here."

Jack hung up the receiver and did a go-as-you-please around the Dutch room, hurdling the chairs. Bobo gazed at him goggle-eyed.

"What on earth——!"

"I've got him!" cried Jack. "I've got him! I did it with my own little wits. Once too often he tried to fool me! He was just a little too nervy trying to pull something in my own hotel!"

"Got who? The old man himself!" cried Bobo amazed.

"Joy and deliverance!" sang Jack. "All honest millionaires can now sleep easy o' nights!"

"But what's going to become of me now?" said poor Bobo.

Jack's transports were interrupted by a ring at the outer door of the suite. He ran to it and flung it open.

Bitter disappointment awaited him.

It was not the famous, much-desired "Mr. B" that he saw outside nor was it a figure that could possibly have taken his shape. Connolly, the house detective, had his huge hand on the shoulder of a slinking, weedy youth with sallow vacuous face, and cigarette stained fingers; in other words, the typical loafer of the Times Square neighborhood. Baldwin was behind the pair, eager to see what would happen.

"Oh, that's not my man!" cried Jack.

There was an awkward silence.

"I followed your instructions to the letter," said Baldwin, eager to justify himself. "You said to arrest any man that asked for that package. This man asked for it."

"Sure," said Jack quickly. "You did right. I'm disappointed, that's all."

"I haven't done anything," whined the prisoner. "What are you going to do to me?"

"Shall I let him go, sir?" boomed Connolly.

Jack roused himself. "Not on your life," he said. "He's got to give an account of himself. Bring him in and shut the door." To the weedy youth he said: "Who sent you here?"

The answer came voluble and craven: "I don't know who the guy was. I never seen him before. Honest, I didn't know there was anything crooked in it. I'm no crook, boss."

"Describe the man who sent you here."

The answer came readily: "A medium old guy, stoutish, not real fat. Had his hair brushed in a funny way, old-fashioned-like, and a little chin whisker."

"That's my man!" said Jack grimly. "Where did you meet him?"

"I was standin' in front of the pitcher theater on Seventh below Forty-Second with some other fellows when a big black limousine car came along and stopped at the curb. We all took notice of it, it was such a long car, long as an ambulance. The door opened a little way, and an old guy leaned out and held up a finger to me.

"He asks me if I want to earn a dollar, and I says sure. So he tells me to go to the desk of the Madagascar, and ask for a package for Mr. Amos Tewkesbury, and bring it to him. But he said he wouldn't be in the car when I got back. He said he'd be standing on the northwest corner of Forty-Second Street and Seventh, and I wasn't to stop when I saw him, but just slip him the package, and take the dollar he'd be holding in his hand. That's all. I didn't see no wrong in it."

"Maybe he's lying, sir," said Connolly.

Jack shook his head. "Sounds like my man," he said.

"What'll I do with him, sir?"

"Let him have the package and let him go," said Jack.

To the prisoner he said sternly: "Your story may be true, but this is an ugly business you've mixed yourself up in. You'd have a hard time proving your innocence in court. The only way you can square yourself is by helping us pinch this crook."

The sallow youth turned a shade paler. "He's stronger than me, and he's heeled," he muttered.

"I don't want you to lay hands on him. I'll take care of that. You follow your instructions just as he gave them to you. Hand him the package without stopping. Go quickly, and don't look behind you."

To Connolly Jack said: "Take a taxi to the corner of Eighth and Forty-Second, and walk back on Forty-Second. You've heard the description of the man I want, and the car he rides in. If he gives me the slip, and tries to escape towards the West, nab him."

It was still raining. Jack snatched up an umbrella and, opening it with his penknife, made a little triangular cut midway in the silk.

"My disguise," he said.

The sallow youth, clasping the package, hurried out of the hotel with Jack at his heels. Jack raised the umbrella and held it low over his head. Thus while his face was hidden from the passersby, he could still see ahead through the little hole. The stretch of pavement between the Madagascar and Forty-Second street was as thronged as it is twenty hours out of the twenty-four, even in the rain.

They had crossed Forty-Third street and were within two hundred feet of the appointed place. Jack was peering eagerly ahead through his peep-hole, when suddenly his umbrella was knocked sideways, and a clawlike hand clutched his wrist. A cracked voice squalled:

"Stop him! He snatched my pocketbook!"

It was a bent little old woman in a queer rusty bonnet over a brown wig. She wore glasses so thick, that her eyes were like little points far behind them. She redoubled her cries.

"He's a thief! He stole my pocketbook!"

Jack crimsoned with anger and mortification. He was helpless. To knock the old woman out of the way would only have been to convict himself of her preposterous charge. In five seconds a great crowd was pushing and shoving around them.

"All my money! All my money!" wailed the old woman, and actually two tears rolled down her withered cheeks. It was the perfection of acting.

A loud murmur of sympathy went up from the crowd, and violent threats were made in Jack's face. He ground his teeth in impotent rage. Anything he might have said would only have made matters worse. He retained the presence of mind to keep his mouth shut.

"Hold him!" cried the old woman. "I'll get a policeman!"

Half a dozen pairs of hands seized Jack roughly. The old woman threaded her way with surprising celerity through the crowd.

Jack permitted himself to say: "You'll never see her again. It's a frame-up to let her and her partner make a getaway."

"Shut up, you thief!" they roared. "Shut up, or we'll smash your hat over your eyes." Those behind who had little idea of what was going on roared out of sympathy.

But the temper of a crowd is subject to abrupt changes. A minute passed and the old woman did not return. It suddenly struck the people that the well-dressed Jack, proud, angry and silent, did not much resemble a purse-snatcher. Jack, feeling the change, said scornfully:

"Do you see her coming back? I tell you it's a frame-up."

The men who had hold of Jack became uncertain, and finally let go. Jack elbowed his way out, and none sought to stop him now. The crowd dissolved. The whole incident had occupied less than two minutes, but that was long enough to do the mischief. The packet presumably had been handed over, and both messenger and principal swallowed up.

Jack hastened over the remaining distance to the corner of Forty-Second street. Neither the sallow youth nor the old gentleman with the imperial was visible of course. Jack hesitated at a loss which way to turn. There was a chance that the old man, having received the money, had turned Westward and so might be intercepted by Connolly, but it was a faint one.

While Jack stood there the traffic officer at that important crossing gave the signal for the East and West-bound traffic to cross, and a double line of cars darted across Seventh Avenue. Fourth in the line of those bound East Jack saw the long black limousine that had been so often described to him.

As it flashed by he had a glimpse of a silk-hatted head with gray hair brushed forward of the ears, ruddy complexion, gray moustache and imperial. Alongside was the rusty black bonnet and the brown wig. The man's head was down, and his attitude suggested he was counting something in his lap. The woman's glance followed his.

It was Jack's first glimpse of his quarry, and his hunting instinct was spurred to action. He made a zig-zag dash across the street under the very wheels of motors and trolley cars. The black limousine was out of his reach, but by great good luck he found a taxicab standing by the curb with its engine running.

He flung himself in, crying: "Four times your fare if you can keep that car in sight. A hundred dollars if I am able to arrest the couple in it!"

The taxi leaped ahead. Jack lowered the front window, and leaning forward, pointed out the right car to the chauffeur. In a wild spurt down Forty-Second street they gained half a block on the limousine. They just managed to get across Sixth avenue before the whistle blew. At Fifth the whole line was held up for perhaps half a minute. The press was so great here, Jack could not see the black car, but he had carefully marked its position, about six cars ahead.

When the whistle blew for the East and West traffic to resume they saw it turn down Fifth with a burst of speed. They followed. In and out of the close traffic the big car threaded its way with a wonderful exhibition of sang-froid on the part of the chauffeur. Jack had a good chauffeur too. But a race through such a crowd is purely a matter of luck. They never succeeded in getting within less than five car lengths of their prize. Jack saw that the black car now bore a Georgia license. He made note of the number.

At Thirty-Fourth street the line was held up again. The whistle had just blown, and this promised to be a longer stoppage. Jack jumped out of the taxi, and ran ahead down the line with fast beating heart.

The black limousine was empty.

Jack gritted his teeth. "The devil's own luck favors him," he thought. "They must have left the car during the block on Forty-Second."

The chauffeur had not seen him. Jack did not approach him, thinking it better to take a chance of following him to his garage. The line got in motion again, and Jack swung himself aboard his taxi as it passed.

At Twenty-Eighth street the whistle blew just as the black car was crossing. It continued blithely down the avenue, the chauffeur waggling a derisive hand outside his car. Jack would have risked defying the whistle, but his way was effectually blocked by other cars in front and on both sides.

"My luck again!" he groaned.

They were held up there while a ten-horse truck bearing a steel girder crawled across the Avenue. When the whistle gave them leave to move again, the limousine had disappeared into a side street. They saw it no more.

Jack had the license number, but an investigation instituted by telegraph only proved as he expected, that that number had been issued to some one giving a mythical address in Atlanta. As for notifying the New York police, he knew very well that within half an hour the license tags on the black limousine would be changed.

24

The most indomitable spirits have their dark hours, and this was Jack's. He returned to the Madagascar feeling that he had come to the end of his resources. It was hard to bear with the commiseration of the hotel detective and clerk on his failure; and he was in no mood to put up with Bobo's selfish complaints.

Bobo's reasoning powers, as has been seen, were of a primitive simplicity. Like a child or a savage he was always under the complete sway of the feeling of the moment. Just now he was, or thought he was, broken-hearted over the loss of Miriam. Forgetting that he had given her up of his own free will, and for good cause, he blamed Jack for all his present misery.

"Did you get him?" he asked when Jack came in.

"No."

To say that Bobo was pleased at the escape of "Mr. B." would be putting it too strongly, but he was certainly not sorry to see Jack's discomfiture.

"Huh! You're too sure of yourself!" he said.

Jack flashed an angry look at him, but said nothing.

"You always think you know more than anybody else!" Bobo unwisely went on. "You're always making up your mind what people are, and telling them what, to do, and all. You want to regulate the universe."

"Still thinking about that girl!" said Jack. "Will you please tell me what Mr. B.'s giving me the slip has got to do with her?"

"I'm just telling you you don't know everything," said Bobo with a superior air.

It was too much. Jack's patience snapped suddenly. "You fool! Your talk has as much sense as barnyard cackle! Is it my fault that you lost your head over an adventuress? This is the thanks I get for trying to save you! For Heaven's sake, go and marry her and be damned to you! But stop grousing about it to me!"

He went out slamming the door, and leaving a much-scared Bobo behind him. Passing through the suite, he crossed to Gyde's old rooms, and let himself through the vault into his room in Kate's house. There was a great change in this room. Under the present régime it was a model of neatness and comfort.

Here Jack lit his pipe and flung himself down, and a measure of peace returned to him. There was comfort in the silence, and in the thought of the locks that secured him from the chatter of fools.

"The old boy wasn't so far wrong when he built himself a refuge like this," he thought.

But by and by when the fragrant smoke had steadied his nerves, he began to tire of solitude. To particularize, he desired the society of a certain person, to wit: the mistress of the house.

In order to see her it was necessary for him to assume the Pitman make-up. Much against his will—he was thinking of putting Mr. Pitman out of the way now, he arrayed himself in that character, and sallied forth in search of Kate.

He found her in her own sunny sitting-room on the floor above. The old-fashioned mother was there too. Mrs. Storer was not in the secret of Jack's disguise. She considered Mr. Pitman rather a common fellow, but was always polite. Now after a few minutes' small conversation, she recollected an errand in her well-trained way, and left the room.

Kate was sewing. The needle became her better than the typewriter. As mistress of a house she seemed to have discovered her true vocation. It may be mentioned in passing that this establishment was a success, and was already paying its way.

"We don't see much of you now," said Kate.

"It's not from not wanting to on my part," he said, watching her dreamily. "But a twenty-four hour day scarcely gives you time enough to play one part, let alone two or three." The sunlight behind her was making a little halo in the edges of her dark hair, and he scarcely knew what his tongue was saying.

"How are things going?" she asked.

The consciousness of defeat still rankled in Jack's breast; he felt a very natural desire to shine in somebody's eyes, so he said carelessly:

"My net is closing around the old man. He can't escape me now. I'll gather him in, when my case is complete."

"Fine!" said Kate.

But Jack could not be sure there was not a faint ring of irony in her voice. He never could be sure of Kate.

"All my lines are working well," he went on. "I had a glimpse of the old man to-day, but I thought it was better to let him go for awhile. I'm not sure of being able to convict him."

"This morning when you left this house I believe you were followed," said Kate.

Jack was not going to admit just then that there was anything he had overlooked. "Oh, I think not."

"Well, I noticed a man standing at the corner looking at this house. His hat was pulled down over his eyes. As soon as you went out he disappeared."

"I take precautions against being trailed," said Jack.

"And I believe somebody has been tampering with the servants," Kate went on. "Yesterday I found Bessie, the upstairs girl, exhibiting entirely too much curiosity as to the arrangements of your room. I shall let her go at the end of the week."

"It isn't possible they could have discovered the secret of this house," said Jack. Something told him he was talking fatuously, but a little devil of perversity held sway over him for the time being.

"You know best of course," said Kate.

This time he was almost sure he heard the ironical note, and he glanced at her uneasily. But the dark head was bent too low over her work for him to read her face. He felt a mighty desire to humble this cool and scornful maid, and changed his tack.

"You're looking very charming to-day."

"Thank you."

He got up, and sat as close to her as he could pull a chair.

"Go back where you were," she said calmly.

"I won't!" he said masterfully.

"Then I will." And she changed to the chair he had left.

Jack glowered at her. "One would think I spread a contagion."

"Well, you know I don't care particularly for Mr. Pitman."

"That's only an excuse. It's me you don't care for."

She laughed tantalizingly. Jack saw now that he had started wrong but didn't quite see how to repair the original mistake. He got up to go. He knew that if he lost his temper, he would be completely at her mercy.

"I'd better go if we're only going to quarrel," he muttered.

"Who's quarreling? Can't you take a joke?"

"It's like a flick of the whip on the raw."

He had sounded the right note at last. She heard the real pain in his voice, and jumped up, careless of where the sewing went.

"Jack, wait a minute! What's the matter?"

He paused with his hand on the door-knob. "Nothing."

"What's the matter?" she repeated. "I insist on knowing!"

"Oh, well, things have gone a bit wrong. What do you care?"

She actually stamped her foot. "How dare you speak to me that way! You came in here like the Lord Hereditary Marshal of England. How was I to know?"

"Well, I didn't want to let on that I had balled things up," he said sheepishly.

"You idiot! Will you ever learn the first rudiments of sense? Sit down here!" She pulled him down beside her Pitman make-up and all. "Now tell me all about it!"

Jack looked at her a little dazed by this sudden change of front. "Why—I thought you were just having a little fun with me."

"Certainly I was. You asked for it. Whenever you take that 'my poor little woman' tone with me, you simply give me a pain. But if you are really up against it—Ah!"

Her voice caught on a deep low note of tenderness. Jack gave up all thoughts of mastery; he would have been quite content to kiss her hand.

"Well, I am up against it," he said quite humbly and naturally—and told her all about it.

She said nothing until he was through; then: "There's no occasion to be cast down that I can see. You and the old man are playing a close game, and he's turned a trick on you. But the game's not over yet."

"He's so darn sure of himself!" grumbled Jack. "He knows what I have on him, but he goes around quite openly in his old black hearse!

Shows himself everywhere. Goes on making his blackguardly collections right under my nose. He seems to enjoy playing with me."

"That's a kind of vanity," said Kate. "I have read that criminals often display it. It is that very thing that will surely deliver him into your hands in the end if you bide your time. Some day he is bound to take a chance too many."

Jack began to feel comforted. "I believe I could have him arrested to-morrow if I gave his description to the police," he said.

"Then why don't you?"

He shook his head obstinately. "I've got to do this myself. I've sworn it.—But how does he know I'm not going to turn over my case to the police? He seems to be able to read my mind!"

"Oh, there's no magic in that. He watches you of course, and anybody who knew anything about you must know that you would feel that way."

There was subtle flattery in this, and Jack began to feel warm about the heart once more.

"Well, he hasn't put me out of the game yet, though on this deal he has certainly called all my tricks. The minute I tried to use Mrs. Cleaver he trumped her. He has called the Pitman disguise, and he must know about my connection with Anderson. If he has spotted me coming out of this house, he must have guessed that there is a way through from the hotel. I'll have to think up an entirely new combination."

"How does the situation stand with the anarchists?" asked Kate.

"Nothing new down there since I told you. I am now a full member of the circle that Emil Jansen belonged to, but so far I have not succeeded in establishing 'Mr. B's' connection with it. I know there is a connection, because the murderers of both Ames Benton and Silas Gyde graduated from that circle. I have to move slowly there."

"Then there is the girl Miriam," suggested Kate. "I believe you could do something with her. Do you know where she is now?"

"Bobo told me she was at the Hotel Bienvenu. But she hates me like poison."

Kate smiled a little. "From what you've told me about her I gathered that she had a weakness of vanity, too. She was piqued because you resisted her charms. Why don't you look her up and well—not resist them quite so hard?"

"Kate!" he said scandalized.

"What?" she said with an innocent air.

"You recommend me to do that!"

"Why not? We don't owe her any consideration, I suppose."

"Oh, it's not that. But if you cared about me the least little bit, you wouldn't be handing me over to another woman."

"That's up to you. I couldn't be jealous of one like Miriam. If you are in any danger from that source, Mercy! I don't want you."

"In other words you know you've got me thrown and hog-tied!" he said scowling.

"Don't be vulgar. This is simply business. You really have a chance of getting somewhere through her. The old man will be sending her remittances now. If you could trace one of those back to its source——"

"Good! That's an idea! I think I see my way, too." His lassitude was gone. A fresh determination filled him. "Kate, you are my good fairy!" he cried. "You have put new life into me! I am going to start to work again this very minute!"

She said nothing, but her eyes were bright.

At the door of the room he paused, holding her hand. "You might let me kiss you before I go," he said diffidently. "Just as a kind of encouragement to go in and win."

Kate smiled. "That's the first time you ever asked me with becoming modesty.—Once. Right here." She put her finger on the dimple in her right cheek.

He did.

25

When Jack got back to the Madagascar, Bobo had gone out. Jack was relieved not to find him. Full of his new plans, he went on down to the office. He was now attired again his proper person as Mr. Robinson of course. He looked up Baldwin at the desk. Baldwin naturally was keen to know more about the mysterious case that Jack was engaged on.

"Baldwin, I've got a new line on my man," said Jack. "Do you happen to know any of the men behind the desk at the Bienvenu?"

"Surest thing you know. I've got a pal there. Name of Dick Starr."

"What's his job?"

"Room clerk. One of the head men."

"Will you introduce me?"

"Sure! When?"

"The sooner the better."

"I'm coming off duty now. I'll go right down there with you."

Starr of the Bienvenu proved to be just such another suave and irreproachable man of the world as Baldwin, but somewhat older. He knew all about Jack; no doubt the two friends had discussed him. While the real secret of Jack's identity was safe, it was understood among those whose business it was to inform themselves of such matters, that the secretary was the real power behind the Norman throne. Consequently he enjoyed more than the usual consideration shown to a multi-millionaire's secretary.

Starr took them into a little room behind the office.

Jack said: "The fact is, I'm doing a bit of detective work for my employer, and one of my clues leads to the Bienvenu. I want your help."

"Anything in my power!" Starr assured him.

"You have a young lady stopping here called Miriam Culbreth?"

Starr nodded. "Some Cleopatra!" he murmured.

"The same," said Jack. "Now some time during the next few days I have reason to believe that a package will be sent her by messenger. Small, flat packet about three inches by seven."

"Packages don't go through the desk."

"But in this case I am pretty sure the boy will be instructed to hand it to her personally."

"Oh, in that case—Want me to have a look in it?"

"Simpler than that!" said Jack. "Just get me that boy's number so I can trace him."

Starr assured Jack that he would be happy to serve him. He seemed a little disappointed that he was not called upon to play a more important part.

They strolled out into the lobby again, and at that identical instant Miriam herself came through the revolving doors. But Jack saw her first.

"Duck, you fellows! Duck!" he whispered swiftly. "Make out you don't know me!"

Messrs. Baldwin and Starr being experienced men of the world, knew how to act. They inconspicuously faded from Jack's side.

Miriam in sables and paradise plumes swam into the Bienvenu like a swan. Not a man in the place but drew a long breath of longing at the sight of her and looked enviously at the man slinking at her heels. Your haughty beauty always brings a man with her like a small dog on a leader.

This man was Bobo.

Jack went up to them with glad smiles. "Hello! This is a surprise!"

It was manifestly a surprise to *them*. Bobo turned a delicate pea green shade, and had nothing to say. The girl smiled charmingly, but her eyes were like two points of ice.

Jack thought: "She thinks I've tracked them here. There's something up. I'll find out what it is."

"We just dropped in for tea," said Miriam languidly.

"Fine!" said Jack. "I'm starving! I'll join you."

She laughed like icicles tinkling. "Hadn't you better wait until——"

"Pshaw! What's an invite between friends!" said Jack. "Come on, I'll blow."

Miss Culbreth was a resourceful person, and eminently self-possessed, but for once Jack had the satisfaction of putting her out of countenance. She turned indignantly to Bobo, as if to call upon him to assert himself, but seeing that she could expect no help from that stricken figure, she hung her head uncertainly. Jack led the pair of them like lambs to the slaughter to the tea room.

Passing the elevators Bobo said huskily: "Thought you were going upstairs to dress."

"I won't bother now," she said.

Jack thought: "Wouldn't leave him alone with me for a farm!"

As a tea-party, the half hour that followed was not a howling success. Bobo crouched in his chair avoiding Jack's eye like a guilty spaniel. Miriam kept her eyes down too, but for a different reason; she didn't want Jack to see the hatred that burned there. The tapering white hand trembled a little in the business of pouring tea.

The onus of keeping things going was therefore upon Jack. Something humorous in the situation excited his risibilities. He experienced a pleasant malice in making out to the others that he saw nothing out of the way. He rattled on like a youth without a care in the world. Anything furnished him with a cue.

"See that old girl in crimson velvet. The famous Mrs. Paul Towers. Used to be Mrs. Peter Vesey. Sold herself to Peter in order to buy Paul, the saying is around town. That's Paul Towers with her. Exactly half her age. Poor devil! He pays high for his meals. They say he has to turn in an itemized expense account like a traveling salesman."

"He's not the only parasite in town," remarked Miriam acidly.

Jack chuckled. "Bless your heart, no! The woods are full of us! What's a handsome young man with delightful manners and not a cent to his name going to do!"

Miriam snorted scornfully.

"But I tell you it's no cinch to be a parasite," continued Jack. "It requires qualifications of a very high order. Firstly, a resolute determination not to work. Any fool can work, but it needs character to idle gracefully. Then a parasite must have A1 cheek, nerve, brass, gall. It takes an unusual man to make a success of it."

"You're forgetting some of the qualifications," said Miriam.

"I daresay. It's an all round man's job."

"Meanness, obsequiousness, conceit!"

"All very fine qualities!" said Jack with inimitable gravity.

They had been at the table about half an hour when a boy passed through the tea room paging Miss Culbreth. Miriam and Bobo both affected not to hear him, but Jack, scenting developments, called him to their table, and indicated Miriam to him.

"Mr. Spragge is calling," the boy said to Miriam. "Said he was expected."

"Tell him I'm engaged, and he needn't wait," said Miriam languidly. "Say that I will let him hear from me."

Jack noticed that Bobo was betraying an extraordinary agitation. Following a sudden impulse, Jack said carelessly to the boy:

"Who is Mr. Spragge, son?"

Fire flashed from Miriam's eyes, but before she could stop the boy he had answered involuntarily: "The reverend Mr. Spragge, sir. Parson lives in the house here."

"Oh!" said Jack drily.

The boy departed.

There was silence at the table. The constraint which had formerly lain upon them was as the gayety of a childish game to this. Miriam had turned very pale, and she was breathing quickly—signs of rage in her. Bobo's chin lay on his breast, and he was visibly desirous of slipping right under the table cloth.

Jack enjoyed his little triumph in silence. A single word would have precipitated an explosion from Miriam. For reasons of his own Jack wished to avoid a general show-down, and he did not speak it.

He presently resumed the feather-brained rattle, and the tension was a little relieved. The simple-minded Bobo cheered up, evidently having persuaded himself that Jack had attached no significance to the mention of the parson. But the girl knew better. She watched Jack with somber eyes, waiting for him to unmask his guns.

When they had finished their tea Jack ostentatiously consulted his watch. "By George! We'll have to be getting back to the Madagascar!" he cried.

"Who's we?" asked Miriam with a sneer.

"Bobo and I. Mr. Delamare's dining with us to-night," Jack lied glibly.

"Is that true?" Miriam demanded of Bobo.

Poor Bobo lacked the backbone to come out flatly for either one side or the other. He fidgetted miserably. "I don't know. Maybe. I forget."

Miriam's luscious mouth had become a thin red line. "He can't go. He has an engagement with me."

"Now that's too bad!" said Jack with deceitful solicitude. "He can't disappoint a big man like Mr. Delamare. Besides, there are important matters to be decided."

Miriam was near the fulminating point. She looked stormily at Bobo. "Well? Have you nothing to say? It's up to you!"

Bobo made a pitiable attempt to assert himself, but he could not meet Jack's eye. "I didn't know he was coming," he muttered. "I can't go now. Anyway you know about everything. You can talk to him."

"There are papers to be signed," said Jack. "I can't do that."

Bobo hung in an abject state of indecision.

Miriam could stand no more. She kept her voice low out of respect to the other people in the tea room, but her words lost none of their force thereby. "Are you going to sit there and let this nobody tell you what to do? If you've got a spark of manliness, why don't you put him in his place? He mocks you to your face! His very look is an insult to me! Are you going to stand for that? Why don't you invite him to kick you while he's at it?"

Jack thought: "Good Lord! Will he still want to marry her after getting such a taste of her quality as that?"

Bobo still hung his head. Jack could not but feel a certain pity for him. After all it was he, Jack, who had got him into this mess.

"If you won't tell him I will!" said Miriam. She turned her blazing eyes on Jack. "Go! And the next time wait until you are asked, before you thrust yourself on your betters! You are only an upper servant. You have presumed on his good nature until now you think you are the master. I warn you you'll find a different kind of person in me! I can keep you in your place!"

Jack received this with a smile. He was thinking: "You are not Mrs. Norman yet, my lady!"

She read the thought as clearly as if it had been spoken. "I'm not afraid of you! You can't stop me in anything I mean to do! I despise you!"

"Well, there's virtue in frankness," murmured Jack. "But let's not rattle the family skeleton in public."

It was true, people were beginning to look curiously towards their table.

"After all, it's a simple matter," Jack went on, "and it's entirely up to Bobo. Bobo, are you coming with me, or are you going to stay here?"

"I'll stay," muttered Bobo sullenly.

Miriam smiled triumphantly.

Jack appeared to give in good-humoredly. "Suits me," he said.

They rose from the table. Out in the corridor while Jack and Bobo were obtaining their hats and coats, there was a brief moment during which they were out of hearing of Miriam.

"Bobo," said Jack firmly, "if you don't come home with me, I swear I'll tell her the truth and leave you to your fate!"

Bobo was like a poor little grain of wheat between two hard millstones. He shivered. "How can I get away from her?" he whined. Obviously he was more afraid of Miriam than of Jack.

"Leave that to me," said Jack.

Miriam was watching them suspiciously. They rejoined her. At the elevator she said offhand to Bobo:

"You may come up. I have a sitting-room."

Miriam entered the elevator in advance, of course. Jack took a firm grip of Bobo's arm.

"Well, good-by," said Jack pleasantly. He squeezed Bobo's arm suggestively.

"G-good-by," stammered Bobo. "I have to go with Jack."

Whereupon Jack turned him about smartly, and marched him out towards the main entrance. Miriam gasped. She could not very well run after them, and grab Bobo's other arm. Indeed, while she stared speechless, the elevator door was closed, and she was whirled aloft. If looks could kill Jack had fallen dead in his tracks!

26

Jack and Bobo returned to the Madagascar without exchanging a word. When they were alone in their rooms, Jack looked at him and said:

"What the deuce am I going to do with you?"

"Best to let me alone," said Bobo sullenly.

"Didn't I convince you to-day that she was a crook?"

"I don't care."

"That was a nice little sample of her temper that she gave us at the table. Do you want to let yourself in for a lifetime of that?"

"I can't help myself."

Jack threw up his hands. There was a silence. Bobo was gloomily drawing an imaginary pattern on the arm of his chair.

"You swore to me you would never see her again," Jack presently resumed. "Yet an hour ago you were on your way downtown to get a license, weren't you?"

Bobo's hang-dog silence was equal to a confession.

"How did you expect to keep it out of the papers?"

"Bribed the clerk."

"Do you know what the penalty is for marrying a woman under another man's name?"

"I don't care."

"What cock and bull story did she tell you to-day to change you again?"

"She told me the truth."

Jack laughed.

"She admitted she'd been working for the old man. But when she found out what his game really was she chucked him. Now she's actually in danger of her life from him."

"Not too much danger, I guess," said Jack. "You still intend to marry her?" he asked.

"I've got to. It's my fate."

"Lord preserve us!" cried Jack in a kind of helpless exasperation. "I really don't see what there is to do, then, but kick you out!"

"You won't do that," said Bobo sullenly. "You bluffed me just now down at the Bienvenu, but I've been thinking it over. I know you won't do it now."

"Why won't I?"

"You can't afford to. It would spoil all your plans."

This was true, but Jack had not given Bobo credit for the shrewdness to perceive it. He tried a new course.

"Do you still believe that Miriam is marrying you for love alone?"

"I don't care!" said Bobo recklessly. "I'm willing to take her on any terms. What chance has a man like me of winning a woman like her ordinarily? It's gone too far now. I've got to have her. She's in my blood!"

Jack looked at him with a kind of respect. "Well, anyhow you're in earnest. I will give you credit for that. But seriously, what are you going to do afterwards? You don't suppose I'm going to lend you my name and my money for the rest of your life?"

Bobo shook his head. "I know the show-down's got to come some day, perhaps soon. But I'll make a sneak before that comes. At least I'll be happy for awhile."

"On my money?"

"Oh, what's a few thousands to you? Anyhow you got me into this."

There was truth in this, and Jack felt certain compunctions. But he was amused at the naïve villainy Bobo proposed.

"I don't grudge you the money," he said smiling. "In a way I sympathize with you, since I see you're really hard hit. But I can't be a party to any such scheme. In the first place as your friend I've got to save you from yourself. You'll get over this, hard as it seems. Secondly, even though she is a crook, she's entitled to be protected from a game like this. Why it wouldn't be a marriage at all!"

"You'd best let me be," said Bobo sullenly. "You can't lock me up, and I warn you I'll do it the first chance I get."

"Don't dare me to prevent you," said Jack softly. "I might find a way."

No more was said about the matter, but Jack continued to think about it. "Bobo put the idea into my head himself," he considered. "Lock him up! Why not? He's no better than a madman for the time being."

They patched up a temporary truce. Bobo agreed not to try to see Miriam that night, provided Jack would let him make a date with her over the telephone. He called her up in Jack's hearing.

"I'll be there to-morrow at eleven. No, I have not changed. Have him there at eleven."

Jack made no further objections. Had Bobo been wiser, his friend's apparent complaisance would have aroused his suspicions.

The two young men dined together, and spent the evening at the theater in perfect amity. Before going to sleep that night Jack perfected his plans.

"Having plenty of money certainly simplifies things," he said to himself.

Jack was always up at least an hour before Bobo. His first act in the morning was to telephone Mrs. Lizzie Regan, his landlady in humbler days, and still his faithful friend.

"Mrs. Regan," said he, "I need your help. Can you give up to-day to me?"

"Sure, Mr. Nor-Robinson, my dear! Anything to oblige."

"Well, come over to the Madagascar, and have breakfast with me."

"What, me! Eat in the Madagascar! I'll have to dress."

"Heavens, no! I'm in a hurry! We'll eat in our suite."

"And me a respectable widow woman! Laws, what would the neighbors say!"

"But you'll come?"

"Will a cat lap cream, my dear!"

While he waited for her, Jack collected every scrap of wearing apparel in Bobo's room, and the closet adjoining, and carrying it all to another clothes closet, locked it up and pocketed the key. Bobo slept the sleep of the hearty eater throughout. Jack then cut the wires of the telephone in his room, and removed the instrument. Finally he locked the three doors leading out of Bobo's rooms, and carried away the keys.

Bobo still slept on while Jack and Mrs. Regan discussed an excellent breakfast in the Dutch room. The honest lady was greatly impressed by her surroundings.

"Sure, it's a proud day for me to be eating in such style along with one of my own boys that I once passed the beans to. Sure if I'd foreseen this day, I would have given you two eggs to your breakfast, though I will say I never tried to stint the normal appetite of a man!"

"My appetite must have been abnormal, I guess."

"Go along! I lost money on you regular!"

"Maybe you won't be so glad you came to-day, when you learn what I want you to do."

"Anything short of murder, my dear. What is it?"

Jack told her the story of Miriam and Bobo—with reservations.

"Sure, if it was me, I'd let her marry him. Maybe it would teach the hizzy a lesson. But I suppose you're right. If more hot-blooded young people were locked up at such times, marriage wouldn't be such a joke in the vaudeville houses."

"I've got to be out a good part of the day on business," Jack went on, "so I've got to have somebody to look after him. I asked you to come firstly, because you know the truth about us, and secondly because I thought if he tried to assault you he'd find his match."

"Sure, I'll soothe him like his own mother.—I brought my umbrella. It's a good strong one."

Before going out Jack went into Bobo's room. The plump youth, yawning and stretching, was just beginning to think about getting up.

"Listen, Bobo," said Jack crisply. "You've got to stay in bed to-day. I've hidden all your clothes. I've engaged a nurse to look after you—and she'll see that you get your meals. You'd best take it quietly, for I'm giving it out that you've been on a tear, and if you make a racket people will think it's the D.T.'s."

"But—what—why——?" stammered Bobo.

Jack slipped out before he had fully recovered his power of speech. He delivered the key of his room to Mrs. Regan.

On his way out Jack sought Baldwin the clerk. "Mr. Norman is sick," he said. "To tell the truth, he's been hitting too swift a pace lately. The doctor has ordered absolute quiet, and I want you to see that he is not disturbed under any pretext whatever, while I'm out. I've left him in charge of a nurse."

Baldwin, the discreet, raised no awkward questions about the suddenness of Bobo's attack, nor where the doctor had come from, but assured Jack that his orders would be obeyed.

"You remember the lovely lady we saw yesterday?" Jack went on.

"Rather!"

"Supposing she comes here and shows a disposition to make a scene, introduce her to Connolly the house detective, see? Tip Connolly off to ask her if she didn't once go under the name of Beatrice Blackstone and do typewriting work for Silas Gyde here. That ought to calm her."

At the newsstand Jack bought a copy of a yachting magazine and from the advertising pages picked out the address of a leading firm of yacht brokers.

A few minutes later he was seated opposite the head of that firm, a trig little man with apple cheeks and shiny pink pate—he need not be named. Every yachtsman knows him.

"I represent a well-known millionaire," said Jack, "before I give you his name, or open my business with you, I must ask you to pledge yourself to regard it as confidential."

The broker agreed without reservations.

"Well," said Jack, "my name is Robinson, and my employer is Mr. John Farrow Norman."

As always, this announcement produced a well-nigh magical effect.

"Mr. Norman is sick," Jack went on, "the fact is he's been going the pace, rather, since he came into his money, and now he's got to pull up with a round turn."

The broker expressed a discreet sympathy.

"He has instructed me to charter a steam yacht for a Southern cruise, a roomy, comfortable boat. The main consideration is to get something that's all ready to go."

"It is fortunate that you came to me, Mr. Robinson," said the little broker solemnly. "As it happens I have the very thing you want. I refer to the *Columbian*, Colonel Oliver Stackpoole's yacht. Perhaps you know her?"

Jack shook his head.

"One of the finest yachts afloat, sir! Three hundred feet long, and a veritable floating palace! Only yesterday Colonel Stackpoole and a party of friends returned on her from a hunting trip to Jekyl Island. I have just received the Colonel's note authorizing me to charter her for the Florida season. She has a full complement of men, a complete inventory of stores, she is coaling this minute, and actually has steam up!"

"That sounds promising," said Jack. "How about terms?"

He agreed without batting an eye to the figure named, and the little broker was sorry he had not asked double.

"Let's go and look at her," said Jack. "If everything is O.K. you shall have a check this afternoon, and we'll sail to-night."

The yacht-broker wished that Heaven might send him such clients oftener.

The *Columbian* was lying at a coal dock in Hoboken. It was a matter of half an hour to reach her in the automobile. Jack fell in love with her at sight, and registered a silent vow, that some day when his work was done he would own her outright—or one like her.

Though really a great ocean-going vessel, her clipper bows, low hull, raking masts and great funnel conveyed an impression of extreme lightness and grace. She was painted black with a green streak at the water line, and her funnel was yellow.

Going aboard, Jack was astonished at the great spread of her decks; almost room enough to drive his car around her; and still more at the size and number of her cabins. Outside, the designer's effort had been to make the *Columbian* as shipshape as possible, but below decks he had aimed to make her passengers forget they were at sea.

On the main deck there was a long suite of lofty rooms; grand saloon, music room, library, smoke room. Overhead forward was the dining-saloon, and a sun parlor aft. All these rooms had open fireplaces, windows, and other comforts not generally associated with the sea. The furnishings were beautiful without being too ostentatious. The sleeping cabins were marvels of spaciousness and luxury.

Jack did not hesitate a moment about taking her. His one regret was that he could not go on the first projected cruise. The fact that the mere signing of his name put him in possession of this wonderful vessel gave him a fuller realization of the power of his wealth than he had yet experienced.

He learned that the *Columbian* would finish coaling during the afternoon. He arranged to have her continue to lie where she was until nine o'clock that night. Thus he could get his party aboard in this out-of-the-way spot after darkness had fallen. The *Columbian* was then to drop downstream to an anchorage in the Bay, and proceed to sea next morning. Her Captain was instructed to see to the necessary clearance papers.

Jack repeated his story of Mr. Norman's illness to the captain. The suggestion was that the millionaire's mind was slightly affected, and they might be prepared for vagaries. The itinerary of the cruise was to include Charleston, Jacksonville, Nassau and Havana.

All arrangements having been completed, Jack returned to the Madagascar. Nothing untoward had occurred in his absence. Miriam had come as he expected, no doubt with every intention of making a scene; but his ruse to confront her with Connolly had worked effectually. She had departed quicker than she came.

Upstairs Mrs. Regan reported all well. Finding his "nurse" proof against the most tearful and passionate appeals, Bobo had resigned himself to his lot. Indeed, who shall say but that he was not secretly relieved thus to have the responsibility of making a decision taken from him.

Jack told Mrs. Regan what he had done. An assiduous reader of the newspapers, it appeared that she knew all about the magnificence of the *Columbian*.

"How would you like to take a cruise in her?" Jack asked.

"Me! Oh law! What a life of adventure!"

"You shall have a stateroom de luxe, with a brass bedstead, and a dressing-table furnished with gold!"

"What me! Lizzie Regan! Oh law!"

"Can you get away to-night?"

"I'd chuck a dozen boarding-houses for such a chance! Sure! As it happens the house is full, and I've got a cook who is not quite feeble-minded. My cousin will run in and keep an eye on things."

"That's settled then. Run along and get ready, and I'll watch Bobo till you get back."

Bobo listened to the plan of the proposed cruise in sullen apathy. Jack could not tell what he meditated doing. In order to be on the safe side, Jack called on Hugh Brome, his lawyer, to assist him with the evening's arrangements. It promised to be a great lark—for everybody except Bobo.

At nine o'clock that night an invalid completely swathed in blankets was tenderly carried out of the private side door of the Madagascar by two friends, and placed in a waiting limousine. A comfortable-looking nurse hovered over him solicitously. Any passerby might have been surprised to hear convulsive giggles from the three attendants—but perhaps he would have put it down to nervousness. Obviously the patient was very sick. But if the wrappings had fallen away from his head, the passerby would certainly have been astonished to see that he was gagged!

An hour later Jack and Hugh Brome stood on the coal dock watching the superb vessel back out into the river.

"Well, he's out of harm's way for awhile," said Jack. "He has no clothes aboard but dressing-gowns and slippers!"

27

Nowadays it is difficult for the great to conceal their movements. In spite of the precautions he had taken, the story of the chartering of the *Columbian*, and the young millionaire's sudden departure on a Southern cruise was in the next morning's papers. Jack silently cursed the yacht-broker.

He had no more than read the story, he was still lingering over his breakfast, when the telephone in the Dutch room rang, and the voice on the wire said:

"Miss Culbreth is asking for you."

"What!" cried Jack. "You mean she's downstairs!"

"Yes, sir."

"You're sure it's me she wants?"

"Yes, sir, Mr. Robinson," she said.

Jack hesitated before answering. To tell the truth his courage sunk slowly into his boots. He would sooner have faced five strong men than the infuriated Miriam. But as soon as he realized he was afraid his obstinacy came into play. He said to himself: "I'm not going to let her bluff me." Aloud he said curtly: "Show her up."

Although she must have set out from home in a rage, Miriam had not on that account neglected her appearance. She wore a little red hat with a cunning flare to the brim, and was otherwise all in black. Her fine eyes were dark with anger.

"By the Lord she's beautiful!" thought Jack. "It's all very well for Kate to talk, but there's a dangerous delight in fighting a woman like this!"

She lost no time coming to the point. "Is this story in the papers about Bobo true?" she demanded, declining to sit.

"More or less," said Jack.

"What do you mean by that? Has he gone away?"

"Just a little trip for his health."

"I don't believe you!"

"Then why ask?"

"You've had him kidnapped!"

"Ahead of you, eh?"

"Spare me your impudence, please!"

Jack bowed low.

"I'll expose you in the newspapers!" she threatened

"Go ahead! You may be sure I know exactly what I'm doing."

His coolness made her pause. She stared at him stormily for a moment "Maybe it's not true!" she said. "Maybe you gave out the story yourself to put me off."

Jack smiled.

"I'll see!" she cried. She darted into the adjoining room, Bobo's bedroom.

Jack let her go. There was nothing in any of the rooms that it mattered if she saw. He heard her opening and slamming the doors, and sat down to his interrupted breakfast. He could see that his cool airs maddened her, and there was a kind of breathless fun in it. He was less cool than he appeared. His heart hammered on his ribs.

She came running back angrier if possible than before. Jack affected to be very much absorbed in an item in the newspaper, which he relinquished with manifest reluctance to rise at her entrance.

"Well, did you find his corpse?"

Miriam's only reply was an inarticulate sound of rage. It was some moments before she could command herself sufficiently to speak.

"Just you wait! I'll get square! I'll beat you yet!"

She turned to go.

Jack suddenly bethought himself that Kate had advised him to make friends with Miriam. Just how far he was moved by a disinterested desire to further his case, and how far by Miriam's angry beauty, it would be well, perhaps, not to inquire.

"Don't go," he said.

She hesitated.

"I'll be bound you rushed away from home without any breakfast. Have some of mine."

Apparently the wisdom of resuming diplomatic relations must have occurred to her too, for she looked over her shoulder with a slow smile. Her eyes were still dangerous.

"Come and sit down," said Jack. "I'll make fresh coffee on the machine."

She swayed towards the table with inimitable nonchalance. Sitting, she gave Jack an inscrutable glance of the strange eyes, and languidly pulled off her gloves.

"By George! You're good to look at!" he said impulsively. It was surprised out of him.

"So are you," she murmured, with a languorous look through her lashes.

It was exactly the wrong thing for her to say; but Miriam persistently misread Jack. So long as she defied him and abused him he was profoundly stirred; he longed to seize and tame her. But when she displayed a disposition to woo him, he suddenly chilled and drew back. He did not let her see it of course. To create a diversion he jumped up to attend to the coffee machine.

"Silly for us to quarrel," she said, when he returned to the table.

"Yes, isn't it?" said Jack.

"Our real interests lie together. If we go on fighting each other, we'll spoil both our games."

It just suited Jack to play up to this idea of their respective positions. "You're right," he said.

"I offered before to join with you," she said.

"But you have me at a disadvantage," objected Jack. "If you marry Bobo you'll have a legal hold over him. Where will I and my job be then? You as good as told me you'd kick me out."

"That was when I was angry," she said blandly. "What a woman says when she's angry doesn't count."

"But you might get angry again," suggested Jack dryly.

She favored him with a slow intoxicating glance of the hazel eyes. "You fool!" she whispered.

"Eh?"

"Can't you see?"

"See what?"

"I couldn't really refuse you anything."

Jack was sorry now that he had asked her to stay. He saw the situation approaching from which no man can extricate himself with dignity and self-respect entire. But he was not sure that he wished to extricate himself. In his confusion he chose the worst possible course: that is, to laugh it off.

"That's good! Five minutes ago you hated me like a rattlesnake!"

"What's the difference?" she murmured. "I hate you because—because you treat me so. When I—Oh, why do you make me say it!"

She was breathing quickly and her eyes were large and bright. Jack wondered how much of this feeling was real, and how much art. But no man wants to disbelieve a woman when she intimates that she loves him.

She suddenly leaned across the table, and took his hand between both of hers. Her proud head was lowered in an affecting way. "Love—! Hate—!" she murmured brokenly. "What's the difference? You drive me wild with your cool airs, your indifference! Sometimes I could kill you! But—but I wouldn't want you any different either. I want you to master me!"

It was a heady draught. Jack's brain reeled.

She raised her head. Her eyes were embers in the wind. "Look at me! Am I not beautiful? You said I was beautiful!"

The voice of the tempter whispered to Jack: "Take her at her word. She deserves no consideration. Kate would have no right to blame you after what she said."

"Look in my eyes," she whispered. "What do you see there?"

The fire of those strange eyes lighted a train of gunpowder in the man. He forgot everything. "Oh—you beauty!" he murmured hoarsely.

They rose simultaneously and leaned towards each other over the little table.

"It's all so simple," she whispered. "Let me marry Bobo. You will still be his master and mine!"

Once more she fatally overreached herself. Every instinct of decency in the man was revolted by the picture she called up. He firmly unwound the white arms that had crept around his neck. He turned away and took a cigarette.

Miriam stared at him frightened and angry. "What's the matter with you?" she whispered.

"You'd better go," he said harshly.

She went to him swiftly. "You can't deny me! You love me! I saw it in your eyes. Why do you fight against me? Look at me. I could be everything to you!"

"Love!" said Jack with a grim laugh. "You're wasting your time now! You almost had me—but you let me peep too far under the lid. Never again! You're too good a hater. I want to keep a whole skin!"

She saw then that she had indeed failed. The humiliation was intolerable. She burst into angry tears.

"Oh, I hate you! I hate you!" she cried. "I *will* kill you if you don't keep out of my way!"

She ran out of the room.

28

The *Columbian* set sail early on a Friday morning. On Monday Jack received the following telegram:

Charleston, S.C.

Came in here last night for coal. At daylight sick man discovered to be missing. Must have climbed through port hole and dropped into waiting boat. Wireless operator gone too. Captain thinks he was bribed by wireless to liberate B. Have discovered that the two of them took the Southern train North late last night. Wire instructions.

Lizzie Regan.

Jack thought swiftly: "Late train North from Charleston last night. That would bring them here late to-night. Bobo would telegraph Miriam of course. She may go to meet him."

He jumped to the telephone, and calling up the Bienvenu, got Starr on the wire.

"This is Robinson—at the Hotel Madagascar, you know."

"Yes, Mr. Robinson?"

"Is Miss Culbreth still in your hotel?"

"Yes, sir, but she's leaving. She just telephoned down for her bill to be made out."

"Could you arrange to have her followed when she leaves?"

"Yet, sir, I have a smart boy here who can be depended on."

"Good! If she goes to the Pennsylvania station that's all right. I will be there. But if she goes elsewhere have a message telephoned to this hotel for me."

"Very good, sir. I will see to it."

Jack hastened into Kate's house and assumed the Pitman make-up. It had outlived its usefulness so far as the old man was concerned, but he had no reason to suppose that he had ever been pointed out to Miriam in that character. At any rate he had no other disguise handy. With a brief good-by to Kate he taxied to the Pennsylvania terminal. All travelers to the South use this station.

Miriam was already there, walking impatiently up and down the concourse. She was heavily veiled, but even so was a sufficiently notable figure. Jack was beginning to be acquainted with her wardrobe, extensive as that was. To-day she was wearing a green hat and black furs that he had seen before.

When the gates were opened for the 10:08 Washington express she went through. Jack bought a ticket for Washington and followed. Supposing that she would ride in a parlor car, he got in a coach, as he did not care to subject Mr. Pitman's disguise to a five hours' scrutiny on the train.

After the train had started, he showed his police credentials to the conductor, and describing Miriam, asked to be informed to what point her ticket had been taken. Word was brought him later that it was to Baltimore. He asked to be told if she got off before that.

But Miriam apparently had no suspicion that she was being followed. In Baltimore she went openly to the Hotel Warwick and registered under own name—or rather, under the name that Jack knew her by. The so-called Mr. Pitman was close behind her.

After putting her bag in her room she reappeared unveiled, and started to walk downtown at a leisurely pace, Mr. Pitman still in unsuspected attendance. He heard her ask a policeman the way to the City Hall. In that building she asked at the Information desk where marriage licenses were to be procured.

Jack smiled to himself. "License number two!" he thought. He did not risk discovery by following her through the unfrequented corridors, but waited within watch of the main entrance for her to reappear.

For the next hour Miriam killed time in Charles Street, the fashionable shopping thoroughfare. She visited several hat shops, and presumably "tried on." Mr. Pitman could not very well follow her into such places. Later a tea room held her for another half hour. At some time during these peregrinations she must have become aware that she was being followed.

Leaving the tea room she hailed a taxi, and ordered the chauffeur to take her to the Hotel Minnert. Jack followed in another cab. When he saw that the hotel was only around the corner, he began to suspect a ruse. She entered by the Ladies' door, and he was less than half a minute behind her.

She was not visible inside. From the doorman he learned that she had walked upstairs. He followed.

On the next floor there were no public rooms but only endless corridors with bedrooms opening off. There was not a soul in sight and he hesitated which way to turn. Finally a chambermaid appeared around a corner, and a piece of silver procured him information.

"Yes, sir, she just went down the corridor on the right. She asked me if there was another stairs, and I told her yes, at the end of that corridor."

Jack hastened in the direction named. At the foot of the rear stairs he found a door giving on a quiet back street. The door-keeper supplied the next link of information.

"Yes, sir, there was a taxi waiting for her. She just drove away."

"Hm!" thought Jack ruefully, "that's a good one on me! Either she knows this place of old, or else she fixed it up on the way with the taxi-driver."

He was not greatly concerned by this mishap, for he knew the time the Southern train was due to arrive in Baltimore, and he expected to meet her again there. The time was six-thirty. He spent the interim in buying himself an overcoat of striking cut, and a tweed hat that would pull down low on his head. These articles changed his appearance not a little. On the way uptown he stopped in at the Warwick, but Miriam had not returned there.

When he got to the station Miriam was not to be seen among the crowd. The train was forty-five minutes late. Informing himself as to which gate the passengers would be discharged through, he took a seat commanding it, and affected to busy himself with a magazine.

As the time for the coming of the train drew near, and no Miriam showed up, a sharp anxiety attacked him. He wondered if he could have erred in his calculations. He knew she had not had time since he lost her, to telegraph down the line for Bobo to get off at Washington.

The train drew in, and the passengers began mounting the steps. Still no sign of Miriam. But suddenly Jack caught sight of Bobo among the passengers and his spirits rebounded.

"Is she going to let me carry him off?" he wondered.

The wireless operator accompanied Bobo, and Bobo was clad in one of his uniforms. As there was about thirty pounds difference in weight between the two—in Bobo's favor, the plump youth cut rather a comic figure, and was acutely conscious of the fact.

As they reached the top of the stairs, a lady clad in deep mourning with a thick black veil concealing her whole head and face stepped forward and laid her hand on Bobo's arm. At first Bobo shrank back from this sable apparition, but she pushed the veil aside sufficiently for him to see her face, and he grinned from ear to ear.

"You fool!" said Jack to himself. "Not to have seen through that!"

Miriam and the two young men went quickly down the way to the side entrance of the station. Jack was not far behind them. In that confusion of people there was little danger of their spotting him. Outside among the waiting automobiles was a big Macklin touring car, and Miriam led the two men towards it. Jack swore at himself again.

"She had the wit to hire a special car, while you have to trust to a taxi!"

He jumped in a taxi. "Follow that Macklin car that's just turning out," he said. "Ten dollars bonus, if you stick to it."

The touring car did not turn South towards the center of town, but headed North by the bridge over the railway tracks. At the first wide street, North avenue, Jack read on the street lamps, it turned East, then North again on another wide thoroughfare which finally brought them out into the country.

"Double fare outside the City limits," the chauffeur said laconically.

"Let her go," said Jack. "I'm good for it."

A short turn through a lane brought them to another main highway.

"Belair Road," said the chauffeur, "main road to the North."

"Have you a full tank?" asked Jack.

He nodded.

"Follow them to New York then if necessary!"

On this dark road the occupants of the touring car soon discovered that they were being followed. They put on speed.

"Give her all she'll take," said Jack.

Fortunately the taxi was of a good make, and the engine was tight and clean. The little car gave a good account of itself. Moreover the road was smoothly paved, which further helped equalize the chances of light car and heavy one. Pursued and pursuer roared down the dark highway with cut-outs open. For several miles the way lay over one steep hill after another. They precipitated themselves recklessly down each declivity, gaining a momentum at the bottom that carried them almost to the top again without slackening.

"This is faster than I'm allowed to run her," said Jack's chauffeur.

"That's all right. I'll be responsible for the damage."

The man grinned and stepped a little harder on his accelerator.

At first the big Macklin car set up a pace they were unable to match, but apparently the driver was unfamiliar with the road, and after he had narrowly escaped flinging his car in the ditch on several sharp turns, he was compelled to slow down somewhat. This gave them an even chance. They kept about a hundred feet behind the red eye of the tail-light ahead.

"We're holding them all right," said Jack's chauffeur.

The words were scarcely out of his mouth when there came a report like a small field piece beneath them.

"Damn that tire!" cried the man.

"There goes Bobo's last chance of salvation!" said Jack.

The blow-out had been heard in the car ahead. They swept out of sight around a bend tooting their horn triumphantly.

It took them the usual half an hour to change tires.

"Back to town I suppose," said the driver when he was ready to start again.

"No!" said Jack. "They might blow up a tire, too. Keep on!"

In a village called Kingsville they stopped long enough to make sure that the Macklin car was still ahead of them. At the next place, Belair, they came upon it resting demurely in front of a dwelling. Since there was a church next door, it was not difficult to guess that this house was a parsonage.

"I thought so," said Jack grimly.

He jumped out and rang the bell. When the door was opened by a maid there was no need for him to make any inquiry. Through an open archway he could see into the living-room of the house. Bobo and Miriam were standing hand in hand before the parson with his book. Even as Jack looked, he finished pronouncing the benediction, and the couple turned around. Miriam had evidently left her woeful headgear in the car outside. She was wearing the dashing green hat again.

Jack, forgetting for the moment that he was disguised, stepped into the room. Bobo did not know him, but Miriam did. Her face lighted up with a wicked triumph.

"What a pity you were late!" she said with mocking sweetness, "I would so much have liked you to be present!"

"What—who—who's this?" stammered Bobo.

"This is Jack. All dressed up! Don't you recognize his beautiful eyes?"

Bobo saw that it was Jack, turned pale, and looked furtively about him for a way out, in case things went suddenly against him.

"Be the first to congratulate me," said Miriam to Jack. "Most of all I want to hear it from you."

Poor Bobo in his skin-tight uniform was an absurd figure of a bridegroom. With humble eyes, he was mutely imploring Jack not to give him away.

Jack had no intention of doing so. Knowing himself to be the real master of the situation, he could well afford to put up with the girl's outrageous triumphant air.

Jack's smile irritated her. She lost her joyful look. The commoner aspect of her broke through. "I'm Mrs. Norman," she said with a disagreeable laugh. She displayed her wedding-ring. "You can't get around that! Remember it, the next time you start out to get the better of me."

"Miriam, for God's sake, don't provoke him!" whispered poor Bobo.

"Provoke him!" she said, raising her voice. "You seem strangely afraid of hurting the feelings of your secretary. He needs to be provoked. He's too big for his shoes! Let him understand that I'm the mistress now, and his chance of keeping his job depends on his pleasing me!"

Bobo almost fainted.

Jack met her eyes squarely. "All right, my lady!" he was thinking. "My turn will come later!" He foresaw that his game in the future would be furthered if he appeared to submit. So he bowed—but he could not quite iron out the mocking smile.

"I only aim to please!" said he.

Miriam looked at him suspiciously.

"What do you wish me to do, Mr. Norman?" he asked Bobo.

To that youth it was like a ray of light breaking through. He lifted his eyes to Jack with a kind of sheeplike gratitude. But he seemed incapable of speech.

Miriam answered for him. "Go back to New York, and wait for us at the Madagascar."

Jack bowed again, and returned to his taxi.

29

Jack returned to New York on the night train. At the hotel he found a message from Starr of the Bienvenu Hotel reading:

"A.D.T. boy 791 came with a package for Miss Culbreth to-day. When he was told she was out of town he took it back with him."

Jack's police credentials smoothed the way for him with the A.D.T. officials, and within two hours of the time he received the message, No. 791, otherwise Tommy Mullulus, was on his way to the Madagascar to be questioned.

He was a small, thin boy with a wary eye that testified to a wide experience of the world, and an insinuating grin that was still childlike. His meager limbs were lost in his faded, flapping trousers, but he had a doughty air far beyond his years. His official age was fifteen; had he not to swear to that to get his "working papers"? But actually he was about two years short of it.

He was disposed to be evasive in answering Jack's questions.

"You brought a package to the Hotel Bienvenu yesterday?"

"Yes, sir."

"Where did you get it?"

"At the office. Fella at the desk handed it to me."

"That means it was brought into the office by the person who wanted it delivered?"

"I guess so."

"Where is your office?"

"1118 Broadway."

"Did you see the person that brought the package in?"

"Didn't take no particular notice."

"Well, was it a man or a woman?"

"I didn't rightly look."

"Isn't it a fact when you boys are waiting for a call, that you size up everybody that comes in to see what kind of a job you're going to get, and what's likely to be in it?"

"We gen'ally does," said Tommy with an innocent air, "but Fat Harris was pushin' me on the bench, and I was pushin' him back, so I didn't take no notice of who come in."

It suggested itself to Jack that the boy was under the spell of a generous tip. To offer him a larger tip was the most obvious course, but Jack, knowing something about boys, hesitated. Tommy would take the money, of course, but it would probably make him suspicious, and therefore more secretive than before. A better way was to win his confidence if it could be done.

"Tommy," said Jack, "the guy that gave you that package is a crook, and I'm trying to land him, see?"

Tommy looked interested but wary. He required to be shown.

"Did they tell you at the office who I was?" asked Jack.

"No more than your name was Robinson."

"Did you ever hear of John Farrow Norman?"

"The poor boy that came in for a hundred million! You bet!"

"Well, I work for him. I'm his secretary."

A noiseless whistle escaped through Tommy's lips. But he still looked a little incredulous.

"You can find that out at the office on your way out," suggested Jack.

Tommy looked impressed by this evidence of good faith. "Say, boss, can I see him himself—Norman I mean?"

"He's out of town to-day. But you'll see him all the time if you work for me."

Tommy was melting fast. "On the level, do you want me to work for you?"

"Surest thing you know!"

"What doing?"

"Oh, just a little detective work," said Jack carelessly.

Tommy was won. "Oh-h! Detective work! That's my specialty!"

"The man who sent that package to the Bienvenu Hotel is trying to blackmail Mr. Norman," said Jack. "We've got to catch him with the goods."

Tommy nodded sagely.

"See if you can't remember what he looked like. Was he a middle-aged man short and thickset, well-dressed, but not sporty, heavy white moustache, and little chin whisker?"

"Sure!" cried Tommy. "That's the very guy! I remember now."

"Well, give me some further particulars then," said Jack to test him.

Tommy considered. "His hair was brushed in a funny way, sticking out like, in front of his ears."

"That's our man!" said Jack. "Has he ever been in your office before?"

"Yes, once in a while. He's a guy you'd remember. Gives big tips."

"When you couldn't deliver that package at the Bienvenu what did you do with it?"

"Handed it in at the office again."

"Then what happened to it?"

"It's there yet. They couldn't return it to sender because he didn't leave no address."

"You're sure he hasn't been after it himself?"

"Not up to the time I left. Us boys watches for that guy."

"Thought you said you couldn't remember him."

"Well, I didn't know which side was on the square then," said Tommy unabashed.

"Good! I'm sure he will come after it, and I want you to go back to the office and watch for him. When he does come in, see if you're clever enough to trail him back to his home or his office, or wherever it is he goes, see?"

"How can I sneak out without orders from the desk?" objected Tommy. "And supposin' I'm out on another call when he comes in?"

"You can leave that to me," said Jack. "From now on you're working for me, and you won't take any other calls, see? I'll have an order sent through from the head office to your branch. But mind you, not a word to any of the other kids!"

"That's all right, boss," said the diminutive sleuth with dignity. "I know a thing or two about this biz. I can easy stall off those pore fish down there."

"Here's something on account," said Jack offering him a dollar bill. "As to your final payment I'll just say this: if you and I pull this off together, I'll offer you a permanent job with Mr. Norman."

"Me workin' for Norman himself! Gee!" said Tommy.

30

A few hours later the bridal couple turned up at the Madagascar. Miriam was beautiful and beautifully dressed, but feeling sure of her position now, she made no attempt to curb her arrogance. She believed that she owned the Madagascar and acted accordingly. The hotel servants cringed—and detested her. Bobo was correspondingly depressed and anxious-looking.

Their unannounced arrival hardly surprised Jack. He was in expectation of a call for funds.

Miriam immediately demanded to be shown through the suite. "So that I can choose which rooms I will take."

Jack, amused by the comedy, accompanied her and Bobo on the tour of inspection. Jack's room, the next room but one to the Dutch room, seemed to please her most. Perhaps it was because she knew it was Jack's room.

"I'll take this for my bedroom," she said, "but the furniture is ghastly. It will have to be completely done over. Bobo's room shall be my boudoir."

Bobo glanced anxiously at Jack. "You can have my room of course," he said quickly. "But this is Jack's room."

It seemed as if she had just been lying in wait for him to say something like this. She whirled on him. "Well, and am I supposed to give way to your secretary? If you're willing to give up the best rooms to the servants I'm not!"

"Miriam is right," said Jack. "I'll move into the two little rooms at the back; Silas Gyde's old suite."

"Hereafter please address me as Mrs. Norman," said Miriam haughtily.

"Certainly, Mrs. Norman," said Jack demurely. To himself he added: "Oh, lady, lady, it's a shame to let you in so bad! When the truth come out the shock will surely kill you!"

"And while we are away," added Miriam, "go to a first class decorator, and arrange to have my two rooms done. I will have the boudoir hung in pale yellow silk brocade, and the bedroom in a softer material, pink. Samples can be sent me."

Jack bowed. "You're going away again?" he asked politely.

"Oh, yes, Bobo just came in to get some money."

Bobo bent an imploring glance on him.

Jack had his things carried into the back rooms, and put all in order there.

"Thank God! I can escape the sound of her voice!" he said to himself. "Where, oh where is that sweet murmur with which she used to woo us! Bobo's awakening has come even sooner than I expected. She might have given him a few days' run for his money. What a story this will make to tell Kate later. But the poor fat kid is in such a deuce of a hole it really spoils the comedy!"

Presently Bobo applied at the door of Jack's sitting-room with a pitiful hang-dog air.

"Come in!" said Jack cheerfully.

Bobo shambled in, and flung himself in a chair. "Don't bawl me out!" he said beseechingly. "I'm just about all in!"

"I'm not going to say much," returned Jack. "But I'm only human. You can't expect me to keep my mouth shut altogether."

"I wish I were dead!" said Bobo.

"Cheer up, the worst is yet to come! There's good comedy in it, I assure you. I'll give you a piece of good advice if you like."

"What is it?"

"Well, when a wife takes that highty-tighty tone towards her husband they say there's only one remedy."

"What's that?"

"Corporal punishment," said Jack, grinning.

"Eh?" said Bobo, staring.

"I believe the English law allows a man a rod no thicker than his thumb for the purpose of maintaining domestic discipline."

Bobo refused to see the joke. He sat in silence with his chin on his breast.

"I suppose you're waiting for money," said Jack.

Bobo nodded.

"I don't want to rub it in, but I'm curious to know if you appreciate the colossal cheek of your coming to me for money after what has happened?"

Bobo nodded again. "What else could I do?"

"I shouldn't be surprised if part of it was actually for the purpose of settling with the man who helped you to disobey my orders."

"Miriam fixed that up by wireless."

"Then I might suggest that it's up to her to settle with the man. You told me Miriam was well-fixed, you know."

"Something has happened," said Bobo. "We went to the Bienvenu before coming here. Some one called her up there. She wouldn't let me hear what she said. She was sore afterwards. Seems her income is cut off or something."

"That's not hard to guess," said Jack. "The old man told her that now she's got you, she can afford to dispense with his weekly contribution."

"Do you really think she's in his pay?"

"Oh, let's don't go into that again."

"Good Lord! What will become of me!" groaned Bobo. "I've got to show her the color of my money, or she'll worm the truth out of me!"

"You'll never tell her the truth. She'd kill you."

"She'll guess the truth, if I don't keep her supplied!"

"You should have thought of that yesterday."

"Don't be so hard on me!" whined Bobo. "What's the money to you!"

Jack felt slightly disgusted. "I'm going to keep you supplied," he said, "within reason. But you'll have to keep that young lady inside the limits that I set. I've no intention of maintaining her like the Queen of Sheba. Tell her your money's in the hands of trustees. Tell her anything you like."

"How much?" said Bobo anxiously.

"Five thousand for the honeymoon. After that a thousand weekly. Not another cent."

"I've got to have the limousine," whined Bobo.

Jack's lip curled. "You're not exactly in a position to make demands. However, you can have the car. It's no good to me."

Bobo commenced to stammer his thanks.

"Cut it out!" said Jack. "I'm only doing it, because it happens to suit my plans. You have disobeyed my orders, and forfeited all claims on me. I reserve the right of course, to show you up whenever it suits me."

Bobo lived in the present. Seeing his immediate needs relieved, he refused to consider the unpleasant future. His eye brightened as Jack went to write him a check.

31

This was the night of the weekly meeting of the Friends of Freedom, Barbarossa's circle, of which Jack was now a full member. On his way to the meeting-place he stopped in at Harmon Evers' place according to custom, to be metamorphosed from Jack Robinson into Henry Cassels, the wild-haired young anarchist.

Jack enjoyed these visits to the wig-maker. Evers was an original. His philosophy never failed him—nor his common-sense. He was so conspicuous for the latter quality that Jack more than once had been tempted to confide in him fully, with the idea of profiting by his advice. It was only the general rule he had laid down for himself, not to tell a soul of his affairs, that had restrained him. As it was, he and Evers had talked over the situation in hypothetical terms. Evers never allowed himself to betray a vulgar curiosity.

Evers' wit and wisdom were usually expressed in terms of hair. His special knowledge was astonishing. He could tell you offhand the style of hairdressing favored by a great man at any stage of his career, and drew ingenious parallels between his hair and his policy. Napoleon's downfall he ascribed to the atrophy of his follicles.

As it was after shop-hours the work was done in Evers' apartment up-stairs, a model of neatness and comfort. Clearly Mrs. Evers' past triumphs on the boards had not unfitted her for the soberer business of housekeeping. Though they showed every evidence of being well-to-do they kept no servant.

"So to-night is lodge-night," said Evers facetiously, as he worked over Jack's hair. "Odd isn't it, how grown men love to club together and surround themselves with all manner of solemn nonsense. The original lodges were in the African jungle. The high officers in secret societies are nearly always bald. Yet hair plays a large part in many rituals. Consider the goat!"

"This is not exactly a lodge that I belong to," said Jack.

"I understand," said Evers. "That was just my little joke. I guess the risks you take, my young friend, and I admire your courage. You have the hair of a brave man. I am always delighted when you return to me in safety to have the make-up removed. It is a valuable work you are engaged on, too. These people are the weeds of our fertile soil; they should be rooted up."

"As to rooting them up I leave that to the police," said Jack carelessly. "I have a special object in view. There are worse things in the world than a lot of spouting anarchists."

"What could be worse?"

"Well, murder as a business proposition."

"Good Heavens! Can such things be possible!"

The meeting-place of the Friends of Freedom was very ingeniously contrived. You entered by the front door of a big double-decker tenement on Orchard street. So many people came and went by this door, that the arrival of the Reds singly and in couples was entirely unnoticed. You passed through the hall of the double-decker into a narrow paved court where a smaller rear tenement faced you.

Entering the latter building, you gave the password at a door on the left of the hall, and assembled with your fellow-members in a large bare room. But this was not the meeting-place. When all were present, and the scrutineers were satisfied, that all had a right to be present, the hall door was locked, a trap in the floor was lifted, and all present silently descended into the cellar. The last man let the trap fall behind him.

Though damp and moldy-smelling, the place was otherwise admirably fitted for its purpose. The walls were of thick rough stone without any openings. A special ceiling had been constructed to keep sounds from rising. In such a vault the speakers could shout themselves hoarse without any danger of giving anything away to the outside world. It is no easy task to find a safe meeting-place for anarchists. In this case the landlord was a member of the circle.

There was another stairway at the rear by which Barbarossa alone was privileged to enter. Jack understood that this stair led to a room in an adjoining house, whence you could gain the next street. It provided a means of escape in case of a surprise from the police.

It was a wild-looking crowd that gathered in the cellar. They specialized in original hirsute effects. Evers the wig-maker could have obtained many new ideas there. But Jack had not attended many meetings before he began to suspect that their wildness did not extend much further than hair. They were noisy, but not particularly dangerous. They seemed to Jack like a parcel of children making believe to be enemies of society. Some of the younger men spoke with a genuine fire, but they were generally squelched by their elders. These elders stood as pat on their formulas as an old guard Republican on his.

This was particularly true of Barbarossa their leader. Anarchy was Barbarossa's meal-ticket, and he worked it for all there was in it. Barbarossa's superb red beard and flaming aureole of hair were his principal stock in trade. He made a magnificent passionate figure on the rostrum. Every word he uttered was received as gospel, for loyalty to him had become a tradition. But to Jack who came to the meetings with a cool brain, Barbarossa's eloquence seemed a pumped-up affair.

To-night the proceedings were held up for ten minutes by the tardy arrival of a member Jack had not seen before, who had sent word in advance of his coming. This was an important man, Jack was told, too busy to attend every meeting. He proved to be a man in his forties, somewhat corpulent, with smooth jetty black hair and small moustache and the clear, pallid skin that goes with such hair. Unlike the others he affected the neat style of a business man. He was addressed as Comrade Wilde.

Jack apprehended a new quality in this man, a more dangerous quality than in any of the others. He watched him closely. Unfortunately the place was none too well lighted. Comrade Wilde held whispered conferences with different members, but took no part in the speechmaking.

Barbarossa harangued the gathering in fiery style on the subject of the iniquities of the Federal Reserve Banking system. Comrade Rado then arose and proposed that the New York branch be blown up as a protest. Barbarossa rebuked him for making such a suggestion in open meeting. It appeared there was a committee to act on such matters. Somebody said something about a "Star Chamber" and a violent dispute was engendered. It was thus at every meeting. Jack suspected Barbarossa of purposely throwing the meeting into disorder. Acts of violence threatened his livelihood. Comrade Wilde listened to the uproar with an ill-disguised sneer.

It was stilled by the speech of Comrade Berg, a mere slip of a youth whom Jack had not noticed before. He rose with trembling hands and ecstatic eyes, and spoke in a voice of soft intensity. His subject was the necessity of purifying themselves for the great sacrifice. The words were not extraordinary; it was the self-forgetfulness, the strange half-insane passion of the speaker that quieted the noisy, ordinary crowd.

"Hello!" thought Jack. "This is the real thing! This will bear watching." Out of the corner of his eyes he observed that Comrade Wilde was likewise attending sharply to the youth.

His speech bore no relation to what had gone before. He had reached such a state of exaltation as to be unaware of what was going on around him.

"We must give up father, mother, dear ones, friends; we must learn to do without love and affection; we must cast out all that makes life sweet to live, so that when the time comes to leave it there may be no unmanly hanging back. We must eat and drink no more than enough to keep life in the body. The world will never be saved by guzzlers. Gross eating obscures the finer spirit of man. In abstemiousness and solitude the true inspiration comes.

"I am young. I have no right to tell men older in the Cause what to do. I am speaking for myself only. I lived alone until the message came to me. I am ready now to give all. When you want an instrument I ask you to use me first."

Barbarossa had been growing more and more uneasy. He now interrupted the youth. "One moment, Comrade. You are out of order. There is some unfinished business from the last meeting. Afterwards we will be glad to hear you. The question that was held over to be put to the vote at this meeting is: Shall we take political action at the next election."

This was a favorite subject of controversy, and the meeting was instantly convulsed again. Berg sat down dazed. He was not allowed to speak again.

"Poor young devil!" thought Jack. "Looks half starved. I'll ask him out to supper."

When they were completely talked out the meeting broke up. The comrades mounted the stairs in amity all controversies forgotten. With their bosoms relieved of much perilous stuff, they yawned comfortably, and began to think of supper.

Jack attached himself to young Berg as they gained the street. "Say, that was a great speech," he said by way of ingratiating himself.

The youth pushed the lank hair out of his eyes and looked at Jack wildly. The light of incipient madness was in his eyes.

"Poor devil! Poor devil!" thought Jack. The sight hurt him. Aloud he said: "Let's go and have a bite of supper."

Berg shook his head.

"Oh, *come on!*" said Jack thrusting his arm through the other youth's.

The tone of genuine friendliness must have reached the cold breast. Berg gave in without further objection.

They entered one of the big bakery-restaurants on Grand street, and ordered coffee and hamburgers. The smell of cooking brought a faint color into Berg's livid cheeks, and his nostrils dilated.

But the hamburgers were not destined to be eaten by them. When he had given the order Jack went into a booth to telephone Evers not to wait up for him, as he could lodge outside in his disguise and come in to change in the morning. Mrs. Evers took the message. When he came out of the booth Berg had left their table.

"Where did my friend go?" Jack asked the waiter.

"I dunno. Guy come in and spoke to him private, and he took his hat and went with him."

"What kind of looking guy?"

"Fat. Real black hair, black moustache, pale face. Dressed neat. Derby and black Melton overcoat."

This was a good description of Comrade Wilde.

"Oh, Damn!" muttered Jack.

He put down the money for what he had ordered and left the place. He spent three hours wandering about the East Side, looking into such places as were still open, on the bare chance of running into his man. All in vain of course. Finally he sought out a cheap lodging and threw himself down exhausted. He was tormented by the sense of an impending disaster.

32

In the morning Jack called up the Madagascar to see if there was any message for him. It appeared that some one had telephoned him several times since the night before. No name had been left, but the telephone number was given.

The number suggested nothing to Jack. He called it, and a voice strange to him answered. He asked if there was anyone there who wished to speak to Mr. Robinson, and after a pause he heard another voice, a squeaky treble.

"This Mr. Robinson? Gee! I thought I'd never get hold of you!"

"Who is it?"

"Whitcomb. You know."

"Whitcomb? I don't know," said Jack perplexed.

"You know, your confidential agent that you gave orders to yesterday."

A light broke on Jack. "Sure!" he cried. "Didn't recognize the name."

"Well you never know who may be tapping the wire."

"Very wise precaution. What is it, Tommy—I mean Whitcomb?"

"I got a report to make."

"Fire away."

"Can't tell you over the phone. It's too important. Say, Mr. Robinson, I got what you sent me after all right."

"Good boy!"

"Want me to come to the hotel?"

Jack not knowing if Bobo and Miriam would be out of the way, said "No." He considered a moment. "Meet me at Harmon Evers' shop, number — East Twenty-Ninth street. In half an hour."

The half hour gave Jack time to get to Evers' and change his make-up. It was not yet eight o'clock.

Evers evinced a strong interest in Tommy when he arrived. "Comical little fellow, isn't he?" he said. "That wiry, blonde hair betokens an enterprising character. These boys of the street learn to think for themselves early."

Tommy and Jack did not discuss their business of course, until they had left the shop. Outside Jack said:

"Do you mean to say you have spotted the house where the old man lives?"

"Not where he lives, but where he changes his clothes."

"Good man! Where is it?"

"Forty-Eighth street, near Seventh avenue."

"We'll go there," said Jack, and looked up and down for a taxi-cab. "You can tell me the whole story on the way. We'll stop at the Madagascar for a gun and a pair of handcuffs in case we meet our friend."

When they were seated in the cab Tommy began his story. "I was thinking over everything you told me, and it seemed to me I wouldn't have a very good show to trail the old man by myself. Maybe he knew my face you see, and anyway the uniform was a give away. So I got my cousin to help me. He ain't working now. He's bigger'n me. We're going partners in the detective business when we get the coin to open up an office."

"I described him the man I was after, and placed him acrost the street from the office, with instructions to follow me if I come up, and pick up the trail if I had to drop it."

"Well, about half past two yes'day, old man come into the office for his package all right. Soon as I see him I slides out and waits for him outside. Say he was cagy all right. He had a hunch he was being trailed. Dodged in one door of the Knickerbocker and out again by another. In the Forty-Second street building he tried to shake me by riding in different elevators, but I stuck to him all right. Me cousin was right there too, with his tongue hanging out."

"He took to the Subway next. Got on an up-town local at Grand Central. I got in the next car because I thought he might reco'nize me, but me cousin sits down right opposite him. Well after we left Times Square station he comes into my car, gives me a hard look, and sits down beside me. Say, me heart was going like a compressed air riveter."

"He says to me: 'Don't you work at 1118 Broadway?' and I says: 'Yes, sir.' He says: 'I guess you worked for me sometimes,' and I looks at him hard and makes out to reco'nize him for the first, and says: 'Yes, sir.' He says: 'You carried a little package for me up to the Hotel Beanvenoo yes'day.' I says: 'Yes, sir. The lady was out, so I brung it back.'"

"'Hm!' says he, like that, and looks at me real hard for a minute, I guess. He's got blue eyes that make holes in you like bay'nits. But he didn't get any change off a me. Then he says real sudden-like: 'Has anybody been trying to fix you?' 'Why no sir!' I says with a baby stare. 'I dunno what you mean.'"

"'Where you going now?' says he. I hadda say somepin real quick. I says: 'I gotta deliver a letter up-town.' 'Where?' 'Seventy-Second street.' He says: 'Let me see it.' I says: "Gainst the rules, boss.' He laughs sneery like."

"By this time the train was pulling into Fiftieth. 'Well I get out here' he says, sticking me with those eyes again. And there he left me flat. What could I do. But I look and I see me cousin is hep, so I know all ain't lost yet. As the train pulls out I see that kid foller him up the stairs."

"Well I chases home, and changes me clo'es. I puts on the toughest rig I got. Then I went down to Mis' Harvest's store and waited 'round. Mis' Harvest keeps a little candy and stationery store under my house. Me cousin and me, we never plague her like the other kids does, and she lets us sort of stick around. We use her phone in our business. We had agreed if we got separated, the one who lost the trail was to go to Mis' Harvest's and wait for a call."

"Me cousin calls me up about four o'clock. He says the old man is sitting in the Knickerbocker bar, drinking and talking to a feller, and if I hustle maybe I can git there before he leaves. Well, I meets me cousin outside the door of the bar, and he says the old man is still inside. He patrols the Broadway side, and I takes the Forty-Second street entrance, and we meet at the corner, and exchange signals."

"Bye and bye old man comes out my cousin's door, and the two of us take after him down Broadway. At Fortieth street, old man turns real sudden and grabs hold me cousin. There was a cop there. Old man says: 'Officer, this boy has been follerin' me all afternoon!' Cop takes a grip on me cousin; say, maybe that kid wasn't scared! Cop says: 'What do you want to annoy this gen'leman for?' but me cousin was mum as a dummy! Cop says: 'Do you want to lay 'a complaint, sir?' Old man says: 'Haven't time. Just warn him, and let him go.' So the cop boots me cousin down the side street, and old man goes on down Broadway. But I was right there steppin' on his heels. He never thought of looking at me in me old clothes."

"Well now he thought he was clear of us all, and he didn't bother about coverin' his tracks no more. He crosses Broadway, and comes back tutter side. He only made one stop. That was in a cigar store. He telephoned from the booth. Then he led me straight to the house on 48th near 7th, an old private house it was, that's been turned into stores and offices. There was no elevator nor nothing.

"I couldn't foller him inside, so I waits acrost the street. He come out in half an hour. Say, I almost missed him then. He's a rapid change artist for fair! Had a big trust on him now——"

"Trust?" interrupted Jack.

"You know, corporation, bow-window——" Tommy illustrated.

"I see, go on."

"But he looked twenty years younger. Real black hair now, little black moustache, white face—like a dude Eyetalian. Had a neat derby on, and black overcoat."

"Good God!" cried Jack. "Comrade Wilde! You're sure it was the same man."

"Certain sure! But it was a peach of a make-up. I wouldn't of got on to it, only he didn't walk like a fat man. He didn't lean back far enough to balance his load if it was bona-fide."

"Pretty good!" said Jack. "I never thought of that."

"Well, I took after him again, but he give me the slip at Sixth Avenue. There was a car waiting for him there—big black limousine——"

"I know it!" said Jack ruefully.

"He hopped it, and went off down-town. There was a taxi there too, but the shover only laughed at me, when I wanted to hire him. By the time I satisfied him I had the price, the black car was out of sight."

"I went back to the house on Forty-eighth. There's a lady's hat store in the basement, and a beauty parlor on the first floor. Up-stairs is mixed offices and unfurnished rooms. It's one of those old style walk-up houses that you can go in and out of, without being noticed. I made out to be looking for a Mr. Webster. By asking round I found out the old man has the third floor rear. There's no sign on the door nor nothing. The other tenants thinks it's a traveler that just keeps his samples there. None of them don't know him."

33

With a brief stop at the Madagascar for the purpose mentioned, Jack and his diminutive assistant were carried to the house on Forty-Eighth street. Tommy led the way to the third floor rear. Above the parlor floor no changes had been made in the old-fashioned residence, beyond letting a few panes of glass in the door panels to light the hall. But the door Tommy indicated was of the original solid wood. Jack knocked without receiving any answer. There was no sound of any movement within.

Jack had made up his mind that the boldest way of entering would be the simplest. He therefore sent Tommy in search of a locksmith while he remained silently on guard in the hall. When the workman appeared Jack explained that he had inadvertently locked his keys in his room, and instructed him to pick the lock. When the man set to work, Jack privately dispatched Tommy down into the yard to keep an eye on the rear windows.

Opening the door was no great task. Jack looked inside with a fast beating heart. His first general impression was of a simply furnished office. He dismissed the locksmith, and recalled Tommy by a signal from the window.

The principal object in the room was an old-fashioned flat-topped desk so placed between the windows that the light would fall over the user's shoulders. The desk was covered with papers, and the merest glance was enough to show Jack that he had here the conclusive evidence that he had been so long in search of. He decided to call in official help now. There was a telephone on the desk, but he hesitated trusting his secret to it. Instead, he wrote a note to the Deputy Commissioner, asking for two plain clothes men to be sent him at once. This he entrusted to Tommy, instructing him to take a taxicab to police headquarters.

The door was fitted with a spring lock of the usual pattern. It had not been injured, and when the door closed it locked itself. As soon as he was left alone Jack set about making a careful examination of the place. He figured that should the owner return, the sound of the key in the lock would give him sufficient warning. He laid his automatic ready to his hand on the desk. He was careful to make no sound that would warn any one who might stop to listen at the door before entering.

First he took a general survey. The two windows of the room looked out on an array of back yards and on the rear of a long row of similar buildings in the next street. One of the windows opened on a fire escape.

At one's right as one faced the windows was an old-fashioned fireplace: across the room were two doors, the lower giving on the stair hall, the upper presumably on the hall room adjoining. The latter door was screwed to its frame.

At the other end of the room from the windows was a large closet. Jack, fearful of being trapped by the return of the owner merely looked in here. It was set out with a bureau and mirror, and from pegs around the walls depended an extraordinary assortment of clothes. Jack saw that there was a complete separate outfit on each peg; fine clothes and mean, native and foreign; a policeman's uniform, and a complete turn-out for a woman. Above the pegs a shelf ran around, and over each peg was a box which presumably contained the smaller articles to complete each make-up.

Interesting as was this exhibit, the papers in connection with the desk quickly drew Jack away from it. Behind the desk there was an object which whetted his curiosity to the highest degree. This was an oaken cabinet with drawers of the kind that are used to contain modern card index systems. Jack eagerly pulled out the top drawer.

Inside was a set of large cards, each headed by a name in the usual manner, and with various particulars as to that individual entered beneath. As the scheme became clear to him Jack's heart beat fast. He could scarcely credit the evidence of his senses. It appeared that he held in his hands a complete record of the operations of "Mr. B." What strange freak of vanity could have led the criminal to collect such a mass of damning evidence!

Here was one card chosen at random.

BLAKELY, CHARLES EVANS

Office: Blakely Bros. & Co., 47 Wall St.

Town house: No. 9 East — St. (Dec. 1st to May 1st.)

Country home: Scarborough-on-Hudson. (Goes up week-ends all year.)

Income: $200,000. (Principally stocks and bonds.)

Personal description: 41 years old; short, fat all over, bald, rosy; known as "Kewpie Blakely." Brown hair and eyes. Wears large, square-cut emerald on left hand pinky. Agent C.D. reports: Blakely is one of the *bon vivants* of the Millionaires' Club, a jolly, open-handed, good-natured fellow, enormously popular. Is a well-known collector of Persian faience. Is happily married and has four children, but is reputed to be somewhat gay. N.B. Reports from female agents do not bear this out. Q. reports Blakely employs a body-guard to ride beside him in his car. Says Blakely never walks in the street. Has a watchman in the corridors of his house at night.

On the other side of the card was a series of chronological entries, some of which were obscure, though the main story was clear enough.

April 17th 19-- Sent form AA.

 18th Instructed Anderson to follow up.

 19th Anderson reports nothing doing.

 23rd Sent form AB.

 25th Anderson reports his solicitor

  thrown out of Blakely's office.

 26th Instructed Anderson let B. alone for

  present. Sent G. M. to Mrs. Cleaver's

  with orders to get next to Blakely.

May 3rd G. M. reports nothing doing.

  Blakely's in love with his wife.

 4th Tried a man instead. Instructed J. L. to

  win Blakely's friendship

  through his love of art.

June 11th J. L. reports success. Is on intimate

  footing with Blakely. Sent

  J. L. capsule with instructions for

  administering.

 15th J. L. reports success. Blakely apparently

  very ill.

 16th Wrote Blakely that he had been

  poisoned, and next time he'd get a

  fatal dose.

 17th Blakely sent his secretary to Eureka

  Agency to subscribe.

The story told by this card was typical. Some of the victims had required more pressure; some had given in easier. Some had fallen behind in their payments, and had required to be "persuaded" anew. Two of the cards Jack turned over, those of Ames Benton and Silas Gyde, were significantly underlined: "*Account closed.*" Jack shuddered.

From the card index he turned to the litter of papers on the desk. On top lay a typewritten communication which bore neither address nor signature, but from the contents was unmistakably to be identified as a report from one of "Mr. B's" agents. It read as follows:

"I cannot give you any definite data as to X's movements around his country place, because his habits are very irregular. He comes out from town sometimes by motor, sometimes by train, and at any hour. Sometimes he stays up in the country for several days at a time, transacting his business over a private telephone wire.

"I understand he laughs at the idea of danger to himself, and is averse to taking any special precautions. I have learned though, that Mrs. X on her own responsibility has engaged guards to patrol their place very thoroughly. It is well known that the Green Hollow Club where he plays golf has long been guarded by a small army under the guise of 'gardeners,' 'greenkeepers,' etc.

"I have not been able to win the confidence of any of the servants in the country. They're a crabby lot. It seems Mrs. X has taken them into her confidence regarding a 'danger threatening their master' and they're all making a great brag of their loyalty, etc. I don't think anything can be successfully pulled off up there.

"But here's a plan. Mr. X sleeps in his town house whenever he is detained late in town. The house is closed of course, and is under the care of two old servants, Tom Monahan and his wife. I learned that Tom was a member of the — district Democratic Club, and I scraped acquaintance with him there. We are now good friends. I have the entrée to the X house (when the master is not there) and can describe it to you fully.

"Yesterday I was sitting in the kitchen with the Monahans, when I noticed that the house in the next street which backs up against the X house is in the hands of painters and decorators. That gave me my idea. It would be useless to try to enter the X house from the front. Monahan has orders not to admit any one whatsoever while Mr. X is there. But there is a door from the kitchen into the back yard which is never locked except at night. I suppose they think that the high board fence around the yard is sufficient protection.

"When X spends the night in town, Mrs. Monahan cooks his breakfast for him, and at half past nine (she is very methodical) carries it up to the dining-room and puts it on the steam table. She does not call her master. He comes down when he is ready. Another thing, Mrs. Monahan does not allow her husband in the kitchen while she is cooking. At this hour he will be in the servants' hall in the front of the basement, reading the paper.

"Here's my plan. Let your man go to the house where the painters are at work—it is No. — East 65th Street, and let him ask the boss painter for a job. The painters are working on the fourth and fifth floors now. He'll be turned down of course, or referred to the office. Now when he comes down-stairs instead of leaving the house, let him go into the dining-room to get the lay of things. The dining-room is the first floor rear. The windows overlook the kitchen and dining-room of the X house.

"When he sees Mrs. Monahan go up to the dining-room with X's breakfast, let him slip down-stairs and out through the yard of the vacant house. He will have a good five minutes or more while Mrs. M is arranging the things, etc. He will find plenty of ladders. Let him plant a short ladder against the back fence and drop into the X's yard. He cannot be seen from the X house unless Mrs. M just happens to be at the dining-room window, which is very unlikely.

"I will enclose a little plan of the X house. Your man enters from the yard by door A, crosses kitchen and goes out by door Z into passage; opens door C into housemaid's closet, where he conceals himself until Mrs. M returns to kitchen. He then goes up the stairs D which brings him to the pantry above. There is a swing door into the dining-room. In front of this door is a tall leather screen. If he waits behind this screen until X gets fairly inside the room, he will be between him and the only exit. If X is already in the room he will have him dead to rights.

"After the accident the chances of your man making a getaway are slim. The entrance hall to the house lies just in front of the dining-room. There are two stairs from the basement. If Monahan runs up through the pantry your man may get out by the front door, if he can open it in time, but if M comes up the front stairs he will meet him in the hall. However, I understood from you that the matter of the getaway was not of the first importance.

"P.S. I have opened this to add that I have just learned X is booked to speak at the A.B.A. dinner at the Astor on Tuesday night. He will stay in town. If you think my plan is good enough you'll have to pull the trick Wednesday morning. The next time X stays in town the painters in the vacant house will be finished."

Jack sat scowling at this document. Another ghastly assassination scheduled! His skin crawled with horror. How to discover the identity of the victim and warn him in time was the problem. It was planned for Wednesday morning——

Suddenly Jack sprang to his feet electrified. This was Wednesday morning. And it must be about nine-thirty now! He pulled out his watch with trembling fingers. The hands pointed to twenty minutes past nine. He had ten minutes! And he had yet to find out whom they planned to kill!

He searched frantically among the other papers on the desk for a possible clue. He uncovered a card which had been removed from the index temporarily. A glance at it was sufficient.

DELAMARE, WALTER DE COURCY.

Of course! Delamare had threatened to defy the blackmailers! Delamare's house was on the North side of East Sixty-fourth Street: Delamare had been the principal speaker at the bankers' dinner the night before: Jack thought of the man's fine courage, his humanity, his humor, his unfailing kindness to himself, and turned sick with horror.

"I have not time!" he groaned.

He fell on the telephone book. Delamare's address was not listed there. Like many a prominent man he did not care to subject his home to the annoyance of calls from cranks and strangers. It is useless to ask Information for such numbers. Jack tried the bank but it was before the opening hour and he could get no answer. Meanwhile the precious moments were slipping.

He snatched up his hat, and ran out of the room careless if all his work was destroyed, so he might save his friend. He had to run half a block before he met a taxicab. That took him swiftly enough to Delamare's house. The inexpressive blind windows told him nothing of what was happening within. It was exactly nine-thirty when he rang the bell. He prayed that Delamare might oversleep to-day.

The door was opened by a middle-aged caretaker, with a somewhat forbidding look, evidently Monahan.

"I must see Mr. Delamare at once!" said Jack breathlessly.

"Not at home. You'll have to go to his office," was the stolid response.

Jack could stand no more. "Good God, man! His life is threatened. I must warn him!"

Monahan was sure then that he had a crank to deal with. He barred the way with his great bulk. "Take yourself off!" he growled. "Or I'll call the police."

Jack almost despaired. "Shut the door and leave me here if you want," he said, "but for God's sake go to your master quickly. Keep him out of the dining-room until you search it. There's a murderer hidden there!"

Monahan's mind moved slowly. He stood staring at Jack full of sullen suspicion.

"Go! Go!" cried Jack.

A shot rang out in the house, seemingly right behind Monahan.

"Too late!" cried Jack.

The sound of the shot galvanized the heavy-witted one into action. Turning, he ran from the door, leaving it open. Jack followed him. The dining-room as he already knew adjoined the hall. As Monahan opened the door there was flashed on Jack's brain the picture of a man standing with a gun in his hand, and another lying face down on the floor.

"Seize him!" he cried instinctively.

But at the sound of their coming, the erect man turned, and Jack saw that it was Delamare with face pale but composed.

"Oh, you're all right! Thank God!" cried Jack. The suddenness of the reaction almost unmanned him. He had to support himself against the door frame.

"You, Robinson?" said Delamare in a low steady voice. "Were you warned of this?"

"Just ten minutes ago. I came as quickly as I could."

"Do you know him?" asked Delamare pointing to the figure on the floor.

"I think so. Turn him over."

Monahan obeyed, and as Jack had expected, he saw the livid, drawn face of the half mad youth he had tried to befriend. The eyes were closed.

Jack nodded. "His name is Berg. Is he dead?"

Delamare shook his head smiling. "Not much. Stunned only. I cracked him on the head with his own gun. He had no strength."

A wave of compassion swept over Jack. "Poor devil! Poor devil!" he murmured. "He isn't the real criminal!"

"I expect not," said Delamare.

Jack suddenly became aware of a dark stain spreading on Delamare's coat sleeve above the elbow. "You're wounded!" he cried.

"Nothing serious. A flesh wound. I can move my arm freely."

"You must have a doctor."

"All right. Monahan, telephone for Doctor McArdle. Then for the police."

By this time Berg's eyes were open. He was muttering incoherently, and rolling his head from side to side on the floor. As Monahan was leaving the room, Jack was struck by an idea.

"Wait a minute!" he said. To Delamare: "If I might make a suggestion——?"

"Go ahead."

"Couldn't we keep this affair to ourselves for the present?"

"Certainly, if it will further your plans."

"This young fellow is mad—or the next thing to it. If we could put him in the hands of a good brain specialist, and have his senses restored by proper treatment, he might make an invaluable witness against the man we really want."

"Good!" said Delamare. "We'll call Doctor Watkins Kent. Monahan, never mind the police. First call Doctor McArdle, and say I have had a slight accident. Say no more than that. Then call Doctor Watkins Kent. Say that Mr. Delamare presents his compliments, and wants to know if he can make it convenient to come to his house at once on a matter of importance."

34

Jack, remembering the critical stage at which he had left matters in Forty-Eighth street, did not wait for the doctors, but left Berg in Mr. Delamare's care, and hastened back. He found that Tommy and the two plainclothes men had arrived in the meantime, but finding him gone, they were hanging around outside the door of the room, at a loss what to do.

This time they broke in the door without ado. At his first glance inside Jack saw that the room had been visited. Though he had been away but little more than half an hour, a clean sweep had been made of the cards and papers. A still smoldering fire in the grate showed the manner of their disposal. The window on the fire escape was open.

"He was inside when you got here!" cried Jack. "He heard you outside. Now he's given us the slip again. Why didn't you watch the back windows!"

The city detectives looked distinctly aggrieved. The spokesman for the pair said: "How did we know what your game was?"

"You knew!" said Jack to Tommy.

Tommy hung his head. "When I came back, and found you gone, I didn't know rightly what to do," he muttered.

Jack saw that it was really nobody's fault. "Oh, well, we'll have to try again," he said.

"You should have called on us sooner," said the principal detective condescendingly.

"Sorry, I didn't," said Jack dryly.

The other missed the note of irony. "Well, lay out your case to us now, and we'll give you some experienced advice."

Somehow the manner of this well-meaning gentleman did not inspire Jack with overmuch confidence as to his perspicacity. Moreover, since his man and his evidence were both gone, he saw nothing to be gained by consulting the police.

"I'm not quite ready to do that," he said good-naturedly. "Sorry to have troubled you for nothing."

The two detectives exchanged a look of scorn. "These amateurs think they know it all!" it said. Only the fact that they knew Jack was a great man's secretary, and therefore a person to be propitiated, restrained them from audible comment.

However, when they found that Jack was disposed to reward them liberally, they changed their opinion of him. Ten dollar bills are wonderful sweeteners.

"How about me?" asked Tommy anxiously.

"Back to the mines," said Jack. "In other words, 1118 Broadway."

Tommy's face fell piteously.

"Mind you," said Jack quickly. "I'm not blaming you for our failure. You did wonderful work. I'll send for you when the trail gets hot again."

He likewise presented Tommy with a green testimonial of his appreciation.

Before any of them got out of the room the telephone bell most surprisingly rang. They all stopped and stared at the instrument as if they expected an apparition to issue from the mouthpiece.

"Wait!" said Jack. "Perhaps there's something here."

He took down the receiver. "Hello," he said ingratiatingly.

The reply came in a tone no less dulcet: "How do you do, Mr. Robinson."

Jack almost dropped the receiver. "Why—what—who—" he stammered.

He heard a light laugh on the wire. "You are surprised. But I was sure I would find you there."

"Who is this?" asked Jack sparring for time—he knew very well.

"Need you ask?" replied the mocking voice. "This is the owner of the desk at which you are now seated."

Jack said to himself, "Mustn't let him think he's putting it over you!" He answered in the same mocking tone. "How do you do. So glad you called me up."

Clapping a hand over the transmitter, he whispered swiftly to the leading detective: "This is the man. Trace the call back. If he's anywhere near, get him. I'll keep him talking."

The detective took a note of the number on the transmitter, and ran out followed by Tommy.

Meanwhile the voice on the wire was saying: "Sorry I was out when you called."

"Very glad to wait until you can get back," said Jack.

"That's nice of you. But I'm mighty sorry, I've been called out of town."

As on a former occasion Jack's recollection was vaguely stirred by something familiar in the man's voice. He supposed that this was the man who had appeared as Comrade Wilde the night before, but as Wilde had not spoken aloud within Jack's hearing, it must have been on some other occasion he had heard this voice. But he could not place it.

When the exchange of ironical civilities began to pall, Jack asked politely: "What can I do for you, Mr. B.?"

"I just wanted a little chat with you. I wanted to congratulate you on your game."

"Thanks!"

"It's been a mighty interesting game that you and I have been playing the last few weeks; a sort of chess game with human pawns, eh?"

"That's right."

"Well, you've won. You have checkmated me."

"Do you mind telling me what you mean by that exactly?"

"I have quit. Burned my records as you see; closed up Anderson and the other agencies; paid off and called in all my operatives."

"Going to retire on your winnings, eh?"

"Quite so," was the calm reply. "But do me the credit of believing that it was not the money I was playing for, but the joy of the game. It was a great game! For three years I have pitted myself single-handed against the combined wealth of this country. I have taken my toll of the millionaires, and not all the power that wealth commands was able to stop me!"

"True enough," said Jack grimly. "I could admire you myself, if you had only left murder out of your calculations."

The man at the other end of the wire chose to ignore the ugly word. He resumed: "I'm counting on the fact that your head is strong enough not to be turned by what I'm telling you."

"I don't quite get you there," said Jack.

"In other words you're too good a man I hope, to be unduly puffed up by the fact that I salute you as the victor, and retire from the game. You will not be foolish enough to think that you have me altogether at your mercy."

"Oh, I hope I know a good player myself when I see one."

"Good! Then you will be content with your victory, which I assure you is no mean one for a man of your years. So long as you have stopped me you will not feel that it is necessary to your triumph to have me apprehended."

"Oh, I didn't say that," Jack answered quickly. "I should have to consider that carefully. I couldn't promise anything offhand."

"Promise?" said the voice quickly, with a touch of pique. "I want no promise. It is nothing to me what you decide. I like you for your sportsmanlike qualities, and therefore I give you fair warning. It is for your own good that I suggest you go no further."

"Much obliged," said Jack dryly, "I'll consider it."

There was still pique in the voice. "Don't get a swelled head, my young friend. It is fatal to clever youths. I've been playing with you the last few weeks. It amused me to see how near I could let you come to me, and still evade you. But if I wished to keep out of your way, you could never get within miles of me!"

"Then why bother about the matter?"

"Because I am tired of the chase. I'm going to settle down into a nice hum-drum life of respectability. I'm not going to put myself to the trouble of running away from you."

"And if I should still keep after you?"

"I'd be awfully sorry," drawled the voice, "but I should really have to put a quietus on you. I could, you know. I've had a dozen chances within the past ten days."

Jack had no reason to doubt the truth of the last statement. He shivered a little. After all, life was sweet.

"I should hate to do it," the voice went on, "you're too good a sport."

"Much obliged," put in Jack.

"But I'd have no choice, really. I must have rest. My doctor orders it."

Jack smiled grimly at the thought of a crook threatened with nervous prostration as a result of overwork. These are rapid times that we live in! He cast about in his mind for the means to prolong the conversation.

"How do I know you're on the square?" he asked. "About quitting, I mean."

"Go see your friend Anderson to-morrow. You'll find him closed up. Mail your employer's check to the Eureka Protective Association. It will be returned to you by the post-office."

It seemed wise to Jack to appear to fall in with the other's suggestions. "I appreciate your friendliness in warning me," he said. "Do you mind if I ask you a question or two. Just natural, human curiosity, you know."

"Ask them and I'll see."

"How did you know I had been here in your office when you came. I had disturbed nothing."

"Perhaps I was there myself at the time."

"Impossible! I made sure of that."

The laugh sounded again. "Nothing is impossible! Think it over!"

"What first put you on to the fact that I was after you?"

"Oh, you want to know too much," was the laughing reply. "Answer me a question."

"Go ahead."

"What first made you suspect the Eureka Association?"

"Mr. Gyde left his heir a statement of their dealings with him."

"Hm! I never thought of that possibility."

"Now answer my question."

"You'd like to keep me here, wouldn't you, until you have time to trace this call back, and send a man to nab me. Sorry I can't oblige. I'm at Grand Central and my train is leaving. Good-bye!"

The detective had not sufficient time, of course, to get his man. Oddly enough the humorous "Mr. B" had told the truth as to where he was. The call had come from the Grand Central station.

35

Locked in his own room, Jack went over and over that telephone conversation, regarding it from every angle, and seeking to establish a new plan of campaign upon his conclusions. He was inclined to believe that "Mr. B" was sincere in his intentions of quitting the game. His dealings with the man had shown him that like all really able liars he used as much of the truth as he could. At any rate he would soon know whether or not he had quit.

But that "Mr. B" would now settle down to a life of respectability, Jack did not credit for a moment. It was all very well for him to talk about being "tired," excitement gets into the blood and one finds oneself unable to live without it. The thing was to figure out in advance what new direction his villainy would take.

Looking at the matter in the whole, Jack could not be very much cast down. It was no small feat that he had accomplished in bringing this man to sue for a truce. For that's what it was, let him make believe all he liked. He, Jack, had stopped him in mid-career, and Mr. B was no ordinary vulgar crook, but a really stupendous figure in his way. And Jack told himself if he could stop the man, he ought to be able to catch him.

He had not the slightest intention of giving up the chase, of course. His adversary's threats had the effect of stiffening his resolution. His present problem was, how to make "Mr. B" think that he had abandoned all measures against him, while he prepared a new surprise. Jack was well assured that he would be closely watched.

Jack's last remaining line of approach to the old man lay through Miriam. True, he had said over the wire that he had called in and paid off all his agents; but that this applied to Miriam, Jack doubted. Miriam would never be allowed to enjoy the pickings of so rich a goose as Bobo was supposed to be, alone. One way or another demands for money would be made. Surely he could find openings here.

The one trump card that Jack still held was that "Mr. B" with all his astuteness still believed that Jack was an obscure and ambitious youth whose sole motive in this affair was to make a name for himself.

Upon these two facts, the connection between Miriam and "Mr. B," and the latter's ignorance of his real identity, Jack built his new plan. It was inspired by the old maxim: "Give a thief rope enough and he will hang himself." After several hours of hard thought, he had it roughed out, but one great difficulty remained to be solved. Supposing he dropped out of sight for awhile, how could he inform himself of what went on in his absence?

After lunch Bobo called him up on the long distance. Bobo and Miriam were honeymooning at Rodney Farms, that exclusive and extremely expensive country resort.

Bobo's honeymoon was probably not of unalloyed joy. His voice was abjectly apologetic. "That you, Jack? How's things?"

"Pretty good."

The friendliness of Jack's tone heartened the other. "I just called up to tell you we were coming back to-morrow for a day or so. Miriam wants to."

"That so?"

"Yes, she fired her maid to-day, and has to get another."

"Yes?" said Jack with more attention. Something stirred in the back of his brain. "Has she got anybody in view?"

"No, she's going to Miss Staley's Employment Bureau. Seems all the women up here get their maids from her. Why do you ask?"

"Oh, nothing."

"It's all right for us to come?"

"Sure!"

"Well, I didn't want to take you by surprise."

"That's all right. As it happens, I want to have a talk with you."

Bobo's voice faltered. "Oh—! You're not going to—— You're not going to——"

"Not yet," said Jack encouragingly. "In fact, I was thinking of loosening the purse strings a bit on certain conditions."

"Oh, if you would! She drives me nearly crazy with her questions, why I can't get more money."

"Well, we'll talk about it to-morrow—while Miriam is out."

Jack's next move was to seek out Kate. To do this it was necessary to don the Pitman make-up, that he was heartily sick of now; he vowed it should be Mr. P.'s final appearance. He found her in her little sitting-room, and first he had to tell her of the exciting events of the morning, concluding with the astonishing telephone conversation. Her face blanched a little, when she heard of the threat.

"Well, you are satisfied, aren't you?" she asked in an offhand tone, "I mean if it's true that he's quit."

"Let him get away?" said Jack surprised. "Oh, Kate!"

Kate hung her head blushing.

"The point is, are you satisfied to have me stop?" Jack demanded. "You know what you said."

"I don't think you ought to take unnecessary risks," she murmured.

This was sweet to Jack. In order to get more of it he made believe not to see her drift. "As to that," he said carelessly, "the risk is no greater than it's been right along."

She shook her head. "No, I feel he means what he says. It was a warning. He has a queer sense of fair play."

The enraptured Jack forgot Mr. B. and all else. "Kitty, do you realize what you're saying!" he cried. "Do you mean you are satisfied I've done my job, and are willing to marry me now? You blessed darling! We could get a license this afternoon. We don't need any further preparations, do we? Oh, what happiness!"

"I wouldn't marry you at an hour's notice—or any man!" said Kate with an indignation, somewhat weakened by the consciousness of her inconsistency. "I need weeks to get ready in!"

"Weeks!" echoed Jack with falling countenance.

"Well, days, anyway."

"But will you, in a week?"

"Will you give up the chase of this man? Turn your case over to the police now. After all it's their business."

A reaction took place in Jack. "Oh, Kitty!" he said in distress. "How can I? All my life I'd feel as if I'd left my job half finished. I'd feel as if I'd been scared off. How could I respect myself? How could you respect me?"

She snatched her hand out of his. At first he thought he had offended her, but presently he perceived that she was moved by quite a different feeling. She was ashamed. She lifted an humble glance to his.

"You're right," she whispered. "It was just a moment of weakness. I wouldn't have let you give it up really, when I had had time to think. How will you be able to respect me now?"

He rapturously repossessed himself of her hand. "Kitty, you silly! Do you think I will be blaming you for loving me a little! How many times have I come to you ready to give up, and had you send me back into the fight again! This just equalizes things a little." He smiled at her teasingly. "You won't be able to be so superior, that's all!"

She looked at him with an odd shy light in her eyes that he had not seen before. "You goose! If you knew!"

"Let's get married anyway," he pleaded. "There's no manner of sense in putting it off any longer."

She shook her head "No. We set a task for ourselves. Let's accomplish it first."

"Well, tell me you love me, and I'll be satisfied."

"You know it. You've always known it."

"But tell me in plain downright English."

She did.

After an interval of divine foolishness, they came down to earth again, and Jack recollected his new plans.

"I've got a difficult and disagreeable job for you," said he.

"What's that?"

"Did you ever hear of Miss Staley's Employment Bureau?"

"Certainly. It's the best-known in town. All the fashionable women patronize it."

"Miriam's going there to-morrow morning to engage a maid."

"Well?"

"I want you to get the job."

"Good Heavens! Let me collect my wits! Lady's maid, I!"

"Look what I've been!"

"Oh, it isn't that I mind! But could I get away with it?"

"Why not? She wants a maid to do for her, I suppose, what you ordinarily do for yourself."

"How will I land the job?"

"Simply go there and register, and pay the fee, and turn down any other offers you may get. I guess they don't get many applicants that could compete with you."

"Silly! There are references to be thought of."

"That's easy. Mrs. Delamare will provide one, and get others if necessary."

"What is the object of my doing this?"

"I'm going to drop out of sight for a while, and I must have somebody to keep me informed of what goes on in Bobo's establishment while I'm away."

"Very well. I'll do it."

The agreement was sealed.

Jack spent the rest of the afternoon in arranging for the necessary references for Kate, in making certain inquiries at the steamship offices, and finally in looking up a friend of the old poverty-stricken days, one Stanley Larkin. He chose this friend because of a general resemblance they were said to bear each other.

Larkin worked in the freight office of a railway. At the sight of Jack his eyes widened in amazement. "Good Lord! if it isn't Jack——"

"Robinson," put in Jack quickly, "for the present."

Larkin was anything but slow. "Sure, Robinson! It certainly was decent of you to look me up in this hole."

"Look here," said Jack, coming to the point at once, "what kind of a job have you got here?"

"Rotten!"

"Is there any reason why you shouldn't give it up for awhile?"

"None whatever, if I could meet my board bill without it."

"Will you make a trip down to British Guiana for me?"

"British Guiana! Am I dreaming?"

"Not that you'd notice," said Jack grinning. "Boat leaves Saturday. I'm going with you part way."

The young clerk balanced the stultifying monotony of life in a railway office against the lure of the tropics. His eyes became dreamy. "Will I go!" he said. "Only give me the chance! It's like a fairy tale!"

"Good!" said Jack. "Let's have dinner together, and we'll arrange everything. It will have to be some out of the way place because I have to take precautions against being followed. Say Pezzi's on West Thirty-Fourth. I'll meet you there at seven."

36

Bobo and the lovely Miriam arrived at the Madagascar next morning. Miriam promptly sallied forth to Miss Staley's to pick a maid, giving Jack and Bobo an opportunity to have a long talk undisturbed. When Bobo learned that Jack's new plans included unlimited funds for himself for the time being, he hastened to agree to everything. Jack rehearsed him carefully in the part he was to play. The principal danger was that Bobo in his enthusiasm might overdo it.

"For Heaven's sake don't look so smug and expectant," said Jack, "or she'll smell a rat before we begin!"

Bobo, it should be mentioned, knew nothing of the part Kate was to play. Bobo had never seen Kate.

Miriam returned successful from her quest, and so far as such a great lady might deign to her slaves, almost good-tempered.

"Yes, I found a girl," she said languidly. "Quite a superior creature. Her name is Mary Dean. She has worked for Mrs. Walter Delamare and Mrs. Willis Estabrook. She'll be here with her things in time to dress me for dinner."

Mary Dean was the name chosen by Kate. "So far so good," thought Jack.

The three of them lunched together in the Dutch room of their suite. Bobo as the meal progressed, became visibly nervous, and scarcely did justice to the timbales of chicken and asparagus tips. Jack watching him, and fearful that Miriam might notice something, gave him the sign to open the comedy, though he had intended to wait until after the meal.

"I want some more money," said Bobo.

"Huh!" said Miriam scornfully. "One would think it was his money you were asking for."

This put Bobo out a little; Jack hastened to give him the next cue. "But I've been sending you a thousand a week."

"What's a thousand a week!" said Miriam. "Our bill at the Rodney Farms was half of that."

"Why didn't you buy the place?" queried Jack sarcastically.

"Is that for you to say?" demanded Miriam.

"I've got to have more!" shouted Bobo—according to previous instructions.

"A thousand was all you said you wanted."

"That was before I married. I need more now."

"Yes, and a whole lot more!" put in Miriam.

This was just what Jack wanted from her. He sought to irritate her still further by addressing himself pointedly to Bobo. "You said it was part of my job to save you from your own extravagance."

"You needn't remind me of that now," said Bobo. "The money's mine, isn't it?"

"You put the management of it in my hands."

"Did he engage you as his nurse?" suggested Miriam.

"You said I was not to give you any more no matter how hard you begged for it," said Jack affecting a stubborn air.

"Oh, for Heaven's sake! This is ridiculous!" cried Miriam. "Are you compelled to go down on your knees to beg your own money?"

"No, I'm not!" cried Bobo, banging the table. "I want money, and I want it quick!"

Jack looked more stubborn than ever. "I'll talk to you afterwards," he said. "We can't discuss business at meals."

"Look here, you'd better understand you'll talk business whenever we want!" said Miriam.

Jack frowned. Still addressing Bobo he said: "We got along all right till she began to butt in."

Miriam turned pale with anger. This, as Jack intended it to be, was an outrageous affront to the dignity she now affected.

"Are you—going to—sit there—and let him insult me!" she stammered to Bobo.

Bobo banged the table again. That table was of inestimable support to him. "No, I'm not! You apologize to her!"

"I won't!" muttered Jack, feigning the sulks.

"Apologize to her!" shouted Bobo.

"Oh, I apologize," said Jack gracelessly.

"That's no apology!" said Miriam.

Jack sprang up and made a sweeping bow, one hand on his breast. "I humbly beg your ladyship's pardon," he said ironically.

Miriam was almost ready to cry now. "Don't you see he's insulting me more than ever!"

Bobo banged the table again. "You treat her with proper respect or I'll fire you!"

"You don't dare fire me," said Jack threateningly.

Miriam caught him up as quick as lightning. "Don't dare fire you! Why not, I'd like to know!" Turning to Bobo: "Has he got something on you? Is that why we've had to put up with his cheek all this while! Oh, I see it all now!"

Jack, while preserving his defiant front, was quivering with laughter inside. The thing was working better than he had dared hope.

"What do you care what he's got on you!" continued Miriam. "Aren't you worth a hundred millions? A millionaire can do anything he wants and get away with it!"

"You're right!" cried Bobo banging the table. "I'm tired of having it thrown up to me. I'm tired of being under the thumb of my own secretary. I can do what I want! I can spend my money the way I want! You're fired, do you hear!"

Miriam smiled an unpleasant smile. Her dearest wish was coming true.

Jack made out to be much taken aback. "You don't dare," he muttered.

"We'll see whether I dare! You pack up your things and get out before night, see? I'll pay you a month's salary to be rid of you!"

"I won't go," said Jack.

"Then you'll be thrown out!" said Miriam.

"I'll tell what I know!"

"Go ahead and tell it," said Bobo. "I'm sick of hearing about it!"

"I'll tell her!"

"Tell me," said Miriam. "I guess I can stand it."

"When we worked in the sash and blind factory together," said Jack with the air of one delivering damning evidence, "he used to swipe his lunch money out of the petty cash, and make phony entries in the cash book to hide it. I caught him at it!"

Bobo hung his head in simulated shame. It was good comedy.

Miriam shouted with laughter. "Is that all!" To Bobo: "You poor idiot! Do you mean to say that was all he had over you to set him up so!"

"Well, I've fired him, haven't I?" said Bobo with an aggrieved air. To Jack he added: "Now you've done your worst, get!"

Jack put on an air of swaggering bravado. "Oh, all right! I'm sick of the job anyhow! I wouldn't work for you now for ten times the salary!"

Miriam laughed insultingly.

Jack arose. He still had to make a good exit. "It's hard enough to take all the work and the responsibility," he said with assumed bitterness, "but when your boss marries a———"

"You'll leave her out of it, or I'll smash you!" cried Bobo.

"Come on! Let's settle it man to man," said Jack. "I'm ready any time!"

"You get out of here!" shouted Bobo. "Or I'll call the house detective!"

Jack went, slamming the door. He proceeded to his own room, chuckling.

Later, while he was packing, he heard a timid knock. Bobo was standing outside with a deprecating air.

"Can I come in?"

"Sure! Where's Miriam?"

"We're safe. She's gone out to see about getting me another secretary."

Jack laughed. "Poor Bobo!"

"It went off all right," said Bobo. "She doesn't suspect a thing!"

"Fine!" said Jack.

"What are you going to do?"

"Take a little trip. British Guiana. Boat leaves Saturday."

"Lucky Dog!"

"What, already!"

"Oh, it was my fate, I suppose."

37

Jack was counting on the fact that the circumstances of his quarrel with Bobo would be faithfully reported to "Mr. B." and that the latter would satisfy himself that he, Jack, actually boarded the steamship for British Guiana.

He moved to a more modest hotel, as befitted his altered circumstances, but on Saturday morning he returned to the Madagascar and loitered in the lobby, ostentatiously bidding good-by to the acquaintances he had made there, whose demeanor, by the way, had noticeably cooled since he lost his job. He did not see Bobo again, but he had a distant glimpse of Kate passing through the lobby, a charming figure in her maid's dress with lace apron and cap, her eyes demurely cast down.

Jack had the satisfaction, at length, of observing that he was the object of a covert interest on the part of a well-dressed, sharp-eyed youth of much the same type as those he had formerly known in "Mr. B.'s" service. When he was sure of this he took a taxi for the boat. Baldwin, who seemed to have a genuinely friendly feeling for him, offered to see him off, and Jack was not averse, of course, to having another witness to his actual departure.

As he and Baldwin stood on the promenade deck of S.S. *Covenas* Jack saw the sharp-eyed one watching from the crowd on the dock. Evidently his instructions were to make sure that Jack did not escape down the gang-plank at the last moment. Stanley Larkin was safely aboard the ship, but according to pre-arrangement he and Jack gave no sign of recognition.

Finally the last gong sounded, Jack and Baldwin parted, the whistle blew, and the *Covenas* started to back slowly out into midstream. On her printed passenger list appeared the names of Mr. Stanley Larkin, bound for St. Thomas, her first port of call, and Mr. John Robinson, booked through to Georgetown, British Guiana. Both young gentlemen were aboard, as we have seen, but as a matter of fact they had changed tickets—and identities for the voyage.

Of that pleasant voyage it is unnecessary to speak, since nothing occurred upon it that bears upon this story. Jack, that is to say the real Jack, went ashore at the island of St. Thomas, where, under the name of Larkin, he booked passage back to New York on the *Lobos*, first returning steamer of the same line.

In St. Thomas he received a cablegram, which read, when decoded:

Still holding my job. Nothing new. Love.
KATE.

In seventeen days from the time he left he was off quarantine again. According to an arrangement effected through Mr. Delamare's good offices, the health officer's boat took Jack off the *Lobos* and landed him on Staten Island, whence he made his way via Elizabeth to Newark without setting foot on Manhattan. This was in case the astute "Mr. B" should take it into his head to have the *Lobos* watched when she docked.

Jack went to a hotel in Newark, where it had been arranged he was to receive Kate's reports. He found awaiting him a day by day account of the life of Bobo's household which did credit to Kate's faculty of observation. It contained, however, no suggestion of what he so much wished to find, the reëntrance of "Mr. B" upon the scene. Only a few characteristic excerpts from Kate's reports need be given.

November 25th: Miriam has embarked on a perfect orgy of spending. All day long, dresses, furs, hats are being delivered at the hotel, not to speak of the dozens of expensive, useless knickknacks that catch her eye in the stores. It is part of my duty to unwrap the packages. Lots of the things she never even looks at when they get home. She buys, I am sure, largely for the pleasure of seeing the salespeople fawn when she gives her name and address. It is a never-failing pleasure to her to announce who she is. Sometimes she takes me with her on a shopping expedition because she thinks I lend style to the outfit. She talks French to me in public. Such French! She bought an automobile to-day, a Vickers-Lee landaulet, price $8,000. She intends to have two men on the box, when she can get their liveries made. A man from Mercer's, the fashionable jewelers, brought an amazing array of pearls and diamonds to the hotel this afternoon. She chose a strand of pearls. I don't know the price. Such unbridled extravagance outrages my New England conscience. I hope you'll be able to put a stop to it soon.

*   *   *   *   *   *   *
*

Nov. 27th: M.'s heart is set on having a mansion on upper Fifth avenue, whence she can institute a social campaign. When she is not at the dressmaker's she is being taken around to see such places. The servility of the well-dressed young real estate agents delights her. She gives Bobo no peace on the subject, but I believe he has avoided committing himself as yet. As she has me fussing over her clothes or her hair almost every moment that she is at home, I hear most of their conjugal discussions.

Nov. 28th: The new secretary came to-day. I dislike him intensely. His name is Leroy Chalfonte. He is a handsome young fellow in a brutal, scornful way, the type that makes fools of many silly women. His manners are superficially good enough, but he doesn't trouble to hide the sneer. I gather that he and Miriam spend the afternoons in the tango parlors. He is covertly insolent to Bobo, who dares not call him down.

* * * * * *
*

Dec. 5th: This is no easy job to hold. M.'s method with servants seems to be that of certain misguided parents with their offspring. I believe it is called "breaking their spirit." When she gets up in a bad temper, positively nothing that I can do pleases. The more patient and willing I am, the greater offense it is. I have found it better to be a little impudent at such times. She expects it, and she can then abuse me with a better face. Sometimes I am sorry for the poor creature. She has never known a moment's real happiness, I am sure. You would think that now she would feel as if her ambition was realized, but no! Mercer's have a pearl necklace worth a hundred and fifty thousand, and she can think of nothing else. I hope you have taken precautions against Bobo's attempting to gratify any such whim.

* * * * * *
*

Dec. 11th: Yesterday Miriam had a talk with somebody over the telephone. She used the instrument in her boudoir. I had a perfectly natural excuse to enter the room while she was talking, but she ordered me out. I made out this much. That somebody was insisting on something that she objected to—somebody that she was in awe of. Thinking perhaps of the danger of somebody listening in, she made a date to continue the talk from an outside 'phone.

This last entry on Kate's report was dated only the day before. Since her communication gave Jack nothing to go on, all he could do was to wait until he heard from her again. She would learn of the arrival of the *Lobos* from the newspapers, and would without doubt call him up at his hotel at the first opportunity.

At nine o'clock that night Jack got his call, and heard the voice that was dearest to him.

"Jack!"

"Kitty, dearest!"

"Oh, my dear, it's so good to hear you! Are you quite well?"

"Right as a trivet! And you?"

"Oh, I'm well. But I can't stand that woman much longer!"

"Poor Kitty! I know. Where are you 'phoning from?"

"Booth in a drug-store."

"Is it safe?"

"Oh, yes! They've gone to the theater, and to dance afterwards. They won't be home until three or after. She insists on my staying up to put her to bed, but they know I go out while they're out."

"Have you any news for me?"

"Yes, I think I have."

"Shoot!"

"You remember in my last letter I said Miriam had had a telephone conversation yesterday that seemed to agitate her?"

"Yes."

"Well, I think I have the explanation. Last night when I was putting my lady to bed—Oh, my dear, you'll never know what I have been through!—Bobo said, apropos of nothing, but only anxious to propitiate her, 'It will be nice to have some relations, won't it?' Miriam replied ill-temperedly: 'I'm not so crazy about it.' 'What's Uncle George like?' asked Bobo. 'Just a business man,' she answered, 'a manufacturer of stoves or something.' 'Well fixed?' asked Bobo. 'He must be or he couldn't have retired,' she answered."

Kate went on: "Well, Uncle George and Aunt Sally turned up for lunch to-day."

"Ha!" said Jack. "What's he like?"

"He doesn't fit the descriptions of 'Mr. B.'"

"He wouldn't! Go on."

"He's a man of fifty-odd, bald, clean-shaven, blue eyes."

"Short and stocky?"

"Yes."

"So far so good. Go on."

"He was very jolly and good-natured; full of jokes: courteous to everybody, even to me. Just the same, Miriam is afraid of him. She is quite subdued when he is there."

"Good! We're getting warm. What's Aunt Sally like?"

"How do you describe an old lady? She's just like another. She probably set up to be a belle in her youth, because she still wears a false front. She's very quiet. Uncle George talks all the time, and she just listens and nods and smiles. It appears they live in Buffalo and have come to New York for a little gayety. They wanted to see dear Miriam's husband, of course, so they looked her up at once. They're staying at the Hotel Abercrombie, but have decided to move to the Madagascar to be nearer dear Miriam."

"What's your opinion, Kitty?"

"I'm not dead certain yet. The most suspicious thing is Miriam's attitude. Why should she be in such awe of her agreeable uncle? That they have not seen each other for years, as they give out, is certainly false. One of Uncle's features fits all the descriptions of 'Mr. B.' that we have received. His piercing blue eyes——"

"Good!" said Jack. "That's the one feature he couldn't change."

"If we were not looking for 'Mr. B.' to appear on the scene, and did not know that he was fiendishly clever, I must say I would never suspect Uncle George. He plays his part to perfection. He lets on to be a prosperous man, and asks no favors of Bobo. I gather that he insists on paying his half everywhere. But to-day I got a hint of his possible game. He and Bobo had a long talk in the Dutch room. I made an excuse to pass through as often as I could, and picked up some scraps of their conversation."

"Well?" said Jack eagerly.

"Uncle George was posing as an experienced and successful man of affairs, see? Without appearing to pry into Bobo's business, he was setting himself to win his confidence in such matters. Bobo is obviously such a fool that Uncle George no doubt anticipates gaining a complete ascendancy over him, and perhaps sees himself in the position of directing all Bobo's affairs. But he's an artist; he carries it off so well, I find myself wondering sometimes if my suspicions aren't all imaginary."

"We'll make sure of that," said Jack.

"What do you want me to do?"

"Get me a scrap of his writing if you can—to compare with what I have."

"I'll try."

"And call me up again first chance you get."

38

The following day was a hard one on Jack, for he had to pass it in inaction and suspense. He thought it wiser not to venture over to New York: an awkward chance encounter might spoil all. He talked to Mr. Delamare over the 'phone, and through him got into communication with the Deputy Commissioner of police. The latter promised him whatever help he needed, which was certainly good-natured, since, at Jack's invitation, his men had twice assisted in a fiasco.

Kate called him up at the same hour as on the day before.

"They're off for the night again. All four of them."

"Anything decisive to-day?"

"No, but many little things have confirmed me in my opinion that Uncle George is our man. He is no less agreeable than at first, but in a curious way I feel his power stealing over us. They have moved to the Madagascar, and have been with us all day. We are already as intimate as possible. Bobo is more friendly to them than their supposed niece. She was in a grinding temper last night after they had gone, and properly threw things about."

"To-day, I fancy, Uncle George must have found an opportunity to give her a call, for she was much chastened. It is a strange and welcome sight to see somebody who can tame her. I could almost like this old man if it were not for some things. He's so sensible! Perhaps that's why he was successful for so long. A sensible crook must be a novelty."

"It is," said Jack.

"To-day they have had all their meals in our rooms. They make me wait on them, because they say I am handier than the men waiters—'and much nicer to look at,' adds Uncle George."

"Confound him!" muttered Jack.

"I don't object to the waiting, of course, for it gives me a chance to hear the table conversation. It is like a comedy. To-day Bobo made a joking reference to the hundred and fifty thousand dollar necklace that Miriam's heart was set on. The old man just looked at her with those icy blue eyes, and she hung her head. The necklace has not been mentioned since.

"Another thing, Uncle George was responsible for firing Chalfonte to-day. Apparently Chalfonte can't be a member of the gang, but a private friend of Miriam's. At any rate his doom was sealed from the moment Uncle George turned up. He was insolent at the table in his usual way, and, backed up by Uncle, Bobo fired him on the spot. Miriam couldn't say a word. Bobo is beginning to think Uncle George is the most wonderful man on earth.

"'What do you want a secretary for, anyway,' Uncle said to Bobo."

"Bobo stammered something about knowing nothing about business.

"'Pshaw!' said Uncle in his hearty way. 'If you want any advice come to me!'"

"Did you get a sample of his handwriting?" asked Jack.

"Yes, by great good luck. I didn't see how I was going to manage it. But he wrote a note in our rooms to-day. I was hoping he might give it to me to post, but he didn't. However, there was a new blotter on the desk, which took a perfect impression of several lines that he wrote. I have just mailed you the blotter. Hold it up to a mirror. The note you see is just a bit of camouflage. He is enclosing a subscription to the Buffalo Express."

"What about their arrangements for to-morrow?" asked Jack.

"I can only tell you about lunch. I know that Uncle George and Aunt Sally are coming to lunch in our rooms because I heard Bobo giving a special order over the 'phone."

"What time?"

"One o'clock."

"Very well. If the handwriting matches up, you may expect us about that time."

"Heavens! How my heart beats when I think of it!"

"You needn't be there if you'd rather not."

"I wouldn't miss it for a farm!"

"Good! Then you can give me a signal. When they are all seated at the table, come down to the door of Silas Gyde's sitting-room and tap three times. On your way back leave the doors open behind you."

Jack possessed three letters in "Mr. B.'s" own hand; that which had fallen on the table in the Alpine Heights restaurant; that which he had found pinned to Bobo's overcoat; and that which had been handed to Mrs. Cleaver in the Hotel Bienvenu. The same hand had likewise kept the card index system. It was a hand of strong individuality, the letters quaintly formed as in antique script, suggesting an orderly, painstaking and somewhat vain character in the writer, who must have gone to no end of trouble to form such a hand in youth.

The piece of blotting paper arrived in the first mail next morning. Held up before a mirror, a single glance was sufficient to identify it. There were the same quaint and artistic characters—unmistakable!

Jack hesitated no longer. He took the first train for Manhattan, and had himself carried to police headquarters in a taxi. To the Deputy Commissioner Jack now told sufficient of his tale to enlist his interest, but withheld the whole, for fear that the official's natural amazement and incredulity might hold things up. The Deputy was satisfied that the genuine John Farrow Norman stood before him, and that was sufficient. Mr. Delamare vouched for it.

Jack asked for eight men, and they were sent for. In the commissioner's office he described to them the man he wanted, and gave his offense as blackmail. A capable sergeant was in charge of the squad. They were to proceed to the Madagascar separately. Four of his men he instructed to wait in the street, in case an escape should be attempted from the windows of the state suite. The sergeant and the other three would assemble in Connolly's room at the hotel and wait until they got word from Jack. Connolly was well known to the sergeant.

Mr. Delamare was anxious to be "in at the death," as he put it, but they persuaded him to wait, and appear on the scene a little later.

Shortly before one o'clock Jack approached the Madagascar on foot from the direction of Eighth avenue. He had had himself set down at the corner, because he thought a taxicab might possibly attract attention in the unfrequented side street. He let himself in by the private entrance leading to Silas Gyde's old rooms. When he was "fired" he had taken the precaution of retaining a set of keys.

Here he waited, pacing up and down the little sitting-room watch in hand. The minutes passed with leaden slowness. He reflected on how much had happened since first he had entered that room with beating heart. No detail of the room was changed: the same expensive furnishings which somehow only created a barren effect—even the kerosene lamp and the heater were still there.

Like all imaginative men on the eve of a decisive action, he became a prey to the blackest forebodings. He remembered how often before the old man had fooled him, when he all but had his hand on him. No doubt his infernal luck would still serve him. They would have changed their plans, and gone out to lunch; or some one had tipped him off—he had his spies out; or his sharp eyes had marked the detectives arriving in the lobby.

In the very midst of these depressing fancies Jack heard the agreed signal, three taps on the door.

A swift reaction passed over him. His spirits soared. "Kitty has not failed me! Everything is all right!" he thought.

He called up the office, and asked for Mr. Connolly. Getting him on the wire, he said:

"Connolly, have you got four men there, waiting for instructions?"

"Yes, sir." The house detective had no idea who was speaking.

"Well, just tell them to take their places."

"Yes, sir."

Jack waited two minutes to give the plainclothes men time to get upstairs. He was thinking: "After all this time, and all these failures, in a minute I shall be actually face to face with him!"

He opened the door into the hotel corridor. Four steps away the door into the end room of the state suite stood ajar. Down the corridor he saw the four detectives taking their places. One was approaching to guard the door by which he entered.

Jack passed quickly and noiselessly through the lower rooms of the suite. In the pocket of his coat he grasped his automatic. He approached the Dutch room through Miriam's "boudoir" since Kate had left the doors open that way. He came upon Kate in this room, standing by a window with her hands pressed tight to her breast to control her agitation. From the Dutch room adjoining came the sound of light talk and laughter.

In passing, Jack touched Kate's cold hand to reassure her—and opened the door. The cheerful sounds of the luncheon party rushed to meet them. He saw the four at the small table. Bobo was facing him and the bald-headed man was opposite Bobo. Miriam had her back to the windows, and the little old woman faced her.

At the opening of the door Miriam turned her head. She was in the act of saying: "Mary, where have you been?" when she saw who it really was, and stopped on a gasp. Bobo looked up and saw, too.

"J-Jack!" he stammered.

With astonishing swiftness the bald-headed man leaped up, knocking his chair over backwards, and, never looking round, ran with head down for the door on the left. This led to the foyer and the main entrance to the suite. The detectives were out there, and Jack let him go. The old lady had covered her face with her hands. Bobo sat like a stone man staring at Jack.

All this happened in a breath. Miriam had sprung up too, and backed away from the table towards the windows. As Jack came further into the room, she suddenly darted behind him into her own room.

Jack was standing listening for sounds from the corridor, when suddenly Kate screamed a warning behind him. He instinctively relaxed, dropping to the floor. There was a shot. The bullet passed about where his head had been, and broke a tankard on the plate rail across the room. From the floor Jack saw the two women struggling for possession of the gun. Springing to Kate's aid, he disarmed Miriam. She retreated to the farthest corner of the room, panting and snarling like an animal.

The sounds from outside were reassuring. There was a scuffle and the bald-headed man was pushed back into the room by two detectives. He still had his head down, but as he came opposite Jack he suddenly raised it with cool and smiling effrontery. It was Jack's turn to be dumbfounded.

"Harmon Evers!" he cried.

It was indeed the philosophic little wig-maker.

39

Jack stared at his adversary open-mouthed. He required an appreciable time to adjust himself to the situation. His face turned grim—but he could see the joke on himself too.

"No wonder you were on to every move I made when I went to you for my disguises!"

"Humorous situation, wasn't it?" said Evers mockingly.

"Was it accident?" demanded Jack.

"Oh, no! I willed you to come to me!"

Jack recollected the boy who had first given him Evers' name.

By this time Miriam had recovered her self-possession. She came out of her corner. Addressing the detective sergeant, she said haughtily: "What is the meaning of this outrage? This"—pointing to Bobo—"is Mr. John Farrow Norman, and I am Mrs. Norman. The gentleman you have your hand on is my uncle, George Culbreth. You shall pay dearly for this!"

She carried conviction. The two detectives looked uneasy. But Jack's amused smile reassured them a little.

"This guy was trying to beat it," the sergeant said.

"I suppose he was going for assistance," said Miriam quickly.

"Well, what did you shoot for?"

"I shot as I would shoot at any intruder into my rooms. Take your hands off that gentleman! I demand an explanation!"

Evers was staring at the ceiling with his head cocked quizzically. He seemed the least concerned person in the room.

The sergeant nodded towards Jack. "We're under his orders, Miss. You'll have to ask him."

"Oh, I know him!" she cried. "A discharged servant of my husband's! He's capable of laying any charge out of spite! You'd better be careful how you believe him!" She whirled on Kate. "And this woman! She let him in! Another unfaithful servant! A nice thing it is when people like us are at the mercy of their servants!"

"Oh, dry up, my dear!" said Evers in a weary voice. "You mean well, but the game is up!"

But Miriam had acquired too much momentum to be stopped right away. "I demand that the management be sent for!" she cried.

"It is not necessary," said Jack. He had caught sight of Mr. Delamare entering from the corridor. "Here is some one who will identify me. Tell her first, who this is."

"Mr. Walter Delamare," said the sergeant with unction.

Miriam, seeing the smile of confidence exchanged by Delamare and Jack, felt the ground slipping from under her feet. Her face blanched. "Well, anyway I am Mrs. Norman," she cried. "Nothing can change that!"

"Tell them all who I am, please," said Jack.

Delamare put a hand on Jack's shoulder. "This is my good friend, Jack Norman," he said. "The late Silas Gyde's sole heir."

Evers' face betrayed no change. Perhaps his intuition had warned him of what was coming. Not so Miriam. A queer gasping cry escaped her.

"Then who—who is this?" she stammered, pointing to Bobo. "And who am I?"

"I don't know the young man's right name. Mr. Norman engaged him to impersonate him, in order to free his hands while he was engaged in running down the murderers of Silas Gyde."

Miriam's proud figure sagged. No further sound escaped her. All the color left her face. She looked old and haggard. Kate thought she was about to fall, and made a step towards her. Miriam stiffened with hate, and Kate fell back.

"What shall we do with this man?" asked the sergeant.

"Take him to headquarters," said Jack. "Watch him well. You've got the cleverest crook in America there."

"Much obliged for the compliment," said Evers coolly. "May I speak to you a moment, alone, before they take me?"

"No, Jack, no!" Kate cried involuntarily.

Jack silenced her with a smile. "Search him for weapons," he said.

The detectives frisked their captive efficaciously. Nothing more dangerous than a pen-knife was revealed.

"Go into the front room," Jack said to Evers. "No use trying a window, because there are four more men in the street." He motioned to the detectives to remain at the doors. He followed Evers.

In the middle of the gaudy blue salon Evers turned with his queer smile. "I suppose you don't want to shake hands with me."

Jack was nonplussed. He felt that he had no business to be liking the man and yet—he did. "One must draw the line somewhere," he muttered. "After all you murdered my benefactor."

Evers was not in the least put out. "Oh, come! Looking at it from a disinterested point of view, old Silas Gyde was not much of a loss to the community, was he? And he wasn't your benefactor until I put him out of the way."

"I can't argue that with you," said Jack stiffly. "Murder is murder!"

"Well, let it pass," said Evers. "That isn't what I wanted to talk to you about. It's my old lady out there. I swear to you on my honor—such as it is, that she never knew what I was up to. She thought it was smuggling, and no woman considers smuggling a crime, you know. She's sixty-three years old and has a heart complaint. Let her go."

"Why, I'll do what I can," said Jack, more and more uncomfortable. "But I can't tell what the trial may bring out."

"There won't be any trial," said Evers quietly.

"What——! You mean——?"

Evers merely smiled.

Jack half turned as if to call for help.

"Wait!" said Evers sharply. "Didn't I give you a good run for your money?" he went on with a genuine note of appeal. "And you've won. Can't you afford to be generous? Don't interfere. Let me pay my forfeit in my own way. The trouble with me was, I couldn't endure the tedium of a respectable life. But I am no quitter. I went into this with my eyes open, knowing the penalty. I was prepared to pay it at any moment."

"I won't interfere," said Jack in a low tone.

"Thanks. One thing more." He held out two keys and a scrap of paper. "These keys are for my box in the Windsor Safe Deposit Vaults. Number and password are written on the paper. Everything I own is in the box. My wife is provided for with an annuity. There are securities to the amount of—Oh, I don't know, half a million, maybe. You can't return it because the records of whom I obtained it are burned. But take it and do some good act. Build a home for indigent millionaires—or anything you like."

In spite of himself Jack had to smile.

"Come on now. Hand me back to the bulls."

In the adjoining room Evers was handcuffed and marched out between two detectives. The old lady picked up her hat and coat, and silently followed them.

The sergeant nodded towards Miriam. "How about her?"

Jack hung in indecision.

"She tried to plug you, didn't she?"

"Oh, I don't mind a little thing like that."

The worthy sergeant looked a trifle scandalized at the jest.

Bobo, who had sat in a daze throughout, lifted a drawn face. "Jack, let her go, please!" he murmured huskily.

Jack looked at Kate, and she nodded imperceptibly.

"Only the one prisoner, sergeant!" said Jack. "I haven't evidence enough against this one."

Delamare, shaking Jack's hand, went with the sergeant, and the two young couples were left alone. An awkward silence fell on them. Jack was afraid to say anything for fear of seeming to triumph over them. Kate signaled to him that the best thing for them to do was to go.

"Wait a minute," said Jack. He turned to the other man with a humorous light in his eye. "Bobo, you and I have been partners in a hazardous enterprise. I can't say exactly that you have always stood by me, but there were extenuating circumstances. And I feel a certain responsibility in introducing you to a life of luxury. So I'm going to establish a trust fund that will pay you twenty-five thousand a year. With care, you and Miriam ought to be able to live on that." He turned to the girl. "Will you stick to him, Miriam? You might do worse. He loves you. It's the real thing—and that's not too common in this wicked world."

Bobo got up. "Miriam!" he said imploringly. He took her hand. She did not pull it away.

"Now, come on, Kate!" said Jack briskly. "Never mind any things!"

He led her down the corridor to Silas Gyde's old rooms. "We'll go through the vault into your house," he said. "The hotel lobby will be seething with excitement by now."

"I wonder if you did right—about Bobo and Miriam, I mean. She isn't likely to do him much good."

"Such as she is, he'd rather have her than anything else in the world."

In Kate's house they paused.

"What are we going to do now?" she asked.

"First I'm going to kiss you," he said, suiting the action to the word. "Then you're going to put on your prettiest dress and hat and we're going down to the City Hall to get a license. Then we'll be married by the first person that's looking for the job. Then we'll take a train for Charleston where the *Columbian* is still awaiting orders, and we'll sail away under the tropical moon with a whole ocean liner to our two selves!"

"But—but———!"

"But me no buts!"

"But you'll have to be here for the trial, I suppose."

"There won't be any trial," said Jack gravely. "Harmon Evers had a vial of cyanide in his vest pocket."

"Oh!" cried Kate. "He must be stopped!"

"I promised not to."

"But is it right to let him cheat the law?"

"He may cheat the law, but not justice! The state will be saved the expense of a trial, and the public a demoralizing newspaper sensation."

THE END

www.ingramcontent.com/pod-product-compliance
Ingram Content Group UK Ltd.
Pitfield, Milton Keynes, MK11 3LW, UK
UKHW042147281224
453045UK00004B/208